A TALE OF TWO COLORS

# the FIRE that calms the STORM

VOLUME V

A TALE OF TWO COLORS

# the FIRE that calms the STORM

VOLUME V

# ANTHONY WOOD

WILL ROGERS MEDALLION WINNER

HAT CREEK

## HAT CREEK

An Imprint of Roan & Weatherford Publishing Associates, LLC
Bentonville, Arkansas
www.roanweatherford.com

Copyright © 2023 by Anthony Wood

**Library of Congress Cataloging-in-Publication Data**
Names: Wood, Anthony, author.
Title: The Fire That Calms the Storm/Anthony Wood | A Tale of Two Colors #5
Description: First Edition. | Bentonville: Hat Creek, 2023.
Identifiers: LCCN: 2023950911 | ISBN: 978-1-63373-882-9 (hardcover) |
ISBN: 978-1-63373-883-6 (trade paperback) | ISBN: 978-1-63373-884-3 (eBook) |
Subjects: | BISAC: FICTION/Historical/Civil War Era |
FICTION/War and Military | FICTION/Action/Adventure |
LC record available at: https://lccn.loc.gov/2023950911

Hat Creek trade paperback edition May, 2024

Cover Design by Casey W. Cowan
Cover art by Albert Bierstadt (1830-1902)
*Guerrilla Warfare (Pickett Duty in Virginia)*, 1862, Oil on panel
Interior Design by George "Clay" Mitchell
Editing by Amy Cowan & Lisa Lindsey

*For Uncle Dwight and Aunt Judy Wood,*
*whose love, support, and hospitality has reminded me*
*that Mississippi will always be home.*

# ACKNOWLEDGEMENTS

WRITING NOVELS CAN often lead an author to sink into a world of fiction that becomes far too real. Authors need anchors to keep them from going adrift in seas of creativity. Two friends and mentors were just that for me. At the risk of sounding selfish, Bob Giel and Velda Brotherton left my life way too early.

One never knows the true value of a friendship until that friend is gone. We think, "Oh, we'll talk when I see her at next year's writing conference," or "He'll be at the retreat and we'll have a good conversation over coffee then."

Then the call comes and reality sets in—they have passed through the thin veil to the other side. And they are sorely missed.

Though always with us in in spirit, I won't forget Bob's "heart as big as the West" love for people and his skill as my development and historical editor. That huge grin under his big cowboy hat will always encourage me.

Velda's sassy and often direct words of wisdom will continue to temper my heart. Her authentic and gentle kindness will be one of my soul's guiding stars to keep the bow of my writing ship headed in the right direction.

Bob, Velda, enjoy your new lives in the place where we all long to be.

**OUTLAW GANG IN A SWAMP**

*An illustration from Harper's Weekly depicting a post-Civil War era outlaw gang hiding out in one of the numerous swamps throughout the South, preying on guilty and innocent alike.*

# DRAMATIS PERSONAE

ANNIE FANNY: Lummy's sassy and frisky snuff-dipping friend who cared for his shoulder injury suffered during a ferry crossing on the Mississippi River from Vicksburg to Desoto, Louisiana in search of Susannah. She was a mess. Lummy crossed paths with Annie at Desoto on his way to enlist in the Confederate Army and when he returned to Vicksburg to enlist in the Union Army, he found her married and owner of Handerson's Café with her husband, Beau. Annie introduces Lummy to her widowed sister, Martha, and her children. Lummy's heart is captured and Annie is still a mess.

CAPTAIN TOM FORD: Leader of the outlaw Choctaw County Home Guard who vowed to kill Lummy for helping the Yankees burn the manufacturing mills in Bankston, Mississippi, and killing Lester, Ford's friend and fellow soldier. He attacks Lummy as he leaves his home to enlist in the Union Army.

COLUMBUS "LUMMY" NATHAN TULLOS: Archibald and Mary Tullos's sixth child born in 1834. As the main character in this series, Lummy leaves his home in Choctaw County, Mississippi and begins his adventurous journey in search of his love, a young slave woman named

Susannah. They eventually marry, but nearly a year into Lummy's service with the Confederate Army in Vicksburg, Mississippi he receives news of Susannah's death. He joins the Union Army to help end the war and finds new love in the process. He returns home in search of peace and quiet.

DAN CREEKWATER: Lummy's Choctaw friend whom he first met on the road to Winn Parish back in 1859. Dan's wisdom of the Universe helped Lummy sort out his recent war experiences and to make his decision to join the 1st Mississippi Mounted Rifles. Lummy shared a camp with Dan in the haunts of McCurtain Creek Swamp after killing Lester, who tried to rape and kill Lummy's family. Dan helped Lummy find his soul again.

ELIHU TULLOS: Lummy's eccentric older brother who stayed home to care for the family and farm in Choctaw County during the war. Elihu became Lummy's greatest ally as he made his decision to join the Union Army. Elihu was the first to experience Lummy's trauma due to his war experiences. He is a faithful brother to a fault.

ELZEY TULLOS: Lummy and Susannah's son who was unknown to him until he traveled to Winn Parish after Vicksburg surrendered. Because of his less than stable state of mind and the possibility of re-entering the war, Lummy decided to leave Elzey with a good family in Winn Parish until such time that he might return.

JASPER NEWTON AND JAMES A. TULLOS: Lummy's two younger brothers who served with the 1st Mississippi Light Artillery, Company C during the Siege of Vicksburg, not far from where Lummy was stationed. They returned to the Tullos farm after the war.

OLD BART: Lummy's "black grandfather" whom he met on Mr. James T. Gilmore's farm. Old Bart helped Lummy through the pain of learning the truth about Susannah's death and rode with him to destroy the outlaw Home Guard gang led by Dawg Smith.

SERGEANT "SARGE" McGUGARTY: Lummy met Sarge at the parole after the surrender of Vicksburg. He encouraged Lummy to join the 1st Mississippi Mounted Rifles, the only white Union regiment from Mississippi in the Civil War. Lummy enlisted and served under Sergeant McGugarty until the end of the war.

SETH: A young runaway slave Lummy took under his wing on his way home to the Tullos farm from Winn Parish after ending Dawg Smith and his outlaw gang's reign of terror. Seth became a member of the family. In helping Seth, Lummy realizes the good influence that the late Mr. James T. Gilmore had in his life.

SUSANNAH: A young slave woman and Lummy's first love taken from Choctaw County, Mississippi to Winn Parish, Louisiana by James T. Gilmore who won her in a card game. Lummy left home to find Susannah in Winn Parish and eventually marries her. He learned while stationed in Vicksburg a year later that Susannah died of measles. Lummy returned to Winn Parish after the surrender of Vicksburg to find that Susannah did not die of the measles. She was brutally raped and murdered by Dawg Smith and his outlaw gang. Lummy made things right by ending Smith's life. Susannah will always have a place in Lummy's heart.

TOM POOLE: Lummy's childhood friend growing up in Choctaw County. They rode together with the 1st Mississippi Mounted Rifles, leading a cavalry detachment to their hometown of Bankston, Mississippi, where Union forces burned the manufacturing mills that were producing military supplies for the Confederate Army.

CHOCTAW COUNTY

And Surrounding Area
1860

# SCAENA

CHOCTAW COUNTY, MISSISSIPPI: Founded and created in 1833 from lands ceded by the Choctaw Indians and named for them. Lummy's parents, Archibald and Mary Tullos, settled there as pioneers in 1835. Lummy grew up in Choctaw County and his family helped start one of the county's first Baptist Churches, New Zion, in 1842. With the war over, he desperately wants to find a peaceful life with his family on the farm there.

VICKSBURG, MISSISSIPPI: An important river port and railroad town that linked the east and west of the growing United States. Lummy boarded a ferry there in search of Susannah and later saw Vicksburg again from across the river as he boarded a steamer to travel south to enlist in the Confederate Army. Returning to the city after training at Camp Moore in early May, 1862, he survived the Siege of Vicksburg and was paroled in July of 1863. He passed through Vicksburg on his way to Choctaw County from Winn Parish after taking down the Dawg Smith gang. He returned once again to the city to enlist in the 1st Mississippi Mounted Rifles and meets Martha, who becomes his new bride.

WINN PARISH, LOUISIANA: Lummy traveled to Winn Parish in search of Susannah. There he found her with James T. Gilmore who won slaves gambling to set them free. Lummy joined his long lost brother and family to work on the Gilmore farm where Ben is foreman. Lummy married Susannah just before he left to enlist in the Confederate Army. Lummy had planned to return to Winn Parish after the war where he and Susannah would start a family and build a life together. Returning to Winn Parish after the surrender of Vicksburg, Lummy learned the truth of Susannah's death and in the process learned that they had a son, Elzey. Life with Susannah no longer possible, Lummy went home to Choctaw County after settling his affairs in Winn Parish. Given his state of mind, he believed it best to leave Elzey in Winn Parish with a good family until such time as he was fit to return for him.

A TALE OF TWO COLORS

the

# FIRE

that
calms the STORM

VOLUME V

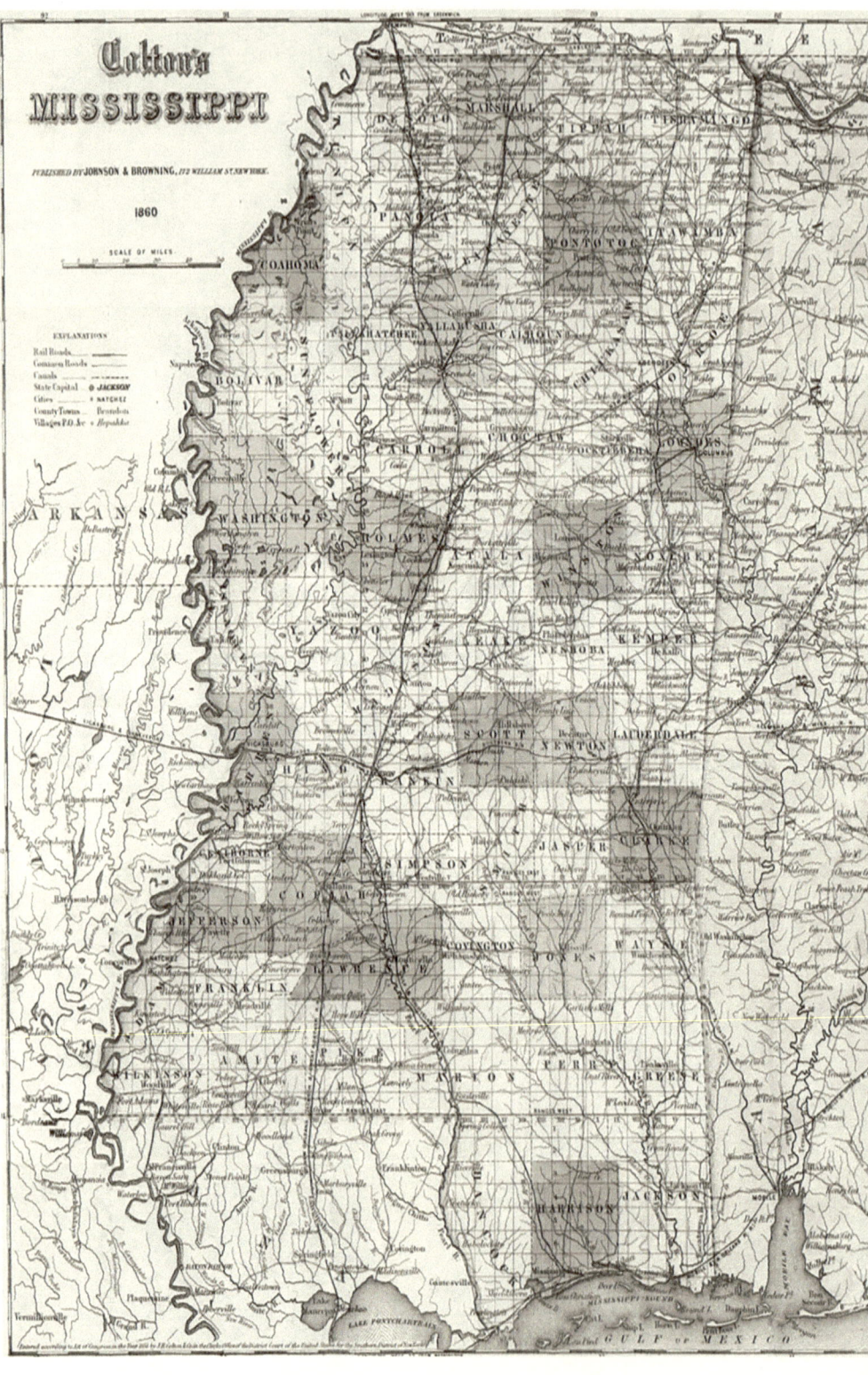

CHAPTER 1

# MY HEART RETURNS
# TO THE HILLS

## LATE AFTERNOON, SEPTEMBER 2, 1866

*Coming home is not just returning to a certain place.*
*It's being in the right place.*

THE SUN FALLS unhurriedly from the sky in an early autumn glow. A gentle breeze swirls through pine branches to lead wispy needles in whispered tunes.

"I like this time of year."

Poole shivers. "Feel that nip in the air. Likely we'll have an early fall, huh, Lummy?"

I look over the Tullos farm. It's so peaceful. I'm feeling cold but not from the weather.

"It seems like just yesterday we laid the family to rest up here."

Poole throws a pine cone. "Yeah, and it also seems like just yesterday Captain Tom Ford almost shot you dead at the funeral celebration last year."

"Yeah, thank goodness Ole Dan Creekwater led them boys on a wild goose chase when I left to go join the Rifes with Sarge."

That was over a year ago. I quickly scan the ridges for signs of movement but let my eyes rest on the half-empty fields below. It's been a good year. Our cotton and corn made well, and prices are good.

Poole picks up a piece of sandstone and throws it at a tree. "Ford ain't been right in the head since the Rebs lost the war."

I break a small piece of fat pine in half and draw in the strong smell of resin. "A crazy man is more dangerous than a sane man."

"Yeah, but...."

"Let's just enjoy the peace in this place and think about the good moonshine the Wood boys'll make with good Tullos grown corn. Ford can wait for a bit."

The funeral last year didn't completely cure my heart of family members lost before and during the war. The annual celebration is over for this year, but not the feelings. Celebrating loved ones gone on to their reward is not much of a reward for the living. Honoring them only brought back sad memories. A dark cloud still hangs heavy over my soul. I guess it always will.

Martha calls, "Lummy, dear, let's go back to the house. The children are ready."

"Be right there." Sweetest woman who ever walked the earth. Besides Susannah. She's in my heart still.

Poole stands up. "What are you thinking?"

"That the fightin' ain't finished. It never will be."

"Hell, we ain't heard nary a sound out of that sorry sack of snakes in a year."

"Yeah, but that don't mean he's not around. A man like Captain Tom Ford doesn't let loose of a grudge for love nor money. He can't. He won't. It ain't his way."

"Then we'll just have to stay alert, like Sarge used to say."

"I always am."

We pack up, and the family works its way down the hill to the dogtrot cabin. My, the sturdiness of the cabin Pa built when we settled this land in 1835. A strength found in strong trees, hard stone, and a determined family. Our family possesses those same traits, making it through the war, surviving difficult times and heartbreaking loss. But we want to thrive, not just survive. That's being a Tullos from start to finish.

We get to the house, and Poole stashes a couple pieces of leftover fried chicken in his pocket. "See ya when I see ya, Lummy dummy. Thanks for having me."

"Let me know if you hear anything."

Poole tips his hat.

Elihu throws a stick at Poole. "Don't be a stranger. Always good to see you, boy."

Poole puts his hand to his mouth like he's drinking from a stone jug. "Just let me know when the muscadine wine is ready."

Elihu laughs. "Grapes of the gods are fallin' from the vines as we speak."

I wave. "Watch your back, boy."

Poole grins and ambles down the road that leads away from our home.

I sit back in Pa's old rocking chair and think about too many things.

Elihu squeezes my shoulder. "I'll leave you to your thoughts." He knows me too well.

Evening passes quietly, and I sit still, but thoughts race through my head like so many flashing ribbons, each one a different color. I can see what memory or pressing piece of business each ribbon represents. I joggle my head like a salt shaker to make it stop. It doesn't.

"Lord, I need a rest—of every kind."

Martha peeks out the cabin door with a smile that always makes my heart leap. "Thinking too hard again, dear?"

"Yeah, when I do, I get those little outbursts I have from time to time. I just can't seem to get some things out of my head. You know, the fight at Vicksburg, taking down Dawg Smith and killing Lester, my hitch with the 1st Mississippi Mounted Rifles, and—"

"It's okay." She sits on my lap and rubs my furrowed brow. "The children are all tucked in. Come to bed now, you've had a long day."

"I will, but I've got too many things on my mind. Be there directly, sweetheart."

"Don't be long, Columbus."

A whippoorwill's call echoes across the empty ridges. A deer browses on corn left in the field after harvest. A shooting star pierces the darkness just long enough to find its home.

I'm home.

An owl flies up into the tall pine next to the barn and asks, "Who?"

I chuckle. "Me. That's who."

It'll be a long time before the effects of the war are lost on me. So much has changed, but the two things that have kept me steady are the love of my family and the peace of working our land. Many times I stopped plowing or harvesting to gaze up at the Tullos cemetery on the hill above the house, reminding myself of where I came from and who I am, Columbus Nathan Tullos. There's also been too many times when I've looked across the field and seen thousands of soldiers charging at me like they did in Vicksburg. It's then I have those uncontrollable fits. Doc Lamb said they should go away. They haven't. And they seem so real. I can't control them. It makes me afraid of what I might do. Of what I'm capable of doing.

Coming home hasn't been as easy as I thought it'd be. War nightmares, farm worries, and the dread of another fight coming have all taken their toll on my nerves. It's hard to sleep. One good thing though, I have nowhere to go but right here. I guess I'm finally becoming a "Pict of the settling kind" like Grandpa Temple used to say. I've not had such a strong desire to be settled since before Susannah died. It's taking longer to find the peace I had growing up in these hills. But it'll come. I want to stay in this place. I will stay in this place—for now.

Grandpa Temple once said, "Sometimes you have to go far away to find yourself so you can come back home." I did go far away, but now I'm back. I crossed a great river once to find peace, love, family, and home, but I brought back a more troubled heart. Maybe I'll find it at the end of a cotton row or on the next ridge chasing a squirrel. My body has returned to the hills. I need my heart to catch up with it. Martha has become my guiding angel to lead me back home.

I look into the starry night and whisper, "Thank you, my Creator. You are everything you promised to be and so much more. Help me to be that to my family, too, Lord."

I wait for a moment to let my soul catch its breath. I find the moon rising above Tullos cemetery hill. I wonder. Is my son Elzey gazing at the same moon rising in Winn Parish? "Lord, let my son Elzey know he's loved. I pray he one day understands that his life is better for having a home there." I pray I made the right decision. I guess that thought will plague me the rest of my life. Maybe I'll see him again, if that's the right and best thing to do.

The air smells musty thick, like the odor of dead and dying leaves pulled back in search of fishing worms. But now, with cotton picking almost over, and life with Martha and the kids blooming, it's time to set my heart on the good things.

AS I HAND out tow sacks to the family so we can get the last bit of cotton picked, I ponder how 1866 has been a good year to get back some of what has been lost when soldiers, blue and gray alike, once scavenged the countryside. Foraging, as both armies called it, was no more than soldiers given permission to plunder what good folks had stored away for their families. They stole from women and children, old men and cripples, the little they had to survive. I'm thankful my only foraging was relieving a few dead Yanks of some things in Chickasaw Bayou when J.A. and I crossed the Mississippi after Vicksburg surrendered. Those boys had gone on to meet their Maker and didn't need that bit of silver and pistol ammunition anymore. That money saved Annie Fanny's life—mine and J.A.'s, too. Sometimes the Lord provides for our needs in strange ways. We did what we did to live. Everybody did. None of it was right. We were all wrong.

Faces around Choctaw County, once gaunt with hunger and misery, are now lit up with smiles over the best cotton and corn crops and prices in years. It gives a man pride and good feeling to look up into the clear blue sky, wipe the sweat from his brow, and thank the Lord for his family and home. That's all most people want.

PUSHING COTTON DEEPER into my sack to make room for more this morning reminds me of Creator's endless sack of blessings. I just need to keep moving to the next stalk, pluck the gift, and be thankful for what Creator offers. I am. Who wouldn't be? I get to pick cotton in the morning as soon as the sun dries the dew from the bolls. That's all I have to do. I don't have to go anywhere or fight anybody. Now that brings peace to my soul.

I'm home. Where what's left of the Tullos family has returned after four years of blood, death, and separation. Where old life has passed on but won't be soon forgotten. Where men who once fought and killed each other, suffered and bled together, returned home in search of peace. Where women and children suffered the worst but kept home alive when the world tried to destroy it. We men nearly did.

But these past months, home has become a place of new beginnings, where hope is strengthened in the scream of a newborn baby. Where family members love and respect each other and simply try to make a day. Where care, honesty, and simplicity command value over chasing after the wind of status and possession. It's where laughter is heard instead of crying.

Home is more than just surviving. It's thriving in the living. Home covers a family in peace like a warm patchwork quilt on a frosty winter's night.

The war ended over a year ago, and though things are slow to recover, we Tullos folk work hard to put our lives back together. We still have the land to farm. Better than that, we have our family. Had it not been for Uncle Rube's treasure, as we all secretly called it, our farm might have been snatched away just for the taxes. The northern bastard carpetbaggers slither around trying to swallow up every farm they can from good honest folk for pennies on the dollar. Talk about not being right. I stand up and announce, "Sneaky snaky bastards anyway."

Young John A., Martha's oldest, who's starting becoming a good farmer in his own right, stands up and asks, "You say somethin', Pop?"

Elihu hits me in the back with a dirt clod. "You better hope Martha don't find out."

I grin and shake my head. "Nothin', John. Just keep on pickin'. We'll take a water break here in a bit." I whisper, "Sorry, Lord, I'm trying to curb my cussin'." We finish the row and rest under the old oak tree Pa used to sit under after a long day in the fields.

I take out the last coin from Uncle Rube's treasure. The rest we used to get the farm back in shape and help who we could. Every dollar we shared with other folks was worth the giving for the friendships we've made and renewed. Most folks are pushing gray and blue from their minds, but some, like Captain Tom Ford, won't let the war end. I don't know that his crazed mind will let him. Forget that hellion for now. I chuckle at a memory of Uncle Rube.

I hand the coin to John A. "That cheap ole moonshiner is still saving people." Then I pray, "Lord, I know Uncle Rube was so tight, I believe he would skin a flea for its tallow. Bless him with a hundred fold return for his gift to our family and others."

John A. agrees. "Amen." He studies the gold double eagle. "Pop, I wish I could've known him."

"Me, too, son. Me, too."

John A. hands the coin back.

Elihu throws a stick at John A., laughing. "Yeah, and I wish I had some of that fine, clear, burn the hair off your tongue moonshine whiskey Uncle Rube was famous for."

I throw a rock at Elihu, who dodges it and sticks his tongue out. "You just hold there for a bit. His nephews, John and Henry, will have a batch made soon enough when we get a load of corn to 'em."

Elihu crows like a rooster. "And not a minute too soon. I truly do like to get my corn from a jar."

John A. looks at Elihu, then me. "You know y'all are all crazy, don't you?"

Elihu puffs out his chest. "And gettin' better at it every day."

I laugh. "Amen, brother, amen."

At day's end the ladies lay out a feast fit for a king and offer the sweetest company a man could ever wish for. I finish before the others and take my coffee out to the porch.

I think of the words inscribed on Uncle Rube's gravestone. Earth has no sorrow that heaven cannot heal. I wonder what sorrow Uncle Rube had so great only heaven could heal it. A lost fortune, good friend, or maybe a forbidden love never truly experienced? No matter, where he is now, I someday want to be. But for now, my heaven is here, on this farm with Martha and the family. I've never been happier or more at peace. I need to let it heal me now. I look into the darkness, where I can almost see his eyes blinking like stars. "Thanks, Uncle Rube."

I breathe in rhythm with the rocking of the chair. I think about how much fun it has been working with my brothers Elihu, Jasper, and James in the field this year. It's just like old times, except for a few people missing.

I doze in and out. I can hear voices. "Lummy, get your ass to pickin', or I'm gonna put one of these cotton stalks to it!"

I call out from my dream, "Pa?" but drift off again, wishing he was still with us. I look around and realize where I am and whisper, "Pa, I miss you."

Soon my head bobs like a fishing cork, and I slip into another dream about us working in the field like I'm living in it now. I hear laughing and joking of grown men who sound like a bunch of young boys in a cotton field. Elihu throws a dirt clod that bursts into a cloud of dust on the side of my head. Jasper and James fall to the ground laughing.

I crawl like a raccoon to get at him. "Why you sorry, lazy, son of a...." I drop my sack and tackle Elihu between the cotton rows. We wrestle like two boys fighting over the last piece of fried chicken at a dinner on the ground at church. John A. and Seth stand up, not knowing what to think about us, but join in the fray. Jasper and James dog pile us, and we tussle around until we're all out of breath. Martha, Jasper's wife Isabel, Ma, and the kids come running, thinking there's a fight.

Someone at the bottom of the pile cries out, "Let me out, I can't breathe!"

Elihu and I yank young Seth up by his armpits, choking and gasping for air. The rest of the family crowds around. Ma puts her hands on her hips. Martha and Isabel follow suit.

"You boys ain't never gonna grow up! I ought'a take a willow switch to your backsides right now. If your pa was here, he'd—" Ma stops like she ran into a wall.

"He'd take that old leather strap and thrash the daylights out of us," James says, laughing.

"Then we'd all bow our necks and get back to work!" Elihu says, sounding just like Pa.

Ma has gone off to some year far away in the past.

I put my arm around her shoulder. "You don't have to go back there to find Pa. He's here."

She smiles faintly and walks up to the house praying, "Them's some fine boys you fathered, Archibald. We couldn't have had better sons. Tell Ben, Amariah, and George what I said. Don't forget Saleta. Lord, I miss 'em all."

With Ma back up at the house, I toss a crumbly dirt clod in a high arch. It lands squarely on top of Elihu's head. It explodes like a cannon shell. And the tussle is back on, including the children. Martha and Isabel just watch, shaking their heads. It's a good dream I don't want to wake from. It's everything I wanted in my new life.

I wake with a start to Martha tugging on my arm. "I must've been dreamin'." I tell her the dream.

"That was no dream, my dear Columbus. That happened just yesterday."

"I guess you could say it's a dream come true then, huh?"

"It was a good time for all of us." Martha brushes the hair back from my forehead. "It sure beats wiping the sweat from your brow after one of your nightmares."

"I am gettin' better, you think?"

"I do."

I get on my knees, and Martha follows suit.

"Thank you for the healin', Lord. And for makin' us a family again."

# CHAPTER 2

# RELEARNING WHAT FAMILY MEANS

## MID-SEPTEMBER 1866

*Becoming family is like shuckin' corn.*
*Once you've done it, you don't forget how.*

COTTON PICKING IS almost done. Soon we'll enjoy "the fruits of our labors," as Pastor Dobbs preached last Sunday at Mt. Pisgah Baptist Church. The Lord gave us good weather throughout the harvest season, and I'm grateful. I spent many cold and rainy gray days and dark nights standing guard in Vicksburg with the 27th Louisiana Infantry. Riding with Grierson on his Winter Raid and the patrols after with the First Mississippi Mounted Rifles wasn't very pleasant either. If it wasn't wet and cold, then it was hot enough to burn the hair off the top of your head. Sarge used to say even the best of soldiers have the right to bitch and moan sometimes. I've got nothing to complain about now. Working all day on our farm in the cool air under a warm sun is a welcome relief from those days. But I won't forget them.

With the war behind us, we're back to the simple life of reaping and sowing. It's the farming life I dreamed about during my years of soldiering—working with my own two hands on my own land and no one telling me what to do, where to go, or when, except maybe Martha. That I don't mind. And nobody shoots at me—at least not yet. I take a deep breath and let out a long, contented sigh.

I scan the farm, taking stock of the work ahead of us. The corn crop still isn't what it used to be. But how could it, with Elihu having little to no help in the fields while we were all away? Good thing the Wood boys came around when they could. Elihu couldn't have got the seed in the ground and the crop out of the field by himself. I need to thank them and talk them out of a jug of their moonshine. Those Wood boys may be mean, but any one of them would give you the shirt off his back in a blowing sleet storm. Had it not been for Seth's help, too, when I left to enlist in the Rifles, the family would've been the worse for it. They could only manage a corn crop, but that kept food on the table and put a little money in their pockets. With the cotton fields left fallow during the war, no wonder the stalks grew chest high full of blooms this year. The soil replenished itself. Working the farm with my family replenishes my soul.

Working with my brother Ben in Winn Parish on Mr. Gilmore's farm seems like a lifetime ago. So much has happened since then. The last time I worked this farm, I broke ground with my pa and brothers just before I left on my search for Susannah.

The dew burns off early this morning. As I take my cotton sack to the field to pluck the big white bolls, I can't help but say, "Lord, thank you."

Elihu and Seth did a fine job getting the corn crop in and out just before Martha, the kids, and I arrived in Choctaw County last year from Vicksburg. With Jasper, James, and me back, putting a cotton crop last spring came just at the right time, or we'd all have been in the poorhouse. With this year's cotton crop doing well and all of us working hard, the year coming, 1867, will be the year we get back on our feet.

Ma, Mary, and Emaline have welcomed Martha and her daughter Margaret into the family like they've always been part of it. I expected no less. Working together to provide meals, homespun for clothing, a clean home, a kitchen garden, and putting vegetables and meats up in jars has brought these women into a fellowship enjoyed by family who love each other.

Martha's sons, always under foot, are a blessing to Ma especially. The children give us all hope for a bright future. Isabel, Jasper's wife, moved in with us not long after we arrived. Isabel had stayed with her aging folks, Jack and Nancy Ray, during the war to help them out. They've passed on now, and the little they left Jasper and Isabel has helped keep us going.

The small dogtrot cabin Pa built still stands strong, but once again is packed like it was when I was growing up. Food is served, and seats are taken wherever a body can find a place around the table or main room. At nightfall, children sleep on pallets that cover the floor, and adults rest on both sides of the hallway. Seth and Elihu moved into the barn to make room for everyone, but more so to find a peaceful night's sleep away from crying children and endless good conversation among the women rattling around pots and pans and taking care of their duties.

Times are still hard, but good people working together survive even better. Pooling our money and labor means none of us have very much, but what we have, we all have it together. Good thing about it, most people in the county don't know the difference because they're in as bad or worse shape as us. I've learned though that happiness, even in the worst of times, is not what you have but who you're with. The war taught me that.

Jasper and Isabel are like two young newlyweds, disappearing when no one's looking, and always call each other little love names like "Angel" or "Honey." I guess I could learn a little bit from them. I'm just glad he made it home to be with her. James, too, though he's yet to become attached in the marital way. It'll take some time for us to get over George not coming home to his Sarah. I think about Amariah, dying of his wounds just up the road in Pensacola, and his sweet wife Amanda passing soon after. People say she died of the pneumonia, but Ma says it was from a broken heart. Amanda really loved that boy. Time is the only healer of such things. Some things for me didn't get the time to heal. But I can't linger on those thoughts. There are too many good things I can turn my mind to now, which Martha reminds me of often. Living with loss had become too much a part of my life before I met her. It just doesn't seem to want to leave my heart. That needs to change.

Little Mary, who is little no more, has become a fine young teacher, having completed her eighth year of schooling. She's worked hard these past weeks getting John A. and Margaret ready for fall school attendance, brushing them up on the three Rs every day. Little James scoots around the farm everywhere and is as nearly impossible to catch as the chickens he chases. And little two-year-old William does all he can to keep up with his brother. Martha's kids have gone to calling me Pop. I like that.

Everyone's found a place in this new family in this new world after the war, except Seth. He sits back sometimes and admires how a family that's gone through so much can still have a good frame of mind. He seems restless though, and I know what that's about.

Seth and I walk up to the well for a cup of well water. He drains his cup and wipes the sweat from his brow. "I sure am learning about how family life ought to be. I've never seen it like this, so much heartache but so much resilience."

James cuts him off, "Resil... what?"

I laugh. "It means to recover well from difficulties, you ignert ass. If you hadn't played hooky from school all them times, Miss Stansbury just might have learned you somethin'. Get back to work before your head explodes like a thunder barrel at Vicksburg."

James stops his corn shelling and leans back on the side of the wagon. "Oh, yeah, Miss Stansbury." His mind disappears into some boyhood dream. "Miss Stansbury. Whew, I sure liked watchin' her write letters and numbers on the blackboard. I especially liked it when she cleaned the chalk off, workin' back and forth, when everything went to wigglin'. Like Pa used to say, 'That poor boy's got a bad case of the red rooster.'"

We laugh, but I hold my hand up. "Young ears, brother, and do pay Miss Stansbury more respect than that."

James nods, grinning. "She was a beauty though, wasn't she, Lummy?"

"Still is and ain't married yet, I hear. You know she's only a couple years ahead of us. At our age now, nobody cares about a four or five year gap between people thinkin' about marriage. Might be somethin' to ponder, little brother."

James scratches his chin slowly. "Might just be, but you know what they say about the best teachers, don't you?" I shake my head. "Married to their work."

I pop him on the shoulder. "Yeah, I've heard the same words said about farmers, too."

I like being with my brothers. It's like old times. I like the good hard work, too. It frees the soul to let the heart swell at day's end when a man can see what he's accomplished. Good work sweats out bad memories. Always has for me.

I like that we work hard and talk little. It's a Tullos thing, I guess. Though I have a thousand things going through my head and talk out loud too much, I don't miss the constant human braying that only stopped when nightfall shut soldier's mouths in camp. Pa avoided common general conversations, calling it worthless idle talk. But when we did talk, it was good.

Corn shelling and cotton picking is done for the day. The sun sinks low in the west. I step up on the porch to sit in Pa's old rocking chair that Grandpa Temple gave him on his last visit to Choctaw County. I rest content for a moment in its familiarity. I wish Pa was here. I close my eyes and see him "gee hawing" the mules breaking ground for a new crop. We had some good times, and the rest? I just push the bad memories out and let the Devil have them back. It's where they need to stay.

A voice begins a familiar old hymn far up on Tullos cemetery hill. Elihu breaks into a sweet tenor version of "Amazing Grace." He usually sits with his back against the cypress marker I carved for Pa's grave. I know he misses Pa, too. The firstborn always does, even more so sometimes I think.

Pa and I were different in some ways but much alike others. That's not all bad. Had he not been so hard on us, I'd probably still be in the bottom of the pit in Vicksburg. Dead. It doesn't excuse his behavior, but bad experiences can prepare a man for worse ones. Pa's hardness certainly prepared me for difficult men.

The old rocker creaks and bumps the floor with every see saw back and forth. It's a comforting sound I've heard thousands of times that reminds me of everything I should be thankful for in this world. It revives memories that must be handed down to children who need to look back and know who, and whose, they are. Too many children's fathers, brothers, cousins, and uncles died fighting each other for causes on faraway battlefields soon to be forgotten. I won't let mine ever forget. Martha's children must know their father Henry died for them in a war not of his choosing… or making.

Each forward rocking motion, I send a bad thought from my soul to a place that soon will be sealed along with the one who caused the havoc and destruction in the first place. That's not Pa, Ben, or even Dawg Smith or Lester. No, that credit goes to the Evil One himself. There's been a place prepared for him.

An abyss I hear, and that's where I send the worst of my past so my future can take hold. With every backward motion, I breathe in the goodness and mercy of the Lord. With every forward rocking of the chair, I breathe out the anger and violence of Satan. My soul is cleansed, at least for tonight.

Elihu continues his song up on the hill, the words floating through the trees over the farm like the smell of good pine resin in the breeze. I see Pa's face in a cloud. And I have compassion.

The same compassion I offer my pa, I must now find for myself and for all I've done. Sometimes I have to force myself to accept how lost I was, but also accept the grace that helped me find myself again.

I think about the words Elihu sings. I have come through many dangers, toils, and snares, and by God's grace I've made it this far. It was grace that brought me home, and it'll be grace that will keep me home. The Lord has promised good to me, and I believe his Word will secure me. I lay my life in the hands of the One who will be my shield and provider, as long as my life endures.

Elihu starts the song again from the beginning, but I have enough to put my thoughts and memories in their proper places. I have peace.

Yellow and red leaves sweep through the trees like a soft falling rain, dancing here and there in the chilly breeze. As light gives way to shadow, I pen a poem.

*Even the best of memories fall to the ground,*
*Like sunlit leaves in the fall.*
*They become part of the earth once more,*
*And there they shall lie, to sweeten the land.*

# CHAPTER 3

# HOME IS IN
# THE HILLS

## LATE SEPTEMBER, 1866

*Where does a man live when his name means "hill," except on a hill?*

MA OPENS THE door and hands me a steaming hot tin cup of leather-brown coffee, lightened with fresh cream from old Lucy the milk cow, and sweetened with honey from Elihu's bee hives. She sits in her chair and rocks in time with me. It's a quiet togetherness that hill people truly appreciate. She hands me a yellowed, worn envelope that bears a postmark of some faded date that ends with 1844. It's from Marion County, where Grandpa Temple, Granny Thankful, and their son, Uncle Silas, lived and died.

"It's from your Grandpa Temple. You know how he loved to tell his stories. You're the one to make sure they don't die with us, son." Memories flash through my mind—Grandpa telling of our ancestors painted blue in the hills of Scotland, Granny Thankful giving me the agate that held my soul true many a day, and wondering what it was like when Uncle Silas fought the British at New Orleans.

I nod, gently folding back the flaps. This is a treasure to be handled carefully with contents that surely will bring light to the past.

Ma pats my arm. "You sat with Grandpa like a baby bird with his mouth open waiting for momma bird to drop in a fresh worm, except for you, it was a new story. You hung on to every word."

"It was his stories about our ancestors that kept me going in the Vicksburg trenches, and with Grierson on the raid. Naming my horse Cloud kept them always in the front of my mind. They keep me on the right road, even now."

"Granny Thankful always thought you'd be the one to carry on the family history. So this is yours now, son."

The pages are faded, but the ink remains in remarkably good shape and readable. "Grandpa Temple wrote that letter to your Pa."

*Marion County, Mississippi*
*March 1844*

*Dear Nephew Archibald,*

    *My time is not long for this earth. I do not feel well these days, but who should expect to at 94 years? I've had a good life, and I am thankful for all God has blessed me with. I want to ensure that the story of our people is not lost on me. My son Silas writes this letter in hopes that you will teach your children about where they come from and who their people were. Silas will do the same.*

    *Archy, you must know where you've been to know where you are, so you can know where you're going. And you know how I love to tell my stories. This will be my last letter. I hope you saved the others I sent through the years. They include all the Tullos tales from the old country told by Grandpa Claudius and others handed down to us. It's a good history, Archy, and you should be proud to be a Tullos, no matter how hard your father was on you, son. Your own family would make any father proud. I'm sorry that Willoughby never gave you his blessing and approval before you left for Choctaw County. I guess even he could use a little mercy now. Find it in your heart for him, son, and say a prayer.*

    *As you know, the Tullos family came to Virginia from Scotland across the ocean in 1661. Claudius, nicknamed Cloud, was just a young man but an industrious one. All of that you have in the letters I mailed earlier.*

    *You have probably asked yourself why we Tullos people tend to settle and feel more at home in the hills. When we settled in the Natchez District of the Mississippi territory back in '11, I wanted live in the hills and bot-*

*toms of Wilkinson County near Fort Adams your Pa visited in 1805. You saw that land when you were just a chap. But your father pushed for us to join him in Pike County after he left Amite County in 1810. We came a long way from Duplin, North Carolina through Effingham, Georgia, to get there. But it's been a good home. Ole Willoughby's wandering foot would've gotten the best of him had it not been for your sweet momma, Anna. I can't say anything, I was right behind him.*

*Archy, that burning desire to live in the hills comes natural because many years ago the Tullos name was spelt Tulloch, which sprung from the old Gaelic word tulach, meaning hillock, or mound. We came from a place named Tulloch on the Firth of Cromarty in a vale that lies between Tullos Hill and Torry Hill. So you see, our Creator begat us in the hill country of Scotland near the River Dee, and we've been drawn to hills and rivers ever since. I have no more than that nephew, but this knowledge may shed some light to help you understand who you are and why our people move and settle often, and need hills and rivers to be at home.*

*I know these tales are not very important to you, Archy. So I ask that you give all my letters to your son Lummy at the right time, when he's old enough to appreciate their value. He's the most interested. Oh, and don't forget to tell him about our pa-in-law, Captain James Mills, who fought in the Revolution. Those Mills, they were good people.*

*That's all for now, nephew. Give my love to your sweet wife Mary and your children. I will look for you, nephew, on the other side.*

*Be blessed,*
*Temple Tullos*

I hold in my hand the last letter from the man who was the only grand-father I knew. And that wasn't for very long. I was only ten when he died. Pa's father, Willoughby, died in Simpson County about the time I was born. From what I've heard, I'm better off having never known him. Ma hands me a small tin box, and I lift the lid to find ten or more faded envelopes with letters inside. I flip through the stack, realizing that in my hands I hold all the stories I heard from Grandpa Temple that have shaped my life. I will read and preserve each one carefully. My heart swells at the thought of being the keeper of the Tullos family history.

Ma snickers and pats me on the back. "Son, you're gonna need somebody to pass this on to."

I wink. "Guess we'll have to go to work on that. Martha's already told me she wants children of our own."

"I can always use more grandchildren around. Don't wait too long. I ain't gettin' any younger, you know."

I lean back in my chair staring at the box and marvel at the value of what I hold in my hands. Little William cries out in his bed.

"I best go see about that crying child. You let the words in those letters lead your mind to wander wherever it chooses. Read them and let pictures be painted in your soul. That's where they need to rest.  Those are the stories that will anchor you in the here and now."

Martha steps out on the porch and stares into fading light, leaning on a porch post. "I'm tired, Lummy. Think I'll turn in."

"I'll be there in a bit. I want to look through these letters."

"Who are they from?"

"The only Grandpa I ever knew, Temple, my real grandfather's brother. Uncle Silas, the one I told you about, he did the writin'."

"The one who fought with Andy Jackson at New Orleans?"

"The very same."

"Your Ma says you favor him, looks and height."

"Yeah, I've been told that all my life."

"What about your real Grandpa? Your Pa's father."

"He may have been blood kin, but he was no grandfather of mine, dammit."

"I didn't mean to upset you, dear."

"I'm sorry, Martha. It's just that he treated slaves really bad, not to mention his children, too. Even Uncle Silas threatened to whoop Willoughby one time about his breeding cages. Remember me telling you about sweet old Miss Lucille who used to put black pepper on my popcorn? That bastard put her in there over and over so she would give him more slave children."

Martha shivers in anger. "Who's in the cage now, Willoughby?"

"I'd rather not talk about all that right now, if you don't mind."

"Sorry, ain't mine to judge what God does with such men."

"Anyway, somebody needs to write these stories down."

"Maybe Mary? She's the scholar of the family."

"Yeah, maybe someday. I just want to breathe them in for now."

Martha kisses my forehead. "Don't be long, dear. Cotton pickin' comes soon as the dew dries in the morning."

"Be there in a bit."

I scan the shadowy ridges. An owl calls to her young ones to come home. The hills called to me, and I came home.

# CHAPTER 4

# HILL PEOPLE

*A man only truly lives where he was created.*

I T'S THE SAME day Susannah was murdered. Ben and Mr. Gilmore, too, for trying to get her back from Dawg Smith. I shudder at the thought of what I had to do to make that right. I try to make myself believe it was a reckoning. It came real close to revenge. I couldn't find solace anywhere when I found out what really happened—that she didn't die of the measles, but by the bastard hand of Dawg Smith. I found no solace, no pleasure in taking Dawg Smith's head using the knife my angry pa made for me when I was but a young man. Pa's anger and violence sure taught me to be unafraid to use it. Only coming back to the hills might bring me any semblance of peace.

I stand up and yell, "Enough of this!" Fortunately, thunder in the west covers my outburst. I return in my mind to Grandpa's stories.

It was always about the hills. Grandpa Temple Tullos said we never were meant to be flatlanders. We sprung from the coastal country of Scotland in a vale between the two hills. He said we were created there. It isn't surprising that Cloud planted himself in the same kind of coastal hills in Virginia's Northern Neck country. He bought and sold land, served as a constable, and worked a thriving cobbler's business and trained apprentices. He even led the building of a new road through the wilderness for settlers. I wish I could've known him. Someday I will.

My life has been defined and shaped by hills as well. Born in the hills of Holmes County, I grew up in these in Choctaw County. That's why Winn

Parish, Louisiana, didn't disappoint me too much. Though the land favored gently rolling hills over the sometimes steep small mountain terrain here, I still felt like I was in Tulach country. Ben's family working Mr. Gilmore's farm and Susannah being there helped.

After my Confederate Army training at Camp Moore, I defended the "city set upon a hill that can't be hidden," Vicksburg. I decided to join the 1st Mississippi Mounted Rifles leaning on my pa's grave marker up on Tullos Cemetery hill. I proposed to Martha in Annie's café on Sky Parlor Hill, a favorite overlook in Vicksburg. I guess we Tullos folk are born with hills in our blood, only happy living in the hills, and will only rest in peace best if buried on a hill.

I sift through the letters in the small tin box. I wonder. Do other people want to know about their ancestors and such things so they can learn who they are? I doubt most people even care. That's why they can find little direction and hope in a world set on fire. Though my life has never traveled in a straight line, these stories have been like pegs in the ground to hold the tent of my life steady in storms that come. Grandpa's stories kept me going in the right direction in my worst moments. They still do. They give my life direction, even now. It's in the hills. It's in my soul.

I believe Creator can pass down things inside us, like my love for the hills from ancestors, in the same way Grandpa Temple handed down the family stories. How can a man feel comfortable anywhere but where God created him in the first place? It's not just having two feet planted on any specific piece of ground. No, it's having your soul set firmly in a place with those who Creator gives you, and where that is. For me, that's Choctaw County, Mississippi.

Traipsing around in the flatlands of the Louisiana delta after the Vicksburg surrender, I never felt comfortable or could get my bearings. If I didn't know how to get my direction from the sun, I would've stayed turned around all the time. Cloudy days made it nearly impossible to navigate. Had it not been for the railroad tracks from Desoto to Shreveport when I left to find Susannah, I never would've found Winn Parish.

That's not true. I would've found Susannah at any cost.

I meditate on the poem I wrote while on the sandbar last year about the wisdom of a great old tree. One line reads, "A great old tree stays where the Lord plants it." My soul is planted in hills, and I want to stay in these hills, our hills, for good. I'm becoming less of a Celt of the moving kind and more of a blue painted Pict of the settling kind. Funny thing though, Martha still won't let me paint myself blue and dance naked around a fire deep in the woods like Grandpa Temple used to tell it. I guess that's more about who you are than what you do. I still might need to do that one day though, in honor of my ancestors, or in preparation for defending them.

My place is in the hills.

In the hills I will live, and on a hill I want to be buried.

But not just yet.

## CHAPTER 5

# POOLE COMES
# FOR A VISIT

### EARLY NOVEMBER 1866

*Old friends are always welcome, even if they bring bad news.*

"NO, POOLE, I ain't heard much of what's goin' on around the county. I've kept my head down and hands to the plough, so to speak. Ma and Elihu just wanted me to get settled first. You know, get the war out of my head. It's takin' longer than I'd hoped, but every day I get better. At least Martha says so."

Poole nods and sips a cool cup of moonshine as we scan the farm from the front porch. The smell of Martha's cooking wafts over us like honeysuckle in springtime.

Poole shifts in his rocking chair. "I guess it can take some time to get your head on straight after all that's happened. What's it been, year and a half now since we mustered out?"

"Yep, June 26, 1865, a date I'll never forget."

"This shine sure is good."

I nod, swishing the smooth moonshine around in my mouth, savoring its flavor. "What is that faint flavor I taste? Wonder what the Wood boys put in this, blackberry maybe?"

Poole leans over and whispers, "Had any more outbursts lately?"

"I really don't want to talk about it, but sometimes. They come and go."

"That's all right, my folks are doin' the same with me. They're just glad I didn't go through what you did in the war, Lummy. You know me, I don't know if my soul could've taken it."

We sit still for moment.

"Can you stay and eat, maybe the night? Sure have missed you, boy."

"And swing my feet under your momma's table again? Hell yeah, I'll stay."

"Well, it ain't Ma's kitchen no more. Ma's been good to slide over for Martha and Jasper's wife, Isabel, to do the cooking now. You know Martha can cook up vittles like nobody's business." I smile. "But Ma Tullos won't have it any other way when it comes time to make her blackberry cobbler. There just ain't none made better nowhere."

"Ain't that the truth?" He pauses to drain his cup. "She ain't sick, is she?"

"No, just a lot of years catchin' up, that's all."

"We'll all get there someday, won't we?"

I backhand him on the shoulder. "I'm just glad we lived to get the chance."

We sit still for a moment again. Poole fidgets. "I want to ask about—"

"I just soon not talk about my son Elzey right now."

Poole takes in a deep breath. "Too hard to talk about?"

"Yeah, kind of. I bounce back and forth like a ball on a billiard table feeling either guilty or that I did the right thing leaving him in Choctaw County. I guess I could go get him."

Poole looks around for any young listening ears. "Probably not a good time to do that, Lummy. Things ain't goin' too good around here right now. In fact, they'll get worse before they get better."

"What do you mean?"

"Surely you've heard about some of the meanness goin' on the county. I know it's happenin' other places, too. At least the newspapers say so, but we live here. And we want Choctaw County to be a good place to live. A place where a man can raise his family and work his farm, or whatever he takes up to do to make a livin'."

I shrug it off like it's no concern of mine. "All I've been tryin' to do is get this farm back in shape. I ain't even been to town. I've caught a few things through the grapevine, but so? What's it to us?"

Poole shifts in his seat. "Things have been brewin' since we left for the Rifles back in '64. Yeah, the men who had power durin' the war are becomin' the powers to be again. You remember ole H.D. Stone, Captain of the Home

Guard in Greensborough? The man couldn't find his boots in a shit storm that morning we burned the town!" I nod. Poole shakes his head. "Can you believe it? The bastard ran for state senator October last year and won. So you know where his temperaments lie."

"With the rest of the ne'er-do-wells who hold to a Lost Cause, which is no cause no more, you're sayin'?"

"Yeah, and Sheriff Platner lost the race to that hard ass Carlson Lindsey in the October election at Greensborough. When court came into session last March, the new Lost Cause sheriff and the circuit clerk resigned their offices on openin' day just to break up court. Judge Cothran had to appoint Major Peery sheriff and Richard Nolin clerk pro tem, as they call it. That means temporary, I think."

I grimace at the news. "I hate to hear that about Sheriff Platner. He said nothin' about that when he showed up at the family funeral last year. Told me he was thinkin' about retirin'."

"Not after Tom Ford almost shot you down last year at the funeral celebration. He ran again saying he may be tired and old, but he's still spry as a turkey gobbler in the springtime. The bucket headed Lost Cause bastards runnin' around in red shirts got him voted out. But he's still around, if you know what I mean."

I sip a little more of my moonshine. "I do."

"Lummy, things are growin' dark when they should be gettin' brighter by the day." He looks around like someone could be listening. "You know they ain't still sure who burned down the Greensborough Courthouse. Nobody's figured it out yet."

"Yeah, Elihu told me when I got back. He said it might have been some arsonist who'd robbed the county of several thousand dollars, or somethin' like that." I kick my foot out and stomp the floor. "And after all we did to keep Captain Beckwith from burnin' that beautiful old brick building. Damn, what a fine piece of architecture. And all those county records lost, hell, I don't even want to think about that."

"At least we didn't do it, and copies of some of that stuff had been sent to the government offices in Jackson through the years, so not all was lost."

I shrug and pour Poole another couple of fingers of moonshine.

Poole raises his cup. "Thanks, this is good stuff. Wood boys can sure turn out a jar, can't they?" I nod, and he takes a sip. "But that ain't the worst of it. Somethin's brewin', and it ain't gonna be good." He catches me up on more happenings around the county. Living close to the county seat of Greensborough, he hears all the news I wish he didn't have to tell me.

Poole drains his cup. "Back in May, the *Jackson Clarion Ledger* reported that there are two warring factions in our county, the Fee Gees and the Hyenas. The Hyenas are led by the new Sheriff Lindsey and that clerk Morehead, the ones who disrupted court that day and want the South to come back alive."

I scratch my head and wonder, "What the hell is a hyena?"

"I did a little checkin' on that, you illiterate son of a... sorry, I'll stop." Poole looks around to see if anybody heard him.

I pound the arm of my chair. "Talkin' out loud again and showin' my ignorance, dammit!"

"Hyenas are heavy-set scavenger dog-like animals with strong jaws and big teeth for tearin' and rippin' their prey. They ain't afraid of nothin', not even a lion. They're a bunch of cowards that get the upper hand by runnin' in packs. Sound familiar?"

Now I remember Old Bart saying something about them. "Yeah, just like Dawg Smith and Captain Tom Ford."

Poole turns his cup up trying to get one last drop of moonshine. "You can bet that's the demon bunch Ford runs with. Dan Creekwater told me at the funeral last year, that bastard escaped hangin' a second time. The man's got more lives than a dern cat."

I hold out the jug. "Want some more?"

He shakes his head. "But that still ain't the worst of it. The Loyal League, some of the folks who used to be in the Union Society H.P. Petty used to lead, they ain't actin' any better either. Back in August, they threatened to burn Greensborough, or what's left of it. Why, I don't know. I guess to keep Ford and his bunch from doin' it first. Did you ever know that lawyer William Pollan. He fought with the Union Army."

I scratch my ear. "That name sounds familiar. Didn't he—"

"Yep, he served as a private in the First Mississippi Mounted Rifles, Company A."

"So what, didn't he get enough fightin'?"

"Don't know if he got to fight at all. You know most of them boys only pulled guard duty in Memphis, and maybe went a short patrol or two. You think we ought to go see him?"

"Yeah, maybe. I just hate to hear one of ours is leadin' the pack and that they ain't no better than the Hyenas they're chasin', you think?"

Poole grimaces. "I do, and it's gettin' out of hand."

"How so?"

"Well, seems Pollan and sixty of his bunch fired on Greensborough just the other day, which still bein' the county seat and all, draws all the worst kinds of people. Some ex-soldiers who don't have a way to make a livin' are lookin' for any fight around just to get paid so they can eat. You remember General Whitley, don't you?" I nod. "He persuaded them to leave. Fortunately, they left without doin' any more harm. Whitley wrote Governor Sharkey about it makin' sure to mention that the sheriff was amongst 'em and tried to keep the peace. They didn't arrest anybody."

I turn my head away from what seems to be a growing concern I want no part of.

"There's more. Remember Jason Niles, that lawyer from Quebec?"

"Yeah."

"He's become the loud mouthed welcomed voice of those who still hold to the Lost Cause."

I pour myself another swallow of shine. "He used to be Elihu's friend. That ended when he heard Jason say Captain Tom Ford was the man to run the county and clean it up."

Poole holds out his cup. "Niles has made it his business to report the name of every man returning home who either left for the north to escape serving with the Rebs or joined up with the Yanks during the war. Either way, he's a weasel rat who wants to keep things stirred up."

I don't want to ask, but I do. "And?"

"He mentioned our names, Lummy."

I set my cup down hard and splash my moonshine. "What?"

"He's tellin' everybody we were with the Yanks who burned Bankston and Greensborough. Says he can't prove it, but he's spreadin' the rumor just the same."

"That ain't good. Ain't good at all."

"I know, but it ain't hard to put together who told him."

"Better not let Elihu hear about that. He'd be worse on Niles than I was on Lester. Did Niles say anything else?"

Poole grinds his teeth just a little. "Yeah, Niles said Captain Tom Ford will be springing a surprise on everybody soon. Don't know what it is, but it can't be good."

I spit. "Captain Tom Ford, that son of a...." I catch myself.

Poole continues. "There's more. The same day Pollan's men did their shootin' in Greensborough, six hundred Fourth Wisconsin Cavalry passed through Kosciusko with a large band of ex-slaves. They plundered several homes and offices in town."

I wince. "That's throwin' a can of coal oil on the fire. They shouldn't have done that."

"Funny thing, a squad of the same cavalry unit arrested a mob who robbed Simon's Store in the same town. And just south of here, the good citizens of Louisville hanged a Negro for allegedly burnin' down the hotel. The Loyal League folks said the Negro had nothin' to do with it."

"I guess it don't take much for the law to get broken down when those keepin' the law don't obey it themselves. That surely ain't good for healing."

"You know that the ones who make the laws don't have to keep 'em."

I feel anger creeping up the back of my neck. "Yeah, and the ones who are supposed enforce them make up new ones."

"People are losin' hope, Lummy. They're hurtin'. There'll be whole families who won't make it through winter. Most are still sufferin' from the war. Not everybody is blessed to have land like your family."

"You know...."

Poole holds up his hands. "I know. Y'all have been so good to help everybody you can. It's just that things are gettin' worse and nobody seems to be doin' anything about it except rascals like Captain Tom Ford who still take what little good folks have left. And if that ain't bad enough, several people who just couldn't take it no more over in Attala County went off into the woods and killed themselves outright."

"That's bad," I moan, "That's real bad, when folks get down that low."

"Yeah, it hurts the heart, don't it?"

"How do you know all this?"

"I read the papers and have friends who keep me informed."

I try to lighten the mood. "You ought to get a job bein' a newspaper man yourself." The bit of humor doesn't work. I didn't expect it to.

"It's a thought, but I ain't got neither the skills nor the patience for it." He winks. "Besides, I'd probably get myself killed for tellin' the truth."

I get up and shake off the bad news. "You wouldn't be the first, I'm sure. Meaning no disrespect, the one who said the truth will set you free was killed for tellin' it." I start for the barn.

"Where you goin'?"

"Let's go see an old army friend, even if we didn't know him at the time."

"Heck no, I ain't missin' one of your wife's good dinners!"

I turn around to join him. "You're right. We'll head out tomorrow right after church."

# CHAPTER 6

# AN OLD COMRADE IN ARMS, BUT A NEW FRIEND

## NOVEMBER 11, 1866

*Just because we didn't fight together then,*
*don't mean we can't now.*

A LATE SUNDAY afternoon sun ducks behind the trees on folks who've had a long day at church. My worship at Mt. Pisgah Baptist Church was cut short for the visit Poole and I need to make. We slipped out during the last song before the sermon. I'm sure Pastor Dobbs frowned, but knew we wouldn't leave but for some important reason. I've come to love that brother.

Poole and I watch William Pollan's house for a good half hour for any sign of mischief. A red-headed woodpecker sounds off flying through the woods. He lands on a dead tree to hammer away for that last beetle for his supper. I love that sound. Its call reminds me of why I live in the hills, and why I will protect them.

We ease down the hill through a pine thicket and call out to the house. The front door creaks open, and the barrel of a Sharps Carbine like the one I carried with the Rifles slowly makes its presence known, aimed at our heads.

"Who the hell are you, and what do you want?"

"Friends. Tom Poole and Lummy Tullos. We served with the First Mississippi Mounted Rifles."

Poole cups his hands and yells, "We want to hunt Hyenas. Heard you can help us find some."

He lowers the gun and waves us in. "Any fool unafraid to wear that blue coat around these parts must be a man I can trust."

Poole straightens his uniform jacket. "No fools here, sir. I put it on when we turned our mounts down the lane to your house. We didn't want you mistaking who we are."

"Good enough, but ain't no sirs 'round here, unless you count my old daddy buried in the Greensborough cemetery. I was a private in the Rifles, too, though a little old to enlist. Come in."

We shake hands, and he invites us in by the fire for some coffee. His frail wife creeps into the room with a wooden tray of meat, cheese, and bread. We thank her. After she goes back into the kitchen, I inquire as to her ailment.

Pollan winces like he's in pain. "She got the pneumonia, Doc says. I'm not sure she'll see the New Year." He hangs his head, wiping tears. "We moved here years ago, built this cabin, and worked this land while I ran a lawyer's office in town. We made it through the entire damn war together, me comin' and goin' from time to time, and neither one of us even got a scratch. To think she could die of that. Hell, it just ain't right!"

His anger is justified. I know it firsthand. And there ain't no one to blame and no comfort for the soul.

His wife peeks around the corner with a faint smile. "It'll be all right, husband, don't you worry your head none. The Good Lord has got us all in his mighty hand." She disappears into another part of the house.

He makes sure she's gone. "He might have all of us in his mighty hand right now, but it ain't where I want to be if it's like this!" He shakes his head. We finish our food in silence.

Pollan finally breaks the quiet. "I just know if it wasn't for all them damn Lost Causers, this county could get back on its feet and prosper. It sure ain't what it used to be, but it's still a helluva good place to raise a family and make somethin' of yourself."

I lean up. "Ain't that the truth?"

He peers into my eyes, waiting, so I talk.

"Mistuh Pollan, I'm Lummy Tullos, and this here's Tom Poole, who we just call Poole. We both served with the Rifles in Company C."

Pollan smiles. "You were with the bunch that ran right smack dab into the whole damn Confederate Cavalry with General Wirt Adams in the lead at the Franklin church, weren't you?"

I raise my arms like I'm aiming a rifle. "Would've taken his ugly ass head right off with a fine Sharps Carbine just like your one poked out that door a minute ago, if I'd got the chance."

He looks down at the gun across his lap. "Yep, I had plenty of back pay stored up and a couple hundred dollars bounty owed me, so I brought this deer shooter home with me. Keeps us in meat." He laughs, propping the gun in the corner next to the chair where he sits. "What happened when you came face to face with old General Adams?"

"We tucked tail and hauled ass like a bunch of scalded dawgs. Our lieutenant ordered us to skee-e-edaddle so we could deliver a message from General Grierson to Colonel Osband and his boys. They sure had a heck of a fight at the creek bridge down the hill from the church house."

Pollan chuckles. "Sure did. Them Negro boys whipped Adam's ass and good, though he'd never admit in a hundred years."

Poole shivers with excitement. "Yes sir, it was a sight to see."

Pollan rubs his clean shaven face. "But you didn't come here to tell old war stories, did you?"

"No, sir. We want to know what's goin' around the county and what we need to do to keep our families and homes safe. We heard our names were bein' tossed about with a few accusations. Just figured I could get the straight story from an old comrade in arms."

"You'd be right, son." Pollan's graying hair and eyes bookended with growing crow's feet make him look much older than he is. This man's weathered many a storm in the courtroom and in life.

"Say your name is Tullos?" I nod. "Well, you're already a marked man, son, you got to know that. You, too, Poole. Your names were already reported as bein' back in the county and havin' fought with the Yanks like I did. Hell, it must've been a year ago. That Niles fella has made it his personal business to point us all out. Nosey bastard, ain't he got nothing better to do with himself?" He points his finger at us. "You two best be extra careful. You got a special target painted on your backs."

Poole looks at me with fear in his eyes. "Lummy?"

Pollan leans forward. "They know you two led the Yanks to burn the Bankston mills."

Poole whimpers, "Everybody?"

Pollan turns to Poole with eyes that bespeak concern. "No, just the ones who matter. I'm surprised they haven't come for you already. Guess they're marshalling their forces."

Poole sits back hard in his chair, rubbing his hands together frantically like he's washing them. I've not seen him this scared. His concern is not so much for himself as it is for his aging folks. Captain Tom Ford has already proven he's no respecter of color or age in his violent wanderings. But this won't be some random raid he dreamed up over breakfast. No, this will be a planned expedition, and his target will be us and our families.

I lay my hand on Poole's arm. "We don't have a lot of time to prepare."

He nods that he's okay. "No we don't, Lummy. But we ain't alone, either."

I slap his shoulder and grin. "That's the spirit." My words speak encouragement, but my heart says worry.

"Mistuh Pollan, we both know we'll be targets, which brings us to the point of our visit. If you don't mind me askin', what is it you're tryin' to do in all of this? You've been slap dab in the middle of everything that's goin on."

"Just keepin' the pot stirred, son, that's all." I'm puzzled. "So maybe we'll draw some attention from Jackson City or Washington D.C. I organized a militia and got it approved by the governor. But so did the Hyenas. Can you believe that? A governor sanctions two opposing, and soon to be warring, militias in the same county? Beats all I've ever seen. It's like he wants to start another war right here in Choctaw County." He shakes his head like a kid trying to avoid medicine his mother spoons him.

Poole turns to me. "Sanc... *what?*"

"It means giving official permission, you know, making it legal and all."

Poole squirms in his chair. "What are you going to do, Mistuh Pollan?"

"Not much else I can do with the Lost Cause bastards startin' to get the upper hand. In the meantime, I'm hopin' some of my contacts up north I've been writing will do somethin' to bring law and order back to this county before men like Captain Tom Ford burn it to the ground. I'd kill that sneaky bastard myself if I could catch him. He's slick and slimy as a slithering snake in a grease pit."

Poole stomps his foot. "You're a lawyer. Can't you do somethin' legal like?"

"No need to get riled up, son. Don't you think I've tried? For a man like me who uses the law and his mouth to make a living, I've never felt more helpless. Hell, you heard what happened in court at Greensborough a while back." We nod. "It'll just happen again. The Lost Causers with their damned Hyenas will get control one way or another."

"So you think burnin' down what's left of Greensborough will help?"

"Hell no, but it's somethin'. I know it was wrong, but the Loyal League can't just sit on its ass while all this is going on. When they asked me to lead the Fee Gees, as the Unionists call themselves, I answered the call." He shakes his head. "Hell, I don't even know what Fee Gees means. Somethin' about some island out in the ocean, you think?" We shrug. "Anyway, something had to be done, you understand?"

"Yeah, somethin' that'll get you hanged, I'd imagine," Poole grumbles.

"That ain't gonna happen. I do know my lawyer friend General Whitley wants peace. If it hadn't been for his convincing words that day, we'd probably had an all-out skirmish right there in town." He scratches his ear. "He wrote Governor Sharkey about it. He had to, and mentioned my name for sure. It's gonna be a long time before Choctaw County has any real peace, boys, so you best get about takin' care of your families and farms."

Poole straightens up. "We plan to do just that."

Pollan stands up. "Watch yourselves boys. They'll come for you at some point. Keep a close eye on your Negro friends, too. He'll go after them first, once he's got you pegged. Ain't nothin' Captain Tom Ford hates more'n anything than what he calls an uppity niggah. More than that, he hates white folks who call them friends. But he sure as hell don't mind beddin' a Negro gal when he's a mind to. You boys take care, and let me know how I can help."

We shake hands and mount our horses.

Poole whispers, "He ain't what people say he is. He's just a man who wants to live in peace."

"Yep, him and bunch of others, I'm bettin'."

"I'm countin' on it."

I pat Cloud on the neck, and we disappear into the night.

# CHAPTER 7

# CLAIMING
# A NEW FUTURE

## NOVEMBER 17, 1867

*The future is what you claim, and work hard at gettin'.*

A YEAR HAS passed since we visited William Pollan. His wife didn't make it to see in the New Year. The wind left his sails along with her passing. I pray for anyone who loses loved ones, but more so for those who lose a spouse. It can break a man in half. A big part of who a man is simply disappears and leaves a big hole right in the middle of him. People don't know what that's like until they go through it. I don't want to ever again.

We had a good service at Mt. Pisgah Baptist Church this morning. Pastor Dobbs preached on troubles in the land and prayed for the Good Lord to intervene. There have been a few incidents this past year, but I stay pretty much out of sight and sound of what's happening around the county. Working a farm ensures that. Elihu, Jasper, and James go get supplies and the mail.

Poole attended church service with us today. While I wait by the wagon for Ma and the girls to finish visiting, and James talking honey to the girls, Poole catches me up on the news.

"William Pollan sent me here to tell you that the Hyenas are gatherin' for the fight he told us about last year. He said they'll bring it soon to those who hold steady to their Negroes and the Stars and Stripes. Pollan doesn't know when or where, or even how they will do it, but he said they want to get things boilin' red hot, then get the credit for puttin' out the fire."

I shake my head. "That kind of scheming could put him in power permanent like. What else?"

"Things are gettin' worse. Back in October, that old hothead drunk, Aleck Caldwell, got into it with somebody, and before you know it soldiers were sent out from Greensborough to arrest them both. Caldwell lit out fast as a bat out of hell, but not before they shot him down. Now his left arm's useless."

"I thought the soldiers were only supposed to guard property and such."

"Hell, most of them ain't worth a shit!" Poole covers his mouth and whispers, "Them boys just want an opportunity to shoot somebody, you know, legal like. You know there ain't nothin' easier to start up trouble and enjoy it than a bored soldier."

"That's like throwin' fat pine on a fire that's already burnin' your own cotton house down. They ain't smart enough to know they're cuttin' their own legs off at the knees doin' this." Heads turns our way, and I quiet down.

"That's it, and folks are gettin' antsy. Times seem to be gettin' harder for most folks. Even though crops in the county have been good, there's still people who can't rub two half-dimes together." He's getting upset, too. I pull him around the back side of the wagon out of sight, and hopefully sound.

"The *Jackson City Clarion Ledger* reported that almost a thousand people in this county alone are on the poor house rolls and gettin' help from the government. That's just pathetic. Hard workin' people don't want a handout. They want good hard work and fair prices for their labor, that's all. And the Negroes only want a fair shake at what any good human bein' wants in this world."

I point my finger at him. "And they have to work ten times harder than we do to get it."

Poole turns red in the face. "Ain't that the damn truth? What the war didn't take then, the damn ruffians like Captain Tom Ford take now. Thievin' sons of—" He stops short. "Oh... sorry, I forgot I was in front of the church house."

Elihu waves his arms and calls everyone back over where Pastor Dobbs makes a passionate plea for the needy as the deacons pass around the collection basket. Few have any money to put in like us, but our family pledges a wagon load of corn to grind for cornmeal and grits. Mr. Allrice and Momma Sophie donate several hams and turkeys, and offer to smoke any meat brought them free of charge to help the poor. Others in the congregation make similar offers, and the deacons promise to spread the goods out fairly.

We load up the women and children for home. Poole waves as he helps his aging folks into their wagon. I need to think more on the news he brought today.

After a Sunday dinner of deer roast, potatoes and carrots, gravy and biscuits, topped off with one of Martha's huckleberry pies, we men step out into the yard this chilly but sunny afternoon. We lean on the split rail fence that surrounds the yard. Elihu lights up his pipe. I look across the field and into the sky to praise Creator for another good crop year. And then I pass the jug to my brothers as we celebrate.

We talk about this year's crops, what we could have done better, and what we hope to accomplish in the New Year. Elihu, Jasper, James, Seth, me, and sometimes Dan Creekwater—when he's not roaming the hills and hollows—make pretty good farm hands, though I do believe we'll lose one of our crew soon.

Seth has made it clear these past few weeks he's become a man in his own right, and being of age now, he wants more. It's only natural. We compliment his work, but he's ready to make a way for himself. His dreams are coming true.

Seth must've come from hearty stock. He's grown to six feet with broad shoulders and big hands. He can certainly pull his weight dragging a cotton sack along the rows or pitching hay into the barn with the rest of us. I had a hard time keeping up with him this year. He's smart. He has a pleasant disposition about him and learns quickly. How could anyone ever have thought him an animal because he's black? It takes a person less than human to make another person less than human, I reckon.

Since I brought him home with me in the fall of '63, Mary has taught Seth to become almost as good a teacher as her. She even had him examined to become an instructor. He passed the tests with flying colors, and Mary received compliments on her good work with him. I wish Susannah, Mr. Gilmore, and Old Bart could see this.

Seth's found his footing and soon will become one of two new Negro teachers in the county. He speaks with an authority that can lead young minds to the awareness necessary for greater things. He's not the scared little runaway slave boy I found in Brashear's Stand on the Old Trace that morning. No, he's a man with purpose and dreams.

I guess when you take a new oath to the Union flag, and to human beings as a whole, the Lord lays a test or two on your heart to see if your word is good. Joining the 1st Mississippi Mounted Rifles proved the first test true, but being part of Seth's life has become one of the greatest blessings the Lord has allowed me. He's come such a long way. A human being will do that if you treat him like one. The most profound things are generally the simplest, I've found.

Seth stands straight and tall in his stature and his beliefs. At supper he announces, "I want every Negro child to have the same education I got and from a teacher as gentle and firm, intelligent and patient, as Mary."

I take another spoonful of cornpone and sweet milk, thinking about little Lucy in Vicksburg with the head full of golden curls. I can still see the sadness in her eyes when she spoke about children, especially Negro kids, who didn't get to go to school. But I also remember the resolve in her spirit when she declared she'd make sure all children had opportunity to get an education when she grew up. There's no telling what a mind and heart like hers will accomplish in this new world. I wish she could know what's happening here and that our family will soon supply the lumber for one of the new schoolhouses.

Seth plans to open a school for black children and has already signed contacts with Unionists who will help him do that. Mr. H.P. Dotson was first in line to lend his support. But that's not all Seth wants.

WE START EARLY to cut and stack wood for the rest of the winter, making several trips to find dead trees and fat pine. We work hard together, and the steadiness of good labor brings peace to my soul. Seth, though, has been fidgety all morning. He's got something on his mind.

After dinner, he and I retreat out into the dogtrot to let our fine meal of squirrel dumplings, corn pone, and black eyed peas settle before we get back to work.

"I got my heart set on having a family, Lummy," he grins. Imagine that, a runaway snatched from the jaws of slavery now having the prospects of a future and a legacy to carry on his new ideas. Sometimes my heart swells beyond what I believe my chest can hold.

"I'm goin' on twenty years old now, and I want to have my own place. But I don't want to leave you good folks. So I have to know. Am I really— you know—family?"

"Well, hell, yeah!" Elihu yells walking around the side of the house with a jug in his hand. "Damn straight you're family, and I'll help make that happen. How about you, brother?"

I kick the dirt. "Like you always say, Elihu, I got nothin' against it."

He laughs and punches my shoulder. Seth listens, but I don't think he knows what we're talking about. Elihu scratches his chin and scans the farm like he's hoping to see a deer in a far off corner of the field in front of the house.

"Under the big shade oak, down by Phoenix Creek?"

I nod. "Yeah, that's a good place."

Pa left that grand old oak standing when he cleared this field back in '42. It's a beautiful tree with a trunk six feet thick and limbs that spread out like a hen covering her chicks with protective wings. Pa loved to sit in the cool shade of the evening after a long day's work. His old straight back chair still leans against it, and I can almost see him sitting there smoking his pipe.

I asked once why Pa left this particular tree. "I just want to remind myself to be like this oak, strong and true, just livin' and growin' where the Good Lord placed me." Then he laughed. "But mostly because I like the way it looks and the good shade it lays out."

Elihu snickers. "Pa was a very practical man."

I'm shocked. "Where'd you learn that word?"

"Well, Seth ain't the only one gettin' schooled around here. I've been payin' attention."

"Well, it's about damn time. You didn't learn nothin' in Miss Stansbury's class, except the shape of her...." Seth clears his throat. "I'm done. Sorry." But we all laugh.

I gaze at the old shade oak, thinking about the poem I wrote about a great old tree. Seth will become a mighty oak that will stretch far into future generations. Like Cloud Tullos was for us.

I fold my arms. "Yep, that'd be the best place. There's a good stand of poplar trees across the creek that'll be easy to log out for the walls. With the sap down, we can get 'em out quicker and let the inside fire finish curing 'em."

Elihu starts scratching in the dirt thoughtfully with a stick. "One room to start, you think? But build it so we can turn it into a dog trot like ours when the time comes?"

Seth cuts him off. "What are y'all talkin' about?"

Elihu taps the stick at his crude drawing of a cabin floorplan. "Why son, you said you wanted to make your own way, be a man and all. That means you got to have your own place to live and land to get started on. Do you know any other way to do it?"

Seth shakes like a kid sitting down to eat a piece of fresh baked pie with cool cream poured on top. He looks to burst with excitement. "Massuh Lummy, you knows no niggah ain't got no chance in hell to own land here."

"What'd you say?" I draw my hand back. "Boy, I'll slap your ass sideways if you ever say that word in front of me again!"

Seth laughs. "Gotcha, didn't I?"

I playfully back hand his chest like I've done my brothers so many times. Seth is my brother. I wish Old Bart could see how his influence has panned out in my life. I miss my old black grandfather. I hope he's doing well over in Texas.

Seth grabs our jackets and draws us close. I didn't know how strong the young man has become. He hugs us tight and cries. "Thank you, Lord, for my two big brothers and my true family." He looks into the sky. "It's all because of you, King Jesus." Seth starts to run off. "I can't wait to tell Ma and the girls."

I throw up my hands. "Hold on there, young man! We ain't done gabbin' yet."

Seth walks back over like a kid who just got a new toy but isn't allowed to play with it yet.

Elihu snickers. "Ain't no use tryin' to hide it. Which sweet flower have you got your eye on?"

Seth is embarrassed. "Miss Chloe, at Mount Pisgah Church."

Elihu grins, and I see Pa in him. "Look, just 'cause I ain't never married don't mean I don't know a bad case of the red rooster when I see it. Why there was a time when I was younger...."

Seth is embarrassed but straightens up. "Aw now, Mistuh Elihu, that ain't no way to talk about me and my darling."

I cover my mouth to hide my smile, but cut Elihu off. "Dang, Seth, she's pretty as a doll in a toy shop."

Elihu gets a little ruffled. "I was just...."

I cut in. "He don't mean no harm, Seth. It's just the way we come up. But Elihu, he's right, when you got somebody special, it's hard to hear stuff like that. When somebody like sweet Miss Chloe shows up, your soul opens up in every way to her. Ain't nothin' like it, brother."

"All right, dammit, you serious sons of bitches! I was just havin' a little fun."

Seth perks up now that he feels respected. "It's all right, Elihu. But yes, I've been talkin' to Miss Chloe for some time, and even got to sit with her at church socials and such. I love her, and I want her for my wife. She's the prettiest thing God ever made and the sweetest woman he ever put on this earth."

"Son, I know exactly what you mean." I remember how he gasped when I showed him Susannah's picture at Brashear's Stand the day we met. I thought his eyes would pop out of the sockets at her beauty, and at the fact that we were married—a white man to a black woman.

Elihu returns to his dirt drawing. "So Seth, now that you're of age, when do you plan to talk to her folks?"

"Don't know. That's why I want to talk to Lummy. He's been married, two times now, and I just thought he could help me think it through."

Elihu taps Seth's boot with his drawing stick. "Good answer, son. He'll help you with the honey lovin' part, and I'll help you with the business of makin' a livin' in these woods and fields."

"I was countin' on that, thank you."

Elihu finishes the crude sketch with a simple design for easy additions as Seth's family grows. He explains the details, and Seth speaks up.

"I appreciate y'all thinking about putting me by the shade oak down by the creek. It's such a peaceful place, with good dirt for a kitchen garden. Digging a well won't be any trouble either."

I look that way. "I've seen you sittin' there many times readin' books or workin' your letters. It is a good place. So Elihu, what about…."

"The land?"

"Yeah, how can we do that?"

"Now that Pa's gone and if Ma's okay with it, I say we redraw the will and leave Seth that piece when she passes. What do you think?"

I stretch my back. "That'll work. That means there's no money involved, and we can do it quietly at the courthouse. Some folks still don't like Negroes owning land these days."

Elihu throws his stick down. "It's a damn shame, but true. We'll just tell that damn nosey clerk that a long lost cousin from down Uncle Silas's way in Marion County moved up and is working with us now."

Seth jumps up and down. "You mean it'll be mine?"

"Lock, stock, and barrel, son. Let's start with ten acres. Work hard, get yourself established. Then you can buy more if it suites you, maybe from us, or from other folks through us if we have to. We'll work it the same way at the courthouse."

He starts to cry. "We sure have come a long way from Brashear's Stand, ain't we Lummy?"

"We sure have, son."

Seth races for the cabin, shouting, "Hallelujah, it's the Year of Jubilee!"

# CHAPTER 8

# A DEDICATION TO
# THE DEDICATED

## JANUARY 1, 1868

*Christopher Columbus crossed an ocean to reach the New World.*
*So has Seth.*

I T'S A NEW year and a new day. The will has been redrawn. Elihu's friend at the land office did the survey, and it took only three weeks to rough out the small cabin. I haven't had this much fun with my brothers in a long time.

I sit in Pa's old straight back chair against the great shade oak. I close my eyes for a moment, and through the veil between the seen and unseen, I can see him reared back, smoking his clay pipe. He gives a nod of approval, and his shape fades into the flickering sunlight trickling through the leafless trees.

A stick cracks, and I turn to see Ma with a sad grin on her face.

"Did you see him?" I'm shocked. "Oh, yeah, God made me that way, too. It's a gift that's kept me sane these long years."

"Didn't know that about you, Ma. So I guess you saw his nod?"

"Yes. I just wish he'd put his hand of blessing on you boys' heads long before he died. But he's doin' it now. I guess you learn a few things about yourself when you cross to the other side."

"There's lot's things we'd all do different if we could see what Pa sees right now, you think?"

Ma wipes a tear with handkerchief. "I do. But like you've said, we gotta walk on this earth like we're sittin' in heaven already with the Lord."

"It's what the Apostle said, Ma, not me."

She wanders back over to play dolls with the girls.

I try to walk on earth like I live in heaven. I whisper, "I'm gonna have to fight like Saint Michael to protect my people, Lord. I may even have to leave my seat alongside Jesus and be the devil for what's coming."

I watch the children playing as my brothers decide what else needs to be done to the cabin. Seth? He's grinnin' like a mule eatin' briars. Martha looks over and gives me a wink. It couldn't be a better day. A calmness sweeps over me like when I used to sit in the Catholic Church garden in Vicksburg during the war. I can feel the saints all around me, cheering for what the Lord has done here.

My vision narrows. The surrounding countryside becomes fuzzy. Then I see them all, standing amongst the living and smiling—all those I love dearly who have crossed over the Jordan River through the thin veil to the unseen.

Something lands in my lap and rolls onto the ground. John A. rushes over, picks it up, and throws the round object at me. I barely have time to catch it, and he plops his hands on my knees.

"Teach us that game you learned in the war, Pop. You know, the one where you hit a ball with a stick and run?"

I study the round ball, tossing it up and down in my right hand. "Not bad, young man. You make this?"

"No, suh. Uncle Elihu got it for me in Bankston. I saved up my pennies and finally got enough. It ain't the best one in Mistuh Wesson's Store, but it's what I could buy. C'mon, Pop. Let's play."

I rub him on the head. "You know I'm gettin' too old for this." It doesn't slow him in the least. It's sunny and the warmest day we've had in a while.

"Aww, come on, Pop, we want to play."

"What about my old war wounds? You don't want them to go to bleedin', do you?"

John A. playfully kicks dirt on my boots like he doesn't believe me, but then becomes very serious, like he's offended me. He feels all over my chest and shoulders like a doctor searching for the source of a bleeding wound.

"They ain't bleedin', are they?"

I pick him up and throw him over my shoulder like a sack of taters. He squeals like a pig as we walk to the small pasture in front of Seth's cabin.

"Heck no! I'm one of the few men who whipped the Yanks and the Rebs all in the same war, and never got a scratch! Find me a good hickory stick three feet long, about three inches thick."

I put him down, and he scampers away like a rabbit bumped off its bed on a frosty morning.

I yell as he disappears into the barn, "One of them axe handles we ain't whittled down yet will do just fine." He already knows what to get.

Martha and Isabel finish putting the curtains up in the lone window that faces the field in front of Seth's cabin, while Elihu and Seth rig up one of our mules to break ground for his kitchen garden. They finish that up quickly and join us in learning how to play the stick and ball game. With Jasper and James already knowing how to play, we split up into two teams and hardly finish a short game when Isabel calls for us to wash up for dinner.

As I clean the dirt from underneath my fingernails with the knife Pa made me, I marvel at what we've accomplished. The ground for the kitchen garden is turned over, the cabin has been furnished as best we could do, and Seth has moved into his own home. And in working together, we've become family even more.

We gather around sawhorse tables to sit on rough oak benches under the great shade oak for the celebration. With Martha's and Isabel's best fried chicken dinner and all the fixings spread across the table, we settle down to a feast a king and queen would be proud to share. And that's exactly what Seth looks like, a king sitting at the head of his own table in his own front yard.

On his left is Chloe, shy, but with a grin that reminds me of Susannah's on our wedding day. Seth rises as we all get seated. He clears his throat like he's about to start a school lesson.

In fine English, he declares, "Thank you all for coming to make this a glorious day of days. The Lord gets all the credit for my new home, but my family gets more thanks than I can give for making it possible. The food is getting cold, but I do have an announcement." He looks at each person. The girls giggle for they sense what he's about to announce. Seth takes a deep breath.

Elihu snorts, "Well, if you don't come on out with it Seth, these girls here are gonna bust wide open!" Everyone laughs.

"All right then. Miss Chloe has consented to become my fiancé." Seth speaks like the grown man he is, and the light beaming in my heart could turn night into day. We give up a cheer.

Poole leans over to Dan Creekwater. "Consented, what's that?"

Dan whispers back, "Heck, I don't even know what a fiancé is."

I elbow Poole. "It means she agreed to marry him, that's all."

Seth gently lays his hand on Chloe's shoulder. "We plan to marry soon, and of course, we expect y'all to be at the wedding. Lummy, would you be my best man?"

"You know I will." Everyone claps, and we congratulate the young couple.

Seth holds up his hands to quiet the small crowd. "I dedicate this new land and home the Lord has given us in honor of Grandpa Cloud Tullos, whose vision and strength I want to inherit and live up to in this world. Hitherto from this time on, this will be called The Cloud Farm. Lummy, would you say the first family prayer over this meal, these fine folks, and our new home?" Seth sits and takes Chloe's hands in his.

"My pleasure, son." Everyone bows, except Dan and Elihu. They're respectful of the Lord but also watchful for any enemy wanting to take advantage of this peaceful gathering.

"Oh, Lord, we're all your children seated here today, thanking you for the bounty laid upon this your table. You have brought us all a mighty long way, but no one more than Seth. Like Columbus travelin' many miles to reach the New World, so has Seth to this, his new world. Like Grandpa Cloud who brought the Tullos family from the old country into the new, Seth has come far in heart, mind, body, and soul. Today, he dedicates his all to you. Lord, give Seth and Chloe a good life, the dreams of their hearts, many children, blessin's on this farm, and loving souls dedicated to you throughout eternity. And to those of you passed on who surround us this day, we thank you for joinin' with us in this moment. In Jesus Name, we all say A-a-amen."

A collective "amen" rises from hearts filled with joy. And we feast.

Afterwards, Elihu and Seth sing "Mine Eyes Have seen the Glory of the Coming of the Lord" to celebrate Seth becoming a land and home owner, and soon to be husband. Ma motions Dan Creekwater over, and she whispers something in his ear.

When Elihu and Seth finish singing, Dan stands up. "I ain't no public speaker by any stretch, but Ma Tullos asked me to say a word about this land and the people who lived here long before y'all came. I heard the stories about your family from Lummy when we stayed in McCurtain Creek Swamp together. I know you good people come from the same woodland folk my Choctaw brothers did. I also know you didn't have no choice on how this land came to be yours, except payin' the government for it. You must know I find no ill will toward you in my heart about that. Anyway, Elihu and Seth, I appreciate the songs you sing. Some say the word 'Choctaw' means 'separation,' others 'flathead' because we used to tie boards on babies' heads. But the meanin' I like most is what my grandmother once told me it means, 'charming voice.' She said it was because we played music instruments very well. Has a good sound to it, I think."

He straightens his jacket and stands a bit taller. "My people are long gone from this land, but our mark can still be seen. Our souls return to rest here when we die, no matter where we are. Some say the reason Choctaw means 'separation' is because one tribe became two. We split from the Chickasaws and became our own people. That meaning has no place anymore. Not in this new land where red man, black man, and white man feast together today as all will do when we cross the river. Because of my family here today, there's no separation between colors. The Lord binds us all together."

Dan sits down, and we give another round of applause. Elihu and Seth stand to sing a hymn sung many times at Mt. Pisgah Baptist.

*Savior, like a shepherd lead us,*
*Much we need Thy tenderest care,*
*In the pleasant pastures feed us,*
*For our use Thy folds prepare.*
*Blessed Jesus, blessed Jesus,*
*Thou hast bought us, Thine we are,*
*Blessed Jesus, blessed Jesus,*
*Thou hast bought us, Thine we are.*

Elihu sits, but Seth remains standing.

He bows his head as do we. "Lord, you are the Good Shepherd. It is you who surely brought us here, and we are yours. Please lead us. Amen."

We all say amen.

Poole elbows Jasper. "Boy, I like a short winded preacher."

We eat until we nearly burst. I have to loosen my belt. Martha brushes her apron and stands to direct cleanup. The men mosey over to the trunk of the great shade oak, and Elihu lights up a smoke.

Ma yells, "You boys get about what you need doin', 'cause we're all goin' to Mount Pisgah Baptist come Sunday."

We turn and salute her like a general. She tosses a well-gnawed corn cob at us. We laugh, and our talk turns to the battles to come. The laughing and joking is cut short.

# CHAPTER 9

# GOIN' TO CHURCH JUST DOESN'T DO IT, NOT FOR ME

## JANUARY 6, 1868

*The Devil slithers in and out of the church house all the time.*

IT'S AN UNUSUALLY warm morning. Sweat wets the back of my shirt as I drive the women and children in the wagon on the dusty road to Mt. Pisgah Baptist Church. My brothers ride horses and mules guarding the front and back of the wagon as we cross deep hollows and top steep hills—perfect places for an ambush. It's a little unnerving riding to church services with loaded weapons across our laps. I blame that on Captain Tom Ford, who isn't above attacking a caravan of pilgrims on their way to worship.

We rein up, tie off the animals, and file into the building like obedient school children. Pastor Dobbs greets us at the door as the choir members warm up their voices.

"Brother Elihu, would you join with the choir this morning and give us one of your solos?"

"Got no problem with it, Pastor. Anythin' for the Lord and his people."

Pastor Dobbs whispers, "You left a little muscadine wine in my wagon, didn't you, son?"

"Two gallon jugs of my finest, Reverend."

"No reverend here, brother, except the Lord." Pastor Dobbs slips Elihu two dollars and then clasps his right hand around mine.

"Lummy, say a prayer at the end of the service, would you, son?"

"Be glad to." I hold his hand for a moment longer. "We've come a long way together, you and me."

Pastor Dobbs smiles and hugs me. "And I'm the better man for it."

We get seated, and church is called to order. Though women and men sit on opposite sides of the center aisle, Martha and I sit together in the back with our children. I don't hold to that old tradition, and the other folks at Mt. Pisgah respect that.

A few announcements are made just before the choir begins its first selection. I let the music and singing wash over me like the waters of the Mississippi when I laid myself under in baptism on the sandbar. Martha slips her hand under the crook of my elbow. I come back to the present.

This is my dream come true, what I have longed for, what I've asked God for—a loving wife and children, a home with land to work, and sitting in church, praising the one who made it all possible. It's the closest thing to heaven I've ever seen.

Without warning, like water from an artesian welling up, I stand up and shout to the roof, "I am a blessed man!"

Martha jerks at my outburst. The church grows quiet. I look down to see Pastor Dobbs's eyes as big as tomatoes, but then they soften. He's come to understand the erratic behavior of men who've lived through horrible things such as war and who lose control on occasion.

"Brother Lummy, do you wish to bring a word to the church?"

I shake my head at first, but I figure it's time to testify to the goodness of the Lord.

Martha takes my hand. "Go ahead, dear, you can do it."

"You don't mind, Pastor? I guess when the Lord says talk, you better talk."

He nods, and the church laughs, waiting expectantly for my words.

"This may take a while."

"Take your time. I can preach my sermon another Sunday. When the Lord fills a man and he shouts like you did, there's not a better message for the church than what he's given you today. Stand up and bless the church, son."

It's like I just got orders from Sergeant McGugarty of the First Mississippi Mounted Rifles. My heart swells at the peace from the words I must speak.

I give my testimony in as few words as I can, from leaving Choctaw County back in '59 until today. I spare no part of the story, leave no stone unturned. Even the worst of it becomes a comfort to me and those whose lives have been shattered by death and destruction, loss of loved ones and livelihoods. At a half hour, I start winding up my speech, most of which I don't remember. It's like someone else is doing the talking.

"Today, I am a blessed man, for all the reasons I just told you. And I plan to hang on to 'em."

Our black members go to talkin' with me, and I preach a moment about the hate and violence increasing in our county. I ask for a show of hands of those willing to stand with me to protect what the Lord has given us against the attacks of the Evil One. Some shout, many say "amen," but all raise their hands.

I finish my talk. "They're comin', and it won't be long." I sit down with that warning.

Pastor Dobbs blesses me and gives a last word of encouragement. We rise to sing Rock of Ages, and I ask Jasper to say the prayer I was supposed to give. I've talked enough.

During the prayer, I step to the back, not to shake hands with everyone like a preacher, but to be first out the door. I need some air.

Elihu follows and leans over as Jasper takes the church up to heaven in prayer. "Did you see it?"

"See what?"

"When you got all lathered up with your preachin', a big ole rat snake slid out of the hole in that corner over there. Must've been six foot long."

I spy the hole he's pointing to. "A six footer, you say? Hmph, that's a good sized one."

Elihu snickers. "Good for keepin' the field mice away, I reckon."

"What'd he do?"

"Made his way down the baseboard without a soul seein' him, but when he peeked around that last pew and saw you railin' on, he stuck his head up like he was listenin'! When you said, 'God will go before us,' that ole snake turned and headed back down the side aisle like a whore runnin' out of a burnin' cat house and slithered back in that hole quicker'n shit through a goose."

One of the good deacons heard a little too much of Elihu's report and gives him a stern look.

Elihu rubs his stomach and whispers the obvious lie, "Sorry, got the stomach troubles."

The deacon nods but gives him a look of *don't say that word in here again.*

Elihu nods, closing his eyes in agreement, but when the deacon turns back around, he sticks his tongue out at him.

"It was his momma who got me called into conference with the good brethren that time years ago for public drinkin' in town. I ought'a whoop his ass for her tellin' off on me." Elihu has the look of a man about to kill a snake.

I can't keep my shoulders from bouncing as I laugh. "Dang boy, cussin', lyin', and threatening a church deacon, all on the same day in church. That's got to be some kind of record."

The deacon scowls at us, but then he can't help but snicker, too. He mouths with no sound, "Now that's funny."

Elihu winks and nods with a grin.

I elbow Elihu at Jasper's last amen. "Let it go, brother, I gotta get out of here. Can't breathe."

Elihu follows me out the door to our wagon parked near the tree line. "That ole snake went right down the baseboard on the women's side. If Ma and the girls would've seen that devilish serpent, we sure enough would've had tongue speakin' and fallin' about the church house like them holy rollers."

I laugh. "Ain't that the truth?"

"I take it as a sign. Say what you want, but I believe the Lord sent a message to you, boy."

"And what would that be?"

"Satan came sneakin', but when he saw you, he ran back to Hell where he came from."

"I don't know about all that."

Elihu punches my shoulder. "You ain't the only one who sits with the Lord, boy. You should know that by now."

"I do. I just ain't lookin' for no more trouble, and I sure as hell ain't lookin for any signs, unless it's a man with a gun comin' at me."

Elihu lays his hand on my shoulder. "You don't have to, Lummy. Trouble's huntin' you like that rat snake searchin' for a mouse."

Elihu walks over to help Ma down the steps of the church house. I squat down to check spokes on the front left wagon wheel. I sense someone behind me and jump as fast as a cat on a mouse.

"Miss Josie, are you all right?" She's lived not far from our place on Null Road since before I can remember. Some say she's over a hundred years old, but no one's quite sure. She doesn't know either, except that she once told me she remembers seeing British General Cornwallis march his troops through South Carolina when she was a child. "He wasn't nothin' but an overdressed fancy peacock sittin' on the ugliest horse I ever did see. We showed him, though!"

She stumbles toward me, her crooked and wrinkling arms reaching out to hug me. I didn't know she could even get this far out of the church house on her own. I step forward to meet her, and she tugs on my shirt. I kneel down. She presses her palms on my cheeks firmly and searches my eyes. I see the strength of an old soldier still carrying on the fight in hers.

"I appreciate you testifyin' today, Lummy. I've watched you grow up through hard and troublin' years with your Pa, not to mention the war and all. You've grown into a fine man who's aware of himself in ways most men try to drink, gamble, or whore away. Not you." She strokes my long hair. "You believe you've done some bad things, even sinful things, don't you, son? That may be true. But you must never forget, there's a whole lot more good in you than bad, and the good in you must win. Sometimes what may seem like doin' wrong is what the Lord commands. Lummy, do what the Lord commands."

I believe I just heard the voice of God speaking to me. "I'm tryin', Miss Josie, but it seems I can't shake the feelin's I picked up in the war. Sometimes they want to undo me."

"I know, son." She presses her hand on my chest. "Just don't forget this. The Devil comes hardest after the ones who hurt him the most." Her eyes immediately glass over like a blind person, and she collapses in a faint. I catch her just before she hits the ground.

A woman's shrill voice screams, "Miss Josie, where are you?" Several ladies rush to help me lay Miss Josie on the ground in the shade. "Oh Lord!

Is she breathing?" After a couple minutes, Miss Josie comes to but has no knowledge of where, or even who she is. I'm puzzled.

Miss Josie's daughter, Jewel, wipes her sweaty face with a handkerchief. "She talked to you. What'd she say? Did she know you, Lummy?"

"She did. Just some things to me personally about doin' God's will."

Jewel looks up in tears. "It's been years since she's said anything to some-body she recognizes." Jewel rocks her grandmother's head in her lap like a sleeping baby and starts singing an old church hymn.

Jasper and James help Miss Josie up and take her to their family wagon. I finish getting ours ready to leave. Elihu helps Ma into the wagon, and when everyone is loaded up, he pulls me to the side.

"Sweet old lady, it's a wonder she didn't fall and hit her head. What was that all about?"

"Nothin'. It wasn't about nothin'."

"Can't be about nothin'. That old lady ain't talked to nobody in years."

"Nothin', I said, dammit, now leave me be." He turns, but I grab his arm. "Sorry Elihu, weren't no call for all that. She just struck a nerve, that's all."

"Can you tell me?"

"Yeah." I stop fiddlin' with the wagon and walk a few steps away from listening ears. "She told me the Devil's comin' after me personally, and to get about doin' what the Lord commands."

Elihu rubs his chin, wondering. He starts again for his horse, but I grab his shirtsleeve.

"That snake you was talkin' about?

"Yeah? What about it?"

"There's a den of 'em in this county, and they're comin'. In fact, they're already here."

Elihu's grin widens to what looks like a quarter piece of watermelon. "Then you know I can dance on their ugly ole heads with the best of 'em!"

"Just don't want you to get bit like last time!"

"One time out of a hundred ain't bad odds with all them copperheads, rattlers, and cottonmouths I've slayed through the years. Besides, ain't you read your scripture about what God said to the serpent?"

I don't want to hear it, but Elihu needs to preach it.

He throws his arm out like an actor. "'Because thou hast done this,' deceivin' Adam and Eve that is, 'thou art cursed above all creatures' and… uh… man will stomp his head, but the snake will strike his heel, or somethin' like that. You know what I'm sayin'."

"I do." I kick the dust. "But it's that strikin' of the heel I'm concerned about. You and me ain't the only ones who could get bit in this fight."

Elihu mounts his horse in one leap. "If you want to kill a snake, you gotta be willin' to risk gettin' bit!"

I whisper, "If it means protectin' my family, I'm willin', and for damn sure able."

# CHAPTER 10

# STILL TALKIN' ABOUT
# THE WAR

## MARCH 6, 1868

*Happiness dependent on another is happiness never found.*

A LOW EVENING sun blazes red through the trees to announce the close of day. Spring plowing is done, and planting time arrives with a bustle of activity. The smell of fresh earth and handling seeds reminds me of Creator's wisdom in how he renews the earth and his people.

The coffee Ma brought steams up a small cloud in the cool twilight as I sit on the porch collecting my thoughts and sorting them out. My heart is calm, yet I'm still a little nervous. The last time I was truly happy without worry was in Winn Parish with Susannah before going to war. That happiness got stolen from me, and I'm still not sure I've recovered. Probably never will completely. I watch the shadows conquer the ridges across the field.

"Lord, I ain't gonna let this happiness be taken from me. Help me."

I've always thought a man needs land and money, a sweetheart or a wife, to make him happy in this crazy mixed up world. At least that's what I was taught by my folks and the church. But after so much loss and learning I have little to no control over what happens in this world, the Lord has taught me happiness is a state of the soul. It's not that the gift of Martha, workin' the farm with my brothers and teachin' the children, and bein' with Ma and the girls doesn't make me happy. It does, beyond what I can express. I've not felt joy like this in years.

I just know it can all be snatched away in the simple pop of a percussion cap or the slash of a short sword. No, happiness is who you are inside, not what you have or who God has sent you. Happiness dependent upon another is happiness never found. It's like trying to hold on to a double handful of river sand. It slips right through your figures the harder you try to hold on to it.

"Even the wind slips through your fingers and laughs at you on its way to somewhere else." I look around to see if someone is listening. "All I can do is enjoy who and what the Lord gives me, for as long as he allows. I can do that. I think."

Nothing on the outside of a man can bring the depth of joy, the peace and contentment I want in this world. That'll only come when I cross the river into eternity, like Pastor Dobbs preaches. But I believe in my heart that a man can get a taste of it now, in this life. But he has to look inside to find it.

So, I'm a better man for the Lord's teaching that nothing from the outside can make me truly happy, and to not let anything from the outside unsettle my soul. This makes me wiser in how I see and handle who and what the Lord gives me. Everything is a gift, even when it seems the world is falling apart. It's the steadiness of soul I need right now. I have it. I'm happy. It's just the sudden outbursts I still have that concern me. And my family.

The door creaks open, and I jump.

"It's a good evenin', ain't it, son?" Ma sits in the rocker next to mine, drying her dishwater wrinkled hands with a damp cloth.

"It is, Ma."

"You seem to be doin' much better these days."

"I reckon I am."

"You and your family bein' here suits you well, right down to the ground."

"Yeah Ma, it does. Time is the great healer, they say. But it ain't just the war I'm gettin' over, you know."

She lays her hand on my arm. "You did what needed doin' to live and keep us alive. You have such a fine family the Lord's given you, son. Your Martha, oh how I've come to love her. She's my daughter now. You know, she reminds me of your sister Saleta, God rest her sweet soul."

"That makes me feel good, Ma." I remember how Saleta's face glowed like an angel's when Pastor Dobbs immersed her in the spring below the hill at New Zion Baptist Church that cold Sunday afternoon. The smile on her face coming up out of the water was like a new dawn sun topping a hill.

"Are you happy, son?'

"I am, and I'm truly thankful, but it's the things I did, the fightin' and the killin', the losin' and the dyin' of good friends and family. I did some bad things, Ma. On both sides of the war." I sit quiet for a moment. "And sometimes I felt nothin' when I did the killin'. If I did feel somethin', it was the anger I let the Devil conjure up in me to stay alive."

"How'd you do that, son?"

I hesitate, knowing this will cause Ma pain. "Thinkin' about Pa bein' so hard on us, Ben bein' such a jackass, and how Lester made light of me lovin' Susannah. Thinkin' about how much I hate bullies kindled that fire. And it worked."

Ma drops her head. "Your Pa wasn't all bad, was he, or Ben?"

"Bad enough, but I've made peace with all that now. It's just they couldn't change to be the kind men I know was inside 'em, that's all. And I kept goin' back to them over and over, hopin' and thinkin', 'Yeah, this'll be the time it's gonna be good. This'll be the hunt, or plowin' this field together, this will be the time.' But I always left sayin' I'd never go back. Their meanness was more than this grown ass man needed to carry." I shake my head. "Sorry Ma, guess I'll always struggle with those thoughts. And the cussin'. Maybe I'm supposed to."

"It's all right, son, I still do, too. I am glad you made peace with your Pa before he passed. Wish Ben had, too. But you must know your Pa always thought highly of you boys. He just didn't know how to show it. Maybe he didn't want to, I don't know. At times he was a bit jealous of you boys doin' better than him, when he should've been proud of what you became. He got that from your mean ole Grandpa Willoughby, who I'm glad you never knew. If you had, you'd understand. Makin' no excuses, but your Pa had it rougher than he ever gave you boys."

"I figured as much. I guess that's why I have compassion on both of 'em. Neither Pa nor Ben asked for the meanness they got."

A tear forms in Ma's eye, and she looks away. "No, they didn't. But that didn't make it right to pass it on though." She sits up straight, wipes the tear, and in the voice of a preacher declares, "I have a long view of things. I know that on the other side, all this will be made right one day."

I cut in. "And it won't matter then so much what happened here because the Lord will open all our eyes?"

Ma swats me on the shoulder. "You just stole my thunder, boy."

I chuckle. "I didn't want to have to take up a collection."

She swats me with her dish rag. "Oh, stop."

"I'm just lettin' you know this boy listened when his momma thought his head was somewhere else."

She smiles, and I take the opportunity to change the subject. "Martha and the kids sure make it easier to change. Ma, I got some good news. You're the first to know. Martha and I are gonna have a child of our own."

The biggest grin I've ever seen on Ma's face breaks to reveal her pearly white teeth. "What? My goodness, that's wonderful! When? I noticed Martha thickenin' up but figured it was just winter pounds she'd put on. Oh my, that makes me so very happy. I'm so thankful for what I got, but havin' a new grandbaby, and your very first, that'll carry me a long time, and...."

I stop Ma's rocking. "Not so loud, Ma. And don't say anything, not just yet."

"How in the world can I not... oh, okay, I won't, son. You and Martha need to make that big announcement. Better do it soon. O-o-oh, I can't wait!" Ma raises her hands, palms facing out, "It'll be hard, but I can keep my mouth shut." She looks to the sky. "Thank you, Lord."

"I don't believe you, Ma, but all right." She swats me on the shoulder with her dish rag. I know women can't keep that kind of secret. I guess that's for good reason. Good news is hard to hold close to the chest these days.

Ma sees my smile turn down. "What is it, son?"

"I do worry about bringin' a new child into this messed up world. I've lost so many people who I loved dearly. Choctaw County's upside down even more now than it was durin' the war. I just don't know, bringin' a sweet little baby into this world of sadness and loss?"

"Son, you gotta trust the Good Lord. If you bring a child into the world, then you must count on Jesus watchin' over that baby. This county will come back to itself one day, and you're here to help bring it back. Faith, son, you gotta have faith."

"I have faith in the Lord, Ma. It's the folks still hangin' on to the Lost Cause that give me doubts."

"Son, you did what you had to do at Vicksburg, with Dawg Smith and Lester, and even at Bankston with the Mounted Rifles. Lord knows burnin' those mills shortened the war and probably saved many a good boy's life, gray and blue."

"Still, most days it don't make it no easier, knowin' what I done. Do I want my little baby to grow up knowin' what I did?"

"It's made you who you are, son. But when you lay it all out on the table, you're still that same little boy in your soul who loved his Creator and his creation. Let him come back."

"But I've lost so many people I loved dearly, Ma."

"I know, son. When I think about that, I remind myself of somethin' Granny Thankful once told me." She hesitates, allowing me to catch up to receive this new piece of wisdom. She looks into my eyes like only a mother can. "Love who the Lord puts in front of you."

I blink at the words, and my heart skips a beat for I believe I just heard the voice of the Lord. I soak in the proverb and visualize in my mind the people God has put in front of me now.

I scratch my ear. "That's all I can do. Hanging on to the losses of the past does nothing but hinder me turning completely loose to give my full heart and soul to God and my new family. I need to love who God puts in front of me and not hang on to hate for the ones Satan took away."

"Count your blessings, son, every day, and thank the Lord so they don't get taken away."

"Your right, Ma." We sit still for a moment. "I still don't want to go into Bankston. I know much has been rebuilt, but I'm sure you can still see the wrecked buildings from the raid."

"They've cleaned much of that up, but—"

"But the ruins are still there—the ruins of good buildings and shattered lives. I just can't go there, not just yet."

"Makes sense for now, son. You probably didn't know it, but Mistuh Wesson wasn't all bad either. When word came that the Yankees were probably on their way to Choctaw County, he gave away most of the cloth that couldn't be shipped to the army in time. You remember Mrs. Prewitt don't you?" I nod. "Her husband was off fightin' with the gray, and she had little to no chance of making things work to live. She rode forty miles on horseback roundtrip to get a bolt of cloth. Mistuh Wesson packed her down with flour and other stuff, too."

I appreciate hearing that, but it doesn't soothe my conscience. "It was a bad thing, burnin' Bankston. I hated doin' it. At least the soldiers handed out flour and wool, some cloth and shoes, as the mills and tannery burned. It wasn't much, but the folks thanked our men for it."

We sit still in the darkness of evening.

"It was the right thing to do, wasn't it Ma?"

"Yes, yes it was, son. People ain't havin' hard times because you burned the mills. They're havin' a hard time because they trusted the wrong cause. Some will keep on strugglin' until they accept that the war is over. Some will lose their lives tryin' to hold onto them notions."

I know she's right. "I want no part of anythin' like that again." In my heart, I know I will.

She pats my arm and gets up to refill my coffee cup. She returns. "It's good to have sugar again."

"Ain't it so."

We sip our coffee for a while with no more words passing between us. We both know a fight is coming. That means I can't turn loose of the anger just yet. Not if I want to have the strength to protect and survive.

# CHAPTER 11

# A NIGHT TALK CUT SHORT

## NEAR MIDNIGHT, MARCH 6, 1868

*The stillness of a good night can be broken by the deepest darkness.*

WE TALK INTO the night about old times and of the truth in Ma's aching heart about Pa's abuse and violence dealt out on her boys.

"I loved your daddy like no other, you must know that. But there was a time, had I the means, I would've left him. But I learned to take it, forget it, and some I don't even remember. I've felt bad about doing nothin'. I tried to make him happy, and me, too. I learned the hard way, words your Granny Thankful gave me, 'Happiness dependent on another is happiness never found.'"

I realize now where I get a lot of my understandings.

Ma presses down her wrinkled skirt. "No, you gotta find joy in your soul. Bein' happy ain't always about things goin' your way or about feelin' good all the time. No, it's mostly not lettin' anything rattle your soul. It's like seeking the kingdom of God within."

I sit up. "What'd you say?"

"Yeah, Lummy, I've been listenin' to you, too all these years. It gives me peace knowin' the Lord will make all this right one day. When the Lord opens our eyes on that great day so we can truly see, we're all gonna think, my, my, look what we missed actin' a fool all those years."

I'm receiving the wisdom of a woman who's suffered much but still finds joy in what the Lord has put in front of her. I take it in, but know our happiness is still not safe.

"Ma, the armies have gone home, but the war ain't over. It'll start up again, except this time it won't be on some faraway battlefield with men wearin' uniforms. It'll be right here amongst us, between neighbors, between families and friends. There's angry folks on two opposing sides in Choctaw County. It ain't gray and blue, though it seems like it. No, it's darkness and light. It's gonna be hard to know which is which when the dust kicks up."

Suddenly a man comes running like a deer chased by hounds. I jump up, pistol in hand, and peer into the darkness. I cock my weapon. Ma sits still. Just as I take aim, Seth leaps up the porch steps out of the darkness and falls to the floor gasping for air.

"He done it, I saw him! Put his pistol to her head and pulled the trigger. Blood went everywhere. Lord God in Heaven if I never see…." He shudders and falls faint.

I splash his face with water. "Who shot who, Seth?"

He sits up and shakes his head like he's got water in his ears. "Captain Tom Ford, he done it. I saw it all."

"Who got shot?"

"Chloe's momma!" I nod. "I went over to ask for Miss Chloe's hand, and about the time I got the words out good, the Devil himself, Captain Tom Ford, and his riders galloped up to the house. We wanted to run, but it was too late. I stepped in front of Chloe and pushed her back into the cabin. They surrounded the house with their rifles and shotguns out. Captain Ford yelled out to Chloe's momma, 'You the one talkin' shit about me, woman?' Chloe's momma didn't hesitate 'cause she wasn't scared."

Seth sucks in another breath. "Chloe's momma walked right up to Captain Tom Ford sittin' on his horse and spit on the ground. She said, 'Shit is shit. You can't take stank out of shit if it's shit. You put a baby in my youngest daughter's belly, and I'm tellin' the whole world about it. Ain't no niggah here afraid of you! You weak ass, beatin' on black folks, little white boy!'"

Ma hands Seth a cup of water. He downs it in one gulp. "Without a warning, Captain Ford pulled out that big pistol and put the barrel to her forehead. We were all so scared. Then Captain Ford yelled, 'Say no more about this or so help me God, I'll scatter your shit for brains all over that cabin.' Chloe's momma stood her ground and without blinking, said, 'You'll need God to help you, for what you've done, you coward. Rapin' my twelve year old child? I won't shut up, not 'til you take up your responsibility to my daughter. And if you want to talk about shit, I ain't never seen it sit so pretty up on a horse!'" Seth drops his head. "Then, he killed her. Chloe's momma fell on the ground with a big hole in her forehead. She didn't even twitch. They all laughed. One said, 'That's one way to get a niggah to shut up!' Then they just rode off."

Ma starts crying, and I can't believe my ears. My face is hot, and my fists are balled up, but I need to keep my head. I have to ask. "So, he knows who you are, don't he?"

He looks up with the eyes of a man who realizes he's just been snake bit. "Only the three of us was there, Chloe's momma, me, and Chloe."

"So he knows who you are. Damn!"

"He does. Why?"

"You need to get Chloe over here now. Take everything of value—food, clothes, bedding—whatever, and get out. James and I'll come with the wagon to load you up."

"I knew you'd say that, but I didn't feel right Chloe stayin' here with us."

"This ain't no time to be actin' like no angel, son. The Devil's about, and the Lord is patient."

"But I've already taken care of it, Lummy. I took her to stay with Mistuh Allrice and Momma Sophie. They just down the road apiece, and so far ain't nobody bothered them."

I scratch my chin. "I don't like it, but okay. You're the man of your family, or soon to be. I'll honor that."

"Sure was hard loading up Chloe's momma in Mistuh Allrice's wagon, but we got her there. Sophie is taking care of the body. Funeral will be in a day or two."

I look at Ma, who nods. "We'll be there, Seth."

"Thank you, Lummy. And about Chloe stayin' with Momma Sophie, I just want to do the best and right thing. You know how sometimes the mind can't overcome what the body wants." He claps his mouth shut, remembering that Ma is sitting at the table. Seth covers his face, embarrassed.

Ma grins through her tears. "Ain't nothin' to be ashamed of, son. It's only natural for a man to want the girl God gives him. I know my boys, and you're one of them."

"Thank you, ma'am. I guess I'm finally old enough to be talkin' with grown folks." Seth sits down and cries like a baby. I let my tears fly for a moment. Ma stands up to go to the kitchen.

"Seth, come eat, and then stretch out on Lummy's bed. You look ragged and need to rest."

"Yes, ma'am. I'll rest a bit, but I can't eat just now. There's just too much swirlin' around in this heart and head of mine. It's makin' my stomach a bit queasy."

"All right, but you'll be hungry when you get up. I'll have something ready for you then."

"Thank you, Ma." Seth's undying good manners are a testimony to his good character and association with Christian people who see him as a human being. He closes the door behind him and lets out a great sigh. "Lord, why are there so many hateful and mean people livin' on your good earth? One day, Lord, one day." His words fade into whispers.

Ma returns to the table and plops down hard on the bench. "I just don't understand such things, why men kill each other, and women? Why would that man do such a thing?"

"There's too many angry men loose in this county. They faced many a bullet on the battlefield and lost any sense of bein' afraid. A man who's got nothing to lose ain't afraid of anything, even dyin', you understand?"

She nods.

"Captain Tom Ford is one of 'em. He didn't fight like regular soldiers did, but he fought. He's like Lester, who ran with the Home Guard, and that Dawg Smith I told you about. They start out as good soldiers for the most part, but the truth of who they really are inside comes out and makes them into men who enjoy killin' and rapin', takin' folks' belongings, and causin' trouble wherever they go. Tom Ford didn't give a second thought about doin' what he did to Chloe's momma. It ain't hard to do if you've got no soul left."

"That poor woman sang the prettiest of anybody I know at Mount Pisgah Baptist Church and was always helpin' out folks poorer than she was."

"I know Ma, but this is just the beginning." I think about Mr. Pollan's words about keeping our black friends close.

Ma wrings her hands. "You're worried about Seth, ain't you?"

"I am. Even though Captain Tom Ford did nothin' to him and Chloe then, he'll think about it. He may be slow, but he ain't stupid. And havin' witnesses around ain't a good thing to leave behind. He'll have to come back for them."

"I don't understand why a white man gets some kind of good feelin' beatin' on a Negro."

"One of two reasons, Ma. You remember those sweet little old ladies at church who taught us children that black people had no souls, don't you?"

She cuts in, "You know I never agreed with them teachin' you that."

I hold my hand up because I know she's about to go to preaching. "I know, Ma, but my point is, if you can make a person an animal, then you can treat him like an animal, or worse. You saw the breeding cages."

Tears form, but she can't talk. Then she mutters out, "Remember our old Miss Lucille who put black pepper on your popcorn? She was put in one of them cages when just a young woman. Your Grandpa Willoughby...." Ma drops her head hard on the table. I check for a mark on her forehead. "I'm all right, son."

"And the second reason is if a white man didn't have a Negro to beat down, who'd be the lowest rung on the ladder?"

"A poor white man, mad as a hornet at the world."

"And those bastards ain't gonna let black folks get ahead of them in any shape, form, or fashion. Somebody's gonna be at the bottom, and it ain't gonna be the likes of Captain Tom Ford. Not if he can help it. The war may be over, the slaves might be free, but the chains ain't been cut yet. Not here in Choctaw County anyway." My skin feels like it's on fire.

"Lummy, now I see how that anger can rise up like the devil himself in a man. Just thinkin' on such things makes my blood burn. It's like your Grandpa Temple used to say, 'If it wasn't for the bullies, this world would be a pretty nice place to live.' And he grew up with the worst bully I've ever known, your Grandpa Willoughby. It was on your Grandpa Willoughby's farm where I saw breeding cages for the first time, right before we left Georgia to come to Mississippi. Lucille was in one of those cages. That's why I made your Pa bring her with us to Choctaw County. Your Pa hated his father for how he treated Negroes. I thought your Uncle Silas was gonna kill him one day over it."

That surely clears up a few things for me. Knowing that makes me proud of Pa.

We sip our coffee and let the words sink in. "That's why your Pa never had slaves. He believed Negroes are human bein's just like you and me."

I set my empty cup down. "Trouble's comin', Ma, you need to know that."

She lays her hand on my arm. "It's been a long time comin', son."

BEFORE FIRST LIGHT, James and I hitch up the wagon and check on Chloe at Momma Sophie's before taking her belongings to Seth's new home. Seth hardly says a word the entire trip. What's to say? The Devil knows just the right moment when to rip away a man's joy. Maybe he can rob a man of happiness in the moment, but he can't steal a man's future.

AS JAMES AND I lead the mules and wagon back up to the barn from Seth's cabin, a familiar sound I've heard many times in the woods around our home catches my ear. I stop at the gate and let James take the rig on. I listen to that steady sound that's like a blue tick hound baying at a treed raccoon. I close my eyes for a moment and clear my head of all thoughts, chasing them away by focusing on the sound from the forest. A big red-headed woodpecker calls, flying from tree to tree.

Suddenly, in my mind I see a cane break down below the large hill in front of me. I smell blood and death, hear men groaning and crying, and taste the dryness of salty sweat and no water. I shiver from a cold not of fear, but from what I'm about to do. Then I see them from the 27th Louisiana Lunette where I stand, rifles in hand. Thousands of blue-suited soldiers all lined up in the brush, waiting with bayonets gleaming in the first small rays of a bloody sun rising. They stand frozen like statues with hollow eyes staring straight ahead in the morning fog. Then I see him.

The old hickory from of the 27th Louisiana Lunette stands tall, but peppered with a hundred bullet pock marks and at least a quarter that many cannon ball holes. On a high limb near his knot hole home, the long bushy red tail of a big red squirrel works his mouth like Sarge yelling out an order. The squirrel bounces up and down, barking at what he spies in the bushes, warning us of the coming danger. All is silent. Until another sound in the woods snaps me back to the present.

It's a squirrel barking high up on the hill near our family cemetery. And I realize Big Red, that huge fox squirrel that warned us of Sherman's assault May 22nd, 1863, has come to warn me yet again. My soul is at peace, but my heart burns red like that bloody sun rising in the hills above the city set upon a hill that can't be hidden on the Mississippi River.

James touches my shoulder, and I jerk awake from my vision. I reach for my pistol but realize the gate on which I lean is not the rifle pit I stood behind that day of battle.

"Vicksburg, brother?" I nod. "What'd you see?"

"That we won't go there to fight this time. Vicksburg's comin' to us. It won't be a blue snake slithering through hills coming for us. It'll be a hyena wearing a red shirt."

# CHAPTER 12

# A NEW HOME FOR A NEW LIFE

## MARCH 30, 1868

*Change can't come quick enough for some folks.*
*For others, it's too quick.*

THE SMALL CABIN we built for Seth down by Phoenix Creek in the long summer shade side of the great oak and his ten acre farm looks like a picture book painting. Seth wears a brave face, despite his sadness for the loss of Chloe's mother. Because of Captain Tom Ford, he'll never enjoy having a second mother like I have in Momma Sophie.

Martha and the girls decorate the lone window with curtains and make sure he has the basics for bedding and cooking. Seth has settled into his new home, and it won't be long before he and Chloe set a wedding date. It'll be a grand event.

Seth's not around as much as usual, but that's a good thing. He's already instructing a few children in their homes, building parents' confidence in his teaching abilities. He's had meetings with parties interested in supporting his work. Staying busy keeps a soul from being pulled into the mud of despair or down the wrong path. He's doing just that.

Seth's learning the art of smoking meats and canning vegetables and jams with Mr. Allrice and Momma Sophie. He stays nights with them after he works with the school children in that area. They can teach Seth much about how to be a good husband.

He laughs when he speaks about his cooking. "Lummy, before I came here, I couldn't even burn water. I like to eat, so I determined myself to learn to cook so I can eat all the things I like, and when I want them. And besides,

Miss Chloe and I plan to take up Mistuh Allrice's smoked meat business when he's ready to lay it down." Of course, he wants all of Ma's recipes, which are pretty easy to learn. He grins. "Who knows, we might open a café in town someday."

Not a bad plan. I bet Annie Fanny would come up from Vicksburg to help them get started, and Susannah's sister, Ruth, could surely do the cooking. That is, if the Lost Causers allow it.

Life for Chloe seems to be on the mend after her mother's passing. But who can ever get over such a thing? I'm surprised how well she and Seth take the loss. I guess after years of violence, abuse, and death, black men and women have developed a resolve and a will to survive no white person can understand. Elihu wanted to get the law involved, but Seth stopped him.

"I appreciate it, brother, but it won't do any good. Same thing will happen again, and more people could get hurt. It'll be this way until men like Captain Tom Ford and his Hyenas get put in cages."

The Negro race is so—what was the word Seth used—resilient? I've learned to push through my own barriers watching my black family embrace what the good the Lord gives in the worst of trials. That's a virtue no white man can rob them of. Watching Martha's children playing in the yard, I notice how handsome Seth and Chloe are together. They'll have the prettiest children.

Seth travels from home to home teaching young and eager minds, all the while keeping an eye open for temporary schoolhouses until a new one can be built. It's not long before two white farmers warm to his ideas and both offer their old cotton houses to be schoolhouses, each in different parts of the county. Seth teaches three days in one place and two the other, and then alternates to ensure the children get equal attention. He's already got eight to ten children registered in each house. But supplies come slowly.

Seth applied for textbooks a while back, but they seem to always be "on the way," the postman says. I think the postman has them hidden away in the back storeroom. Elihu can't stand the thought of that, and neither can I.

Late one afternoon, we ride into Bankston to pick up the mail, trying not to be noticed. I sit in the wagon with my hat pulled down and my long hair covering both sides of my face. It's the first time I've been in Bankston since I helped burn the mills, and I don't want to be recognized. Elihu leaps off the wagon and stomps through the open door into the post house.

As the wrinkled old gray-haired postman checks General Delivery for Tullos mail, Elihu bursts out, "There goes a snake!" Elihu jumps the counter chasing after the supposed snake and beelines to the storeroom that he suspects holds Seth's textbooks.

He pushes the door open as the postman yells, "Hey, you can't go in there!"

"But that copperhead slithered right under this door. Can't have him sneakin' around in here. Somebody's gonna get bit."

The clerk tries to close the door, but Elihu blocks it with his foot.

Elihu spies the boxes of books. "What's this?" He sees the mailing label which reads Seth Tullos. For a second, Elihu is taken aback, but proud that Seth has taken on his new family's name. He collects himself and turns to the postman, who beats him to the punch.

"You're committin' a crime boy. That's the U.S. mail you're messin' with."

Elihu walks to the postman, fists clenched. With noses touching, Elihu stares down on him with eyes that could kill all by themselves. "Damn straight that's the U.S. mail. And it sure as hell ain't yours. How long you had them books, you worthless damn government paid U.S. postman?"

The old man tries to come up with an answer but has none.

Elihu barks, "Yeah, thought so. That turtle's drawn its head back into the shell." Elihu loads the four boxes into our wagon. The postman peers out of the window afraid Elihu will report him to the government office across the street. Elihu walks back inside.

"I'll say this only once. Don't ever withhold mail from anybody again. Ever! You hear?"

"I'm sorry. I didn't want to Elihu. It's just, well, that damned Captain Tom Ford threatened me. Said if I gave your boy them books, he'd catch me outside of town somewhere and hang me as a traitor." The postman shivers like a cold snake just slithered down his spine.

"I understand, but it ain't no excuse." Elihu points out at the street. "Look out there. See them nosey eyes lookin' with their gossipin' tongues already waggin'? When that bastard Ford hears about it, and he will, you tell him the truth. Elihu Tullos came and took what the post office should've done already gave us. If he's got a problem with that, tell him to come see me. He knows where I stay."

The postman nods, ashamed. "Is that your brother Lummy out there?"

"What's it to you, old man?"

"Captain Ford knows who he is, and knows he's back. Jason Niles put his name in the Greensborough newspaper months ago."

"Tell me somethin' I don't already know."

"He said your brother's the turn coat traitor who burned Wesson's mills, and he's gonna hang him for it."

"When hell freezes over, old man. That's big talk comin' from a skunk bellied, shit eatin', fish mouthed, dumb ass fool, don't you think?"

The old man shrugs. "I'm just sayin'."

"You've said enough."

Elihu slams the door on his way out and hops up on the wagon next to me. He says nothing until we get out of town. He pulls out a small jug. "I need a drink." He takes a swig and hands it to me.

I shake my head. I need my wits about me. I give the mules a gentle tap with the reins, and we bump on down the road.

Passing a familiar spot a mile out of town, I peer up a long lane to see Josiah on the porch of his one room cabin. I back the wagon up and head up the hill where Josiah stands up waving.

"What's the smartest old man I've ever known got goin' on today?"

Josiah, the most intelligent man I know, never got credit for running Wesson's huge Semple engine that powered his mills. Josiah never had any training, and Wesson was too proud to admit that a black man could figure out how to run and maintain the engine when no white could. Wesson called him, "Chat," short for chattel, just to keep Josiah in place. It was good to see Josiah when I helped burn the mills. It was also good to see Wesson running around in his nightshirt in the firelight shadows, screaming and cursing about his mills burning. I still find no pride in what I did. But visiting with Josiah for a moment while sat in a rocking chair on the porch of the Bankston Hotel was like putting sweet cream on a good helping of Ma's blackberry cobbler.

Josiah grins and starts down the porch. "You see what I'm doin', boy. Absolutely nothin'."

We backslap a hug, and Elihu climbs down from the wagon, moonshine jug in hand.

"You boys come take a seat." Josiah spies the jug in Elihu's hand and starts coughing, trying to clear his throat like he's been sick. "My throat is some kind'a dry, Mistuh Elihu. You got just the right remedy for such an ailment right there in that jug."

Elihu laughs and holds out the jug. "Sure do. Finest shine the Wood boys ever made from the cool clear waters of Aaron Wood's Spring." Elihu tips the full jug to carefully pour a stream of the fiery liquid into Josiah's tin cup.

Josiah takes a long, slow draw from his tin cup. "Um umph, that's good stuff." He finishes off the last drops, but waves off a second offer from Elihu. "Won't make it to church on Sunday if I take another sip. Just forget to take that jug with you when you head home, please suh."

"Yours to keep, old man. Just hang onto the jug if you want me to refill again it some time."

"I'll guard it with my life, good brother."

I sip a swig and wait for any news Josiah is willing to share.

"What brings you boys out this way? Lummy, I know it's been a while since you've been back, but you shouldn't be in town, not just yet."

"Had to come in sometime. Figured today was good as any."

Josiah shakes his head like he's trying to get water out of his ears. "T'ain't safe, son. Trouble's brewin' like good beer, but I fear the taste will be far less than desirable. The word's out. I knew it'd come, son. You shouldn't have been in town the night the mills were burned."

I sit on the steps, rubbing my hands together like I'm washing them. Why, I don't know.

"Wesson recognized you, Lummy. He saw you with your sergeant when the flames kicked up and he ran out in his nightclothes cussin' up a storm."

"I figured as much. But that was war."

Josiah holds out his cup for a refill. "Still is for him and other folks about. Guess I need another taste, please, suh."

Elihu pours Josiah two fingers more. "What're people sayin', Josiah?"

"That Captain Tom Ford and his no count Hyenas, wearin' them damn red shirts, are gonna get you back for burnin' the mills."

Elihu shakes his head. "I hate to hear that."

I swirl the moonshine around in my cup. "Ain't nothin' we didn't already know, brother."

Josiah holds his cup to his mouth, but before he takes a sip, he says, "But more so for killin' Lester, I think. He and Ford were best friends from kids on up, sort of like you and that boy Poole."

I bang my cup on the porch, bending it a little. I start to say I'm sorry, but Josiah waves off my apology. "Damn, this is not what I hoped to come back to after tryin' to do right in the war."

Josiah smiles weakly. "Doin' right has its consequences, son. Is that the right word? Yeah, consequences, that's it."

I look at Elihu, "There just ain't no end to this stinkin' shit, is it brother?"

"Not in this world, it seems."

Josiah leans up and holds out his hands, motioning for me to place mine in his. His voice deepens, and I start to pull my hands back, but he grips them tighter.

"Son, I've been around a long time. I've seen some crazy things in my time, things not of this world. Things that'll make a strong man shudder and a Sunday preacher run." Josiah looks right to left, then back into my eyes. "Lummy, there's devil gods in these hills and swamps. They sneak in and out of good folks homes in town and out. They even create trouble in the best of churches. Some of them preachers carry on, spittin' out what rich folks want to hear, with their hand stuck out behind 'em to get paid so nobody can see. I guess that's what you call not lettin' the right hand know what the left is doin'."

I laugh, but Josiah doesn't.

"I've seen the devils in the swamp where Dan Creekwater lives, around graveyards, in town after dark, followin' behind folks travelin' on the road.

Green wisps of smoke with eyes of fire that can pierce a man's soul, slippin' through the night lookin' for who they can hurt. They can't be killed, but they can be driven off. And Captain Tom Ford is the key."

With a few more words but no more moonshine, Josiah tells us about the devilment Captain Tom Ford wreaks on the good citizens of the county. He finishes as dark creeps over the ridge.

Elihu stands up. "It's time we head back, Lummy." He hands Josiah the half empty jug. "I'll be back with another next time I come to town."

"Thank you kindly. Y'all be careful and watch out for them haints."

Josiah waves as we wander down the narrow path from his cabin to the road. Elihu shifts on the hardwood wagon seat to wave again to the man who just made his hair stand on end.

"Lummy, you think that moonshine makes him see ghosts?"

"A man sees what the Lord allows him to see. If Josiah said he saw them, who am I to argue with what a man sees, moonshine or not? Josiah doesn't get drunk. He only sips occasionally."

"So, what we're up against ain't of this world?"

I backhand his shoulder and smile. "It's always been that way, boy, don't you know?"

"Then we need some help."

"I've already started talking to the Lord about it."

"What'd he say?"

I pause. "That he'll send his angel soldiers at just the right time."

CHAPTER 13

# WHEN THE WORLD BURNS TO THE GROUND

## APRIL 5, 1868

*Some dreams don't need to be interpreted.*

THEY CAME TWO hours before dawn in the darkest and coolest part of a moonless Sunday night. When sleep is deepest and dreams are heaviest. I awaken with a start from just such a dream.

In my dozing state, my older brother George Washington Tullos, who fought with the 15th Mississippi and died at Franklin, Tennessee, comes marching toward me in his crisp, neatly pressed uniform. He looks the perfect soldier ready for battle, except that he's covered in blood—from head to toe.

"Go outside." He echoes, "Now! Now, now...."

Groggy, I wake to Elihu shaking me hard. Finally, I come to.

"Get your guns, quick!"

I don't take time to dress. I pull on my boots and run to the front porch in my long handles to see the night lit up like daytime.

The cabin we built for Seth across the field by Phoenix Creek is ablaze with the flames licking at the old shade oak. I blink, not believing my eyes. I rub my left arm with my right. My skin is on fire.

We race to the burning cabin with Jasper and James right behind us. We close in on the house, too far gone to save. The school books Elihu and I picked up at the Bankston Post Office are scattered everywhere. Elihu taps my elbow with the back of his hand and points.

Seth hangs by his neck from a big limb of the big shade oak twisting and turning in the cool damp wind whipping through the night. The flickering firelight from the burning cabin reveals the shiny wetness of his blood drenched night shirt.

Elihu drops to his knees shaking his head. Jasper wipes his watery eyes. James doubles over to puke. And I think my body will explode like an underground mine at Vicksburg.

I shake and I scream the rebel yell we boys shouted in battle. "Why?" It does no good.

The roof of the one room cabin collapses with a loud crash, and so does my peace. My soul shatters like a clay water jug dropped on a rock. Nothing but pieces left.

I raise my arms into the darkness of the moonless night. I scream like I haven't since Susannah died. The words aren't understandable. I think I'm going to faint.

I collect myself and see a note nailed to the great oak. It reminds me of when Poole and I nailed a similar piece of paper with our initials to the Choctaw County Courthouse on the Greensborough door the morning after the Bankston raid. The message left on the old shade oak is short but clear.

## THIS IS WHAT HAPPENS TO NIGGAHS AND THEM THAT TREATS THEM GOOD.
## TF

Flashes of Dawg Smith race through my mind. Memories of Lester cloud my thinking, but the message is not the only thing clear—whose initials TF belong to.

*Tom Ford.*

During the war, Ford made it his business to conscript and hunt down good Union men who wanted no part of secession. He used black and tan hounds to track and catch them. He's confessed to hanging a number of good men loyal to the twentieth star on the true American flag. He's been known to say how proud he is every time a Yankee lover's neck snaps like a twig. He almost caught and killed my good friend, H.P. Dotson, who fled north to save his family. Now he's killed Seth, and all the dreams he and Chloe had. The man is a murdering rascal. Even Grierson's chief scout Chickasaw called him notorious. And that wasn't a compliment.

On Grierson's winter raid, Captain Beckwith's 4th Iowa men captured him near Bellefontaine the morning before we burned the Bankston factories. The guards dragged him away, but not before he recognized me. He said something about me killing his best friend Lester and how he was going to cut me up for catfish bait to use in the same creek where Elihu and I dumped Lester's body. He called me a blue-suited, niggah lovin' turncoat. I couldn't let that one go by. I embarrassed him terribly with something about him mating with his black and tan bitch dog, but that didn't stave off his threats. The threats meant nothing until he shouted as the guards dragged him away that he'd get me later. He knew why we were in Choctaw County.

Ford screamed at the top of his lungs that day, "I know you're here to burn Bankston, and I know where your damn family lives, you damn niggah lovin' Tullos!"

Captain Beckwith said I need not to worry with Captain Ford again, for he was sure the man would be hanged that same day. I told him I wasn't worried and that I knew this county better than he did. After he was taken away, I thought I'd be shed of that demon, only to find out later he somehow escaped the special guard ordered to watch him. And then he showed up at our funeral celebration the first August I was home after the war.

Now he's come back. Like he promised. He knows what I did and where I live. Where my new family is. And there's nothing we can do right now but watch Seth's cabin burn to the ground.

Elihu stands up and dusts off his knees. "They're callin' us out, boys."

Jasper shakes in anger and clears his throat, "They ain't gotta call me twice, dammit!"

James spits and washes out his mouth out with creek water. "When do we leave? That bastard's got to die."

I say nothing for a couple minutes but know what needs to be said. "If we're going to do this, we've got to do it right. And make it stick. There ain't no other way if we want to come out of this thing alive with our families."

Elihu stares at Seth still hanging. "Let's get our little brother down." Nobody moves. We're all still in shock. "Now, dammit! I can't have him hangin' there like that no more."

Jasper and James gently lower Seth to the ground, then look at the blood on their hands.

My stomach turns sour as a strange feeling comes over me. I try to shake it off. It's not flash in the pan anger in the heat of a moment. I know what this is—the slow burn, ears pinned back, hackles on the back of my neck raised, determined, quiet, calculating rage that powers demons. Heat rises in my soul. My face burns hot. And not from the flames of Seth's burning cabin.

Elihu puts his arm around me. "It powers angels, too, like Saint Michael, Protector of God's people. It's time, so tell us what to do, brother."

Jasper puts his arm around James. "Yeah, Lummy. We don't know anything about fightin' on horseback. We were artillerists."

James chuckles. "Maybe we can steal a cannon."

Nobody laughs.

I count the cost of what we're about to do. It only takes a couple minutes. "All right then. It won't be easy and sure as hell won't be pretty."

My brothers nod.

I look into the darkening clouds as the fire dies down. Where's the help, Lord? We need it now.

## CHAPTER 14

# WHAT TO DO, WHEN THE WORLD'S ON FIRE

### APRIL 12, 1868

*What you won't admit, you can't use for good.*

WE BURY SETH up on the hill with the rest of the Tullos family a week after his murder. I have few words to say over my good friend and brother. I'm glad Pastor Dobbs took the largest part of the service. I couldn't have held back the tears.

Pastor Dobbs finishes with the Twenty-third Psalm, often used, but always appropriate. There's no back slapping, no grand feast for the guests, no well-wishing for the living. No, sadness blankets the small crowd like a wet and musty old worn out quilt.

Everyone turns to leave. Martha asks if I'm ready to go back to the house. I shake my head. I need time with my friend. I look down on the beautifully carved cypress marker with a Bible carved in it. Seth surely loved to read. Then it hits me. The Twenty-third Psalm.

That was the first piece Seth read out loud to the family after Mary taught him to read. That was such a happy night at Sophie's home before I left to join the Rifles. He was so proud, and so were we. Seth brought his reading to the supper table that night as a gift to his new family.

Psalm Twenty-three, a powerful piece of Scripture. Words a writer could pen in trust with the ink of confidence. Words to invoke action. Action I must take now.

I recite the text out loud and meditate on the words. I quiet my spirit and push away all thoughts from my soul but the words of the psalm. I ask for understanding. I figure if the writer received wisdom to put his thoughts on paper, I can expect the Lord will give me wisdom to understand them.

The Shepherd certainly has guided me, given me what I need, and much of what I want. I have green pastures now, even still waters. My soul has been restored, and I'm doing my best to follow his lead on the righteous path. But I hesitate there.

I have walked through the valley of the shadow of death, too many times—coyotes in Louisiana, the Vicksburg siege, killing Dawg Smith and Lester, riding with the 1st Mississippi Mounted Rifles, burning the mills in my own hometown. King David must've walked the same valley many times as well. I'd like to ask him now, *Where does it stop? When does it end?* From what I've read in the Good Book, it never did for David either.

I'm weary of walking in the valley of the shadow of death. And no, dammit, I don't fear any evil. I've always felt the presence of the Lord even in my darkest and most difficult hours. Just because a man feels like he's been abandoned doesn't mean that he is.

Some say the reason Jesus cried out, "*Why hast thou forsaken me?*" while still on the cross was because his Father turned his back on him. They say God can't look upon sin.

Horseshit.

The Father looked right at him and was never closer to his son bearing the weight of the sins of humanity than in that moment. God doesn't leave us in our worst or even most sinful moments. And he knows I've had my share of both. If he turned his back on us in our worst moments, how could he coax us back to him? The One who knows me the best loves me the most. He certainly knows me. No, somebody wrote Jesus became sin so we wouldn't have to stay covered up in it. I'm counting on it. That, and forgiveness.

I kick the dirt. It's probably not a good idea to curse while talkin' about scripture. We're all just a bunch of wicked ungrateful children in regular need of the rod of discipline like Pa once used on me and my brothers. A rod, or whatever he could get his hands on.

I'm having a hard time finding the staff of comfort in this moment. I guess I still need that rod of discipline. What man with any sense of humility in his soul doesn't? I need to be whipped for what I'm thinking about Captain Tom Ford right now. But I feel something else.

I sit and lean against Pa's grave marker I carved out of a cypress stump when I lived in McCurtain Creek Swamp with Dan Creekwater. I lay back to watch tall pines reach for the sky, brushing each other in the gentle breeze. This is a quiet, peaceful place. The smell is pungent but soothing. But something stirs my soul, weakens my stomach, and makes my head ache. It's a feeling I've not had for some time. Just what is it? I really don't want to think about this.

I'm not afraid of fighting to protect my own, or even dying for that matter. I proved that at Vicksburg, with Dawg Smith and Lester, and burning my own home town. So, I have nothing more to prove. But what is this feeling?

Suddenly Martha's face floods my mind. Then I see a new log home. Children play at my feet as I sip a tin cup of Elihu's fine muscadine wine. Hymns drift over the ridges from a new church house we Tullos boys built. Then it hits me like a red sun breaking through the dark dawn forest. It's the future for a man who's become a Celt of the settling kind and a Pict free to paint himself blue and leave his marked stones in the deep woods he never plans to leave kind.

Now I know exactly what plagues me. I want to deny it, but that's just pride talking. I shake with a bit of anger like I did in the trenches at Vicksburg. But it's not anger that stirs me. No, it's something else. I don't want to say it, so I shout it.

"Okay, dammit, I admit it! It is fear."

Then it comes to me. What I won't admit, I can't use for good. I sound like the Catholic priest back in Vicksburg. I sure could use a few minutes talking with him right about now.

It's the fear of losing what I have, the chance to live life as I had always hoped, what Creator has always intended for me. It's knowing I have to become someone else again, something not natural to who Creator made me to be, to survive what's coming.

Fear can be a good thing. I'd always thought our Pa beat fear out of us when we were little. But that's not what this is. It's not something to rid myself of or even be ashamed of. It's a good fear, the kind that will keep my soul. It's the awareness that will make me sharp, clearheaded, and survive. I see that now. Fear can be my friend. I accept it.

I have much to lose now because Creator has blessed me so well. I don't need anger to protect me anymore. I'm glad to let it go. Hope and new memories of a good life and future are enough to keep me moving forward. I can't lose this new life, not this time.

I look to the clouds. "Susannah, will you help?"

Has Creator laid out a feast in the presence of my enemies? How could he, when I've killed them all? He did for King David after he slew the giant and defeated the Philistines. Granny Thankful's thoughtful words ring true in my ears. "Son, there's a thin veil between the seen and the unseen, between those who've gone on and we who are still in the land of the living." That includes enemies, too.

I throw a rock at a tree, remembering young David with his sling. Choctaw County is still full of damn Philistines. So, what do I do about the Goliath named Captain Tom Ford?

I look down upon the great shade oak next to Phoenix Creek and remember what I wrote about a great old tree while on the sandbar. That tall Mississippi River cottonwood beside the river was no stranger to storm, flood, and drought like the great old oak below.

But the old cottonwood's limbs were never used for such a murderous purpose like that of the great shade oak. Even from here, I can see where the bark on the limb was rubbed off by the rope that hanged Seth. That scar will take a long time to heal. Just like mine.

And the damnable misery of it all? The oak never asked to be an instrument of death. Not like that. Sometimes a great old tree is used for things never intended by Creator—devilish things.

It's the same with human beings. I know, because I'm one of them. And now I'll have to do things never intended to be done by me. Again. Now.

CHAPTER 15

# FOR THE PRICE
# OF A HAM

APRIL 16, 1868

*Restraint drains more energy than fussing and fighting.*

THE RICKETY OLD two-wheel mule cart stumbles down the road filled with broken pieces of flat red sandstone. It's the same road Mr. Allrice and Mrs. Sophie have traveled for decades now, delivering their famous smoked hams and turkeys, sausage and canned meats the town folk enjoy. The road to Greensborough is long and bumpy, but this stretch is flat and straight as an arrow, shaded by limbs of every kind of tree.

They wanted to bring Chloe along to get her out of the house, but she's still grieving Seth's death. It's been only a week. As they ride along, Mr. Allrice and Momma Sophie sing, "Swing low, sweet chariot, comin' for to carry me home."

Mr. Allrice cups his ears to catch the sound of horses slowly moving in the pine thicket off to his left. He keeps singing. "I looked over Jordan and what do I see? Comin' for to carry me home? A band of angels comin' after—" He stops the wagon abruptly and reaches for his old scattergun as he continues the tune, "Comin' for to carry me home—"

A shot rings out in the quiet woods, throwing Mr. Allrice from his wagon onto the hardpan road. He wheezes and yells, "Run Sophie!" He writhes around, feeling his chest, and pulls back a bloody hand. He lies back, wondering why as darkness overtakes him.

He awakens to the sound of familiar voices. "Sophie? Where's my Sophie?" I calm him down, and Mr. Allrice asks for water. I give him just a little.

"She's fine, Mistuh Allrice, Momma Sophie's fine." I say nothing about the cuts and bruises she suffered. Though barely conscious from a hard blow to the head, she told us the dreadful story. I'm just thankful the men wreaking terror did no more harm to her than that.

I lift Mr. Allrice's quivering head with my palm, his eyes shifting back and forth. "What happened, Mistuh Allrice, who done this to you?"

He tries to lean up on one elbow, but winces with pain and collapses back down on the bed of the wagon. "I don't know why they did this to us, son. But I heard them talkin'."

"What did they say?"

"They mentioned you, Lummy, your friends, and somethin' about school books and Seth. They laughed at my hard breathin' while they waited for me to die. I didn't know what happened to my Sophie. They helped themselves to my hams and turkeys, but I couldn't say nothin'. It got dark, and they gave up when I shallowed my breathin' to almost nothing. Guess they thought I was dead."

I hold my hand hard over his wound hoping to stop the bleeding, but it ain't working.

He sits straight up in a flash. "Where's Sophie, I told her to...." And he collapses.

I catch him and lay him down gently. "But can you tell me what any of them looked like?"

"Do I need to, son?"

I shake my head. I know who they are, Captain Tom Ford's gang.

We get Mr. Allrice to his home where Ma is waiting. We lay him on the table much the way Ma described how the doctor operated on Amariah on our kitchen table the night he died. I don't want to think about that. Isabel brings hot water and bandages.

Ma winces at the bullet wound. "Elihu should be on his way back from Bankston with the doctor anytime now."

Mr. Allrice tries to raise his head but can't. "Where's my Sophie?"

Momma Sophie hobbles over, refusing any help. "I'm right here, dear."

Mr. Allrice pulls Sophie's bloody face close and looks into her eyes. "I was singin' my favorite song, Sophie, you know, the one about them angels come for to carry me home. Wasn't no angels who came to get me today, unless it was the Devil's demons."

"And I was right there singin' with you the whole time, old man."

The light in Mr. Allrice's eyes starts to fade.

Sophie cries out, "Oh, husband, please don't go, not now. Lummy and Poole was the angels the Lord sent to come get you. You home now, husband, safe in the arms of Jesus."

Mr. Allrice comes to, smiling after a few seconds. He coughs and spits blood, but relaxes back down on his pillow. "I saw it Sophie, it was beautiful."

Sophie wipes his sweaty forehead with a cool rag. "What did you see, my husband?"

Mr. Allrice, with crystal clear thought in the voice of a prophet declares, "I was standing by the Apostle John, and we looked up into heaven. I saw all manners of folks praisin' God together. There was a great multitude, which couldn't be counted. Them folks was from every nation and every tongue spoken on earth. They stood before the throne, before the Lamb of God, wearin' white robes and carryin' palm leaves in their hands. They cried out all in one voice, 'Salvation to our God who sits on the throne, and unto the Lamb!'"

It's the heavenly scene Mr. Allrice shared with us the first time we ate in his and Sophie's home. With these last words, Mr. Allrice closes his eyes and passes from this earth. Sophie sits down hard on the bench at the table and cries. She wails. We all cry.

The good folks sitting outside come in to prepare the body for the funeral. The service is set for the afternoon two days after his death, mostly due to the untimely heat. It's a long two days.

MA AND THE girls travel today with my brothers to the cemetery as I go help Momma Sophie make the last journey with her husband. I walk my horse up the narrow path to find a small gathering of friends and neighbors. The one mule, two-wheel cart sits ready to carry Mr. Allrice to the burying place. Men stand by waiting, but no one looks at me as I dismount. Their eyes are all downcast. No one speaks. I walk to the small porch where Sophie sits in her rocking chair. I take off my hat and wipe the sweat from my brow.

"Momma Sophie, you ready?" She doesn't answer. She sits motionless, staring straight ahead.

"Momma?" I slowly make the steps up the porch and kneel down beside her. I close her eyes and kiss her forehead.

"You go on now, Momma Sophie. Mistuh Allrice, Chloe's momma, Seth, and Susannah, they're all waitin' for you." I lay my head on her lap and cry. My soul slips away like the moon behind dark clouds.

The double funeral that starts out sad becomes a grand celebration. Even though I can't get in the mood, I do like the festival way my black family makes something good out of something really bad. We sing, we cry, we shout, but no one questions the Lord. My black family knows better than any that life on this earth pales in comparison to what Chloe's momma, Sophie, Mr. Allrice, Seth, and Susannah now enjoy.

My brothers widen the sides of the simple pine box so both Mr. Allrice and Momma Sophie can be buried together. I've never seen that done, but I believe it appropriate. As others file by to make their way home, I sit by the double grave.

Elihu walks up hesitantly, shaking his head. "All for the price of a damn ham. Hellfire and damnation, we'll get that bastard." He walks away without looking back.

Martha kneels beside me. "Lummy, they're all together now. Where they are now, we want to someday be." She lays her head in my lap, and I stroke her soft hair. I'm reminded of when Dorcas did the same when she and I visited Ben's grave in Winn Parish. The pain is the same. No. It's worse.

I do hope one day we'll all know that heaven starts right now—when the veil between seen and unseen becomes so thin in the hearts of men and women that our spirits walk in and out with the Lord's presence guiding us to be good human beings.

Martha whispers, "It could happen, if we but sit still with the Lord. It's a matter of the soul."

The obvious lesson is if a man walks on earth like he lives in heaven, he should be a better man. Martha shifts likes she's getting comfortable for a nap. Lord knows she needs one.

Without warning, the pain of loss seizes my heart and stings like a big red wasp. Pa, Amariah and Amanda, Susannah, Ben, Mr. Gilmore, Granville, Hog Fart, George Washington, Chloe's momma, Seth, now Mr. Allrice and Momma Sophie. Their faces steal my mind and won't turn loose. Maybe it's because I don't want to turn loose. Maybe the Devil just stole my heart. The Lord knows I need to become a devil to fight that demon Captain Tom Ford.

My chest tightens. Grief replaces anger without warning. Soldiers at Vicksburg who tried to kill me, Dawg Smith, Lester, their faces crowd out those of my loved ones passed on. I want to calm myself. I'm not sure I need to right now.

Martha raises her head. "Are you all right?"

I look deep into her eyes and hold her close. "I'd like to ask if I have even a chance of heaven for what I'm about to do."

She lies back down. "Lummy, you're already in heaven, don't you know?"

I stroke her smooth cheek. I wonder. Can I walk like Satan here on earth and still be seated in heaven with Jesus? I'll find out soon enough.

# CHAPTER 16

# NOW IT'S COME
# TO BLOOD

### APRIL 25, 1868

*Nothin' conjures up the Devil's ways more than family blood spilled.*

WE LAY MOMMA Sophie and Mr. Allrice to rest. It's not easy going back to our regular routines. I'm mad as a stirred up hornet, but what can we do? I'm holding back against the Devil's temptations, waiting on a word from the Lord. I catch myself wringing my hands, thinking about what I should do next. Spring is in full bloom, and I try to keep my mind on my work. It ain't easy.

Captain Tom Ford taunts me and my brothers, trying to draw us into a fight on his terms. He doesn't know three of us survived the Vicksburg siege and know how to fight. Like a hunter waiting to take a deer, we also know how to sit still and wait. But taunting time is over, now that blood's been spilled. Family blood is red, no matter if the skin is black or white. But once we strike back, then the battle is on. I do fear what it might lead to or where it could end.

I'm glad Susannah's little sister Ruth came to the funeral. She favors her sister so much it's like seeing Susannah all over again. That's not easy. Now she's all alone—no mother, stepfather, or sister. I didn't think she'd stop crying at the graveside. We all cried that day. I'm thankful old Miss Rachel took her in and makes sure Ruth keeps her job cooking at the Bankston Hotel. So far, no one has connected Ruth with me and burning of the mills.

I haven't visited Bankston except to get the school books with Elihu, and for obvious reasons. The suspicions about Poole and me being involved with the Yankees the night of the raid are now told as truth. What can I say? It is the truth.

I'm not afraid of their talk, but it's gone beyond that now. The main reason I don't want to go to town is seeing the ruins of the mills and manufactories we destroyed. They remind me of the death and destruction already visited on my family because of what we did. I won't go back to town anytime soon, like Josiah warned. I've plenty to do to keep me away anyway.

But my youngest brother James hasn't listened to my warnings about traveling alone and staying away from Bankston.

James took a fancy to Ruth at the funeral and has asked questions about me and Susannah. I tell him about my secret love life with Susannah that stretched from when we were kids through my years in Winn Parish. I tell how I couldn't speak at all about her to friends and family. My teeth clench still when I share stories of having to bite my tongue on many occasions when Negroes were spoken of as animals. My shoulders tense as I tell of the ribbing and being called a "niggah lover" on the streets of my own home town. I hang my head in pain as I retell the stories of killing Dawg Smith, Lester, and others I fought, but mostly about times I didn't speak up against hateful men and women. Those were the times when I walked away ashamed.

James listens to my warnings, but is not deterred. I fear for him. He can be reckless and all too willing to take chances. I witnessed that fighting alongside him in the trenches of Vicksburg. He laughed as he lobbed grenades over the parapet at the Yankees with minie balls whistling around his head. All I can do is warn him.

I lay out the differences he must accept if he chooses the path that leads to her doorstep. He argues that it's a new world like I've always talked about. I tell him it ain't so just yet, not in Choctaw County. I warn that a mixed race couple won't be accepted here for a long time, and that their children will suffer berating as well. In Mississippi, if you have even a speck of black blood, you're considered a Negro. I warn him to be careful. He grins like a school boy who avoided a whipping for yanking a girl's pigtail.

"Then I'll move north where people are all right about such things."

I try to make him see the truth. "You don't understand. If you would've told the average Union farm raised or city-reared boy soldier marching south that he was fighting to free the darkies, as they called them, he would've turn right around and went home."

"Well, I guess I'll just have to find that out for myself."

"I'll talk to Mistuh Dotson. Maybe he can connect you with some of his friends in Illinois who'll take y'all in." I stop with that. Real love takes many risks. Hell, I took many to be with Susannah. I give up, but he won't. I didn't.

It's Saturday afternoon, and we take it a bit easier for our work is done for the week. We laze around, having stuffed ourselves with one of Martha and Isabel's fine meals. I enjoy sitting on the porch, smelling the rich tobacco smoke my brothers puff from their clay pipes. The children play in the yard, and the ladies finish clearing the table. I notice the wood pile getting low, so I ask John A. to give me a hand. He follows me like a clumsy puppy dog yapping a mile a minute about how he'll catch the biggest fish when we go down by Big Bywy Creek later this afternoon. Ma wants fish for supper, and that suits me just fine.

John A. chops an armload of kindling, and then he runs a few pieces of cord wood to the house. A man rides away from the house. It's James on one of our mules. He's kicking up a pretty good dust cloud. Everyone knows he's headed to see Ruth.

Elihu walks out of the barn shaking his head, growling, "Damn that boy, he's gonna get hurt goin' into town by himself." He stops at the woodpile to gather a load of wood in his arms.

"Where's he goin'?" I already know the answer, but I have to ask.

"You dumb ass boys and your damned black beauties." Elihu throws a stick of wood back in the pile. Hard. He's got nothing against loving a Negro woman. He's just afraid of what the Hyenas might to do to James if they see him with Ruth.

I try to lighten his mood. "Hell, we get it honest. It's all Uncle Rube's fault, don't you know? That black gal he was sweet on that he never told nobody about? Ma said she was a beautiful flower to behold."

Elihu frowns. "You ain't got me fooled, boy. Love may drive your hearts, but it's the red rooster in his britches that clouds the pine knot James hangs his hat on. James ain't careful like you was. He ain't stupid, but he's actin' like he is right now."

"I know, but what can we do? He's a grown man, and I've talked to him about Ruth a number of times. He listens, but when a man's heart is set, well, you know."

Elihu stomps the ground with his right foot. "I just don't want to bury my little brother before his time, dammit. That's all."

He's right, and I also know I can't go on living like nothing happened to Chloe's momma, Seth, Mr. Allrice, and Momma Sophie. Part of me wants to act like it never happened, but the better part of me knows I can't let it go. Time is short for what's coming, so I just try to enjoy a peaceful afternoon fishing with my son. I'm just glad my other son, Elzey, is safe in Winn Parish. I hope.

John A. and I catch a mess of fish—three keeper bass, ten bream, and two good sized catfish. It's enough for a fine supper put alongside fried potatoes, canned green tomatoes, and corn pone. Sharing life with a son, teaching him the ways of the woods, how to hunt and fish, it just don't get any better than that. Seth was that for me. Oh, how I do miss him already.

We eat 'til we nearly burst. We gather in the dogtrot to catch the breeze and sip a little of Elihu's muscadine wine. I try to smile at the kids laughing and Elihu's jokes, but I still have a hard time thinking about the folks we've lost. I can't chase it out of my mind. It's because it's not over. In fact, it's just getting started. William Pollan warned us Captain Tom Ford would come after our Negro friends first. Ford's done that. More is coming, and soon. I will be a part of it. To the death.

Martha stays closer than usual. Her eyes reveal a worried soul. It's the same look she had when I boarded the steamer to Memphis with the 1st Mississippi Mounted Rifles. It's the kind of worried look that I might not come back.

I don't say anything, and she doesn't ask. But my mind's working alive like a beehive.

I ask Elihu for just a bit more wine when I spy a rider barreling down the road to our house. I can't make out who it is, but he reminds me of Old Bart. I step out to the edge of the porch, hand on my pistol.

It's Old Josiah.

"Lummy, you gotta come quick! Right now!"

*James.*

"They hurt him. They done hurt him real bad."

"Who hurt James?"

Josiah rubs the tears from his eyes as he dismounts.

I leap off the porch and shake Josiah by the shoulders. "Who, man? Who hurt James? Where is he?" I know, but I have to hear it.

Josiah kicks his boot around in the dust trying to catch his breath. "Captain Tom Ford. You know, the man who hunts men with bloodhounds."

"Elihu, Jasper! Get out here!"

Everyone hurries to the edge of the porch.

Ma finally emerges, rubbing her aching knees. "What in the Devil's goin' on?"

Josiah coughs and clears his throat. "That's exactly what's going on out here. The Devil's doings, Missus Tullos."

Ma turns. "Martha, Isabel, and you girls, y'all get back in the house. I'll come tell you in a minute."

They retreat into the house, but Ma stays. "I don't want my girls no more afraid than they need be."

I give Josiah the rest of my muscadine wine. "Sit down. Rest while you're talkin'."

He swallows hard, trying to choke out the words at the same time. "James came by the Bankston Hotel to see Ruth. You know I been watchin' after that little angel like she was my own daughter since her folks passed. Nobody's bothered her until James got caught sneakin' around tryin' to see her. You know that boy. He just ain't as careful as you was back in the day."

Elihu elbows me. "Just told you that."

"Now ain't the time, brother." I can hardly contain myself waiting for the worst of it.

"He and Ruth snuck off to the livery stable just to talk. That boy treats her just like you did Susannah, as a gentleman. I saw the whole thing. They hardly got behind the stable when Ford and his gang came from the saloon, all full of whiskey and talking loud. They caught James as he helped Ruth get away. She made it. He didn't."

My fists ball up, and I want to hit something. I slap the porch post with my hand. Hard.

Josiah whimpers. "Lord, they beat that boy to within an inch of his life. Captain Tom Ford kept yellin' at James about how this was payback for you burning the Bankston mills and killin' Lester. Oh, Lummy, they clubbed him with sticks, rifle butts, and pistol handles. He tried to cover up, but they split his head wide open pretty bad. Blood went everywhere. I ran up quick as I could, but they put this old man down quicker than shit through a goose. I'm so sorry, I tried."

"You done all you could." I pat him on the shoulder and pull back my hand wet with blood from a wound on the back of his head. "You're hurt!"

"T'ain't nothin'."

I help him up. "You get up on that porch, old man. Jasper, come help. Ma!"

She's standing right behind me. "I'll take care of Josiah. You go find your brother."

Josiah stumbles up the porch steps, his arm wrapped around Jasper's shoulder. Josiah stops. "They dumped him in McCurtain Creek near the swamp. Captain Ford laughed about how he was gonna leave James there like you left Lester and...."

I don't wait for the rest. Elihu, Jasper, and I race to the barn to mount horses, taking no time to saddle them. Martha rushes out of the house with extra pistol ammunition and my ten gauge shotgun. I stuff the pistol in my belt, and we ride off like we're headed to a fire. We are. To a fire the Devil started.

# CHAPTER 17

# THE DEVIL SLITHERS THROUGH STILL WATERS

## MIDNIGHT, APRIL 25, 1868

*In the most peaceful of places, the seeds of discord are sown.*

W E TREAD THE low water creek to lessen the sound of our coming until we get near the swamp. We rein our horses up on top of the creek bank to listen for any movement or voices of men still hanging around. We sit still for a moment.

McCurtain Creek Swamp was a place of healing for me when I hid from the Home Guard after killing Lester just before I joined the Rifles. The vastness of this swamp reminds me of my trip to the sandbar. There I sensed the greatness of Creator in the wide expanse of the Mississippi River as he filled my soul with his Spirit.

But even the Devil can slither his way into the most peaceful of places and sow discord. A cotton mouth glides on the top of the slow moving creek waters. Fitting. The Devil's already here.

There's a slight rustling on my right. I raise my ten gauge shotgun to see a familiar silhouette in the moonlight. Dan Creekwater.

"Lummy? Figured you be along directly. Haven't seen you in a spell. Wish it was at a better time, but you best come quick. Your little brother's at my place."

We take the trail I traveled many times into the dark hollow of McCurtain Creek Swamp few dare for fear of never returning. There's no good reason for people to think that except the superstitions they choose to believe. But it works for Dan Creekwater, and it did for me.

We pass through the switch cane patch that hides Dan's camp. The aroma of smoked raccoon brings back good memories of sitting by the fire and talking out my soul's troubles with this wise old man. I doubt there'll be any good memories from this visit tonight. We hop off our horses, and Jasper is the first to look James over.

I check James's head wound. "Do you think we can get 'em home tonight?"

Jasper shakes his head.

Elihu takes out a small bottle of whiskey and tries to get James to drink. He chokes down a sip and comes to, his eyes searching around like he can't see. I wave my hand in front of his face, but he has trouble focusing his eyes.

"Can you see me, James?"

He stares at me for a moment, then grins just a little. "Yeah, you ugly ass dawg faced bastard... ooh... that hurts like hell." He reaches for his head that has a gash to the bone six inches long and an inch wide. I grab his hand before he gets dirt in the wound.

Dan brings hot water from the fire. "I did nothing but make him comfortable until I got water boiled and you boys gettin' here."

"I appreciate it, Dan. You did what you could."

"I'm ready to do more if you trust me."

"You know I do." I want this old warrior with me with what's coming.

"All right then. James, this is gonna hurt like hell, but we can't let that wound get infected. It'd kill you."

James nods and takes a big long drink of whiskey. "Ahh, that's good shine. The Wood boys make that batch?"

Elihu nods. "The best there is."

Dan reaches for a leather pouch. "Elihu, wash the wound with hot water and this clean cloth as easy as you can."

Elihu pats the gash with the water soaked rag to clean off the dried blood. James tries to rise up against the pain, but I hold him down.

Dan pulls s few small items from the pouch, then threads a small needle. "Lummy, you pour some shine on the wound. Jasper, Elihu, you boys hold him down."

James screams and jerks as I dribble the fiery liquid across the wound, careful not to let any get in his eyes. I give him another long drink. He smiles a bit. The moonshine must be dulling the pain.

Dan places his hand firmly on James's head. "Good job."

In just a couple of minutes Dan has the wound sewed up tightly, and James looks to feel better already. He goes to singing and talking about how much he loves Ruth. We just leave him be until the moonshine finally puts him to sleep. We decide to wait until morning to take James home.

"Jasper, take word to Ma and the girls. They'll be worried sick if we don't tell them he's all right. And they don't need to be by themselves. Watch yourself. Captain Tom Ford ain't done with his mischief just yet. He'll be comin' to spill more Tullos blood."

# CHAPTER 18

# McCURTAIN CREEK MORNING

## MORNING, APRIL 26, 1868

*Ain't nothin' like the dawn breakin' through cypress trees
on a cool still morning.*

I AWAKEN TO a big red-headed woodpecker tapping on a dead tree searching for a beetle bug breakfast. His hammering rings through the swamp like so many workmen framing a new house.

I lay still, trying to forget the evils of the night before. The quiet fills my soul, and the gentle breeze brings the smell of fresh rabbit roasting on the fire. Then I sit up looking for James.

"He's all right," Dan assures me. "Didn't move all night."

I check his wound. "Thanks, Dan. Don't know what we Tulloses would do without you."

Dan takes the rabbit from the fire. "Ain't nothin' you wouldn't do for this old red man. He'll have a scar, but he'll live. Piece of rabbit?"

I take a leg and enjoy its smoky flavor.

Elihu walks back into camp fixing his britches. "Just left a deluxe catfish dinner in them bushes back over there. Best not go that way for a day or two."

I throw my rabbit bone at him. "Damn boy, can't you see we're eatin'?"

"Yep, and I'm ready for a piece of that rabbit."

I sip the rich dark coffee Dan boiled up and watch James reach to rub his head.

Elihu catches his hand. "Don't do that just yet, son. You gotta let it heal."

James tries to sit up, barely making it to his elbow. He reaches for the cup of coffee Dan offers. "What happened to me?"

I ask, "What do you remember?"

"I sneaked off with... Ruth!" He tries to get up but falls back down. "Is she all right?"

"I think so. Josiah said she got away. Tell us what you remember."

"I'd just got Ruthie around the back of the livery and kissed her when I heard hollerin' and cussin'. I spied Captain Tom Ford comin' our way and told Ruthie to get goin'. But it was too late. They rushed us like Yanks coming up the hill at Vicksburg. We wasn't botherin' nobody. They grabbed me and tried to get Ruthie, but somebody came runnin' in and threw his body at the men pawing all over Ruthie with their nasty hands. He knocked them down. Ruthie broke free, then it all went dark for me. I don't even remember how I got here." He looks around and tries to get up again. "Where's Josiah? It had to be him who saved my Ruthie."

I hold him down, and Dan fetches a little moonshine to calm him.

"How'd I get here?"

Dan sits down beside James. "I heard them boys laughin' and yellin' at the edge of the swamp. Before I knew what was goin' on, they dumped you in the water. I howled like a pack of wolves, and it must've scared them. They ran off. Just knew I'd find you dead, boy."

"I'm surprised they didn't slit my throat."

"They were just about to when I run 'em off."

"I remember somebody hollerin' like they'd been shot. But I heard no shot."

"I put an arrow into one's shoulder, and before they could pull pistols I let loose another one into the loudest one's hip just above the saddle. They couldn't tell where the arrows were comin' from, so they lit out like a bear was after them. They must've thought the haints were chasin' them."

I pull another piece of rabbit from over the fire. "Hell no! Weren't no haint. It was a bear after them. Of the Choctaw tribe!"

James pats Dan's arm. Dan nods, chewing on a rabbit leg.

I throw my rabbit bone into the fire. "If you can, we need to get you home. There's things need doin'."

Dan stops chewing. The look in his eyes is enough to stop a man dead in his tracks.

I don't blink. "Can't let this go by, Dan."

Elihu stands up wiping rabbit juice on his pants. "I'll get the horses."

Dan reaches for his bow and quiver. "What you gonna do now, Crazy Deer Dancer?"

I think he's making a joke about the Choctaw name he gave years ago, but not so. He has the look of man ready to peel the hide from the top of his enemy's head to the bottom of his feet.

"Chloe's momma, Seth, Mistuh Allrice, Momma Sophie, and now this? I want to kill 'em all. If I'd done it when first blood was drawn, maybe they'd all still be alive." Tears blur my eyes.

Dan takes my shoulders in his big hands. "You can't go there, son. They did the killin', not you. You ain't had much time to do anythin' about it."

"They're all just as much family as James here. They're my blood."

James softly touches his wound. "We all are. Jesus made it so."

I kick at the air and slap my hands together. "Why'd I wait, dammit?"

In a small voice, James whispers, "Lummy, you know what day it is?"

"Hell, I don't know."

"Resurrection day. You know, Easter, when Jesus came up out the grave." James's memory is muddied. Easter was two weeks ago, but I say nothin'. I don't want to be reminded of anything good right now. I'm too angry at the world and at myself. He grins. "I reckon some folks can't stand us bein' happy all together like it will be in heaven."

I throw my cold coffee into the fire. "Well, heaven sure as hell ain't nowhere on this earth. If it is, I can't see it."

Elihu hands me the ten gauge shotgun. "You will soon enough. We just gotta help the Lord a little with this one."

Dan slurps his coffee. "Remember what I said about the meanin' of the word Choctaw?" I nod. "It ain't about sweet voices no more. It's about separation—their heads from their bodies."

I pull the knife Pa made me and thumb the edge of the blade. "I know how to do that."

# CHAPTER 19

# SINGLED
# OUT

## EARLY AFTERNOON, APRIL 26, 1868

*Ain't nothin' like bein' the talk of the town,*
*whether they're right or not.*

W E GET JAMES safely home to find Poole on the front porch pacing like a father waiting for his first child to be born. The look on his face is as if the child just died, wondering if the mother will soon follow. I'm glad he's not married. Though it's the greatest blessing any man can have on this earth, it's a worry he doesn't need right now.

"Came as quick I heard."

"How'd you find out so quickly?"

He rubs the back of his neck. "Captain Tom Ford and his damn ruffians came through Greensborough today as people got out of church. I was helpin' my folks into the wagon when I saw a crowd forming around the old burned down courthouse. Ford was wavin' a piece of paper around talkin' about two men who helped the Yankees burn Bankston and Greensborough. He was talkin' about us, Lummy." I hear the fear in his voice.

"Did he call out our names?"

"No, but he might as well have. You know Jason Niles already made known the names of the men who fought for the Union, especially those who switched sides. People are already narrowing it down to us." Poole looks to puke.

"Come to the edge of the porch, boy, and let it go."

He heaves, but nothing comes up. He's not scared. He's just worried about his aging folks. Ma brings him a cup of cool water to wash out his mouth and cool his throat.

I hand him a kerchief to dry his mouth. "What happened next?"

"Ford hopped up on the back of a wagon and went to tellin' that he knows exactly who the initials belong to on the note we wrote. People started lookin' around at their neighbors, tryin' to figure out who he was talkin' about."

"He said, 'Not tellin' who they are or even what the initials are right now, but you know these men. These scoundrels of low character ran off and joined our enemies when they were needed at home fightin' Yankee aggression!' When he said that, the crowd roared like they was a mob or somethin'. Never seen people get so agitated so fast. I pulled my hat down when Captain Ford nodded at me like he was placing his mark on my back.

"A Ford man shouted, 'Let's find 'em and hang 'em!' Another yelled, 'And skin 'em alive!' Then a commanding voice like the Lord himself spoke. It was Sheriff Platner, who ain't sheriff no more. He spoke like a brush arbor preacher."

"What'd he say?"

"He shook his fist, 'What's done in war stays in war. Ain't a man here who carried a clean musket in those days. Even the Home Guard did things that'd make a preacher cuss. You want names? I'll give you their names. Right now!' Somebody threw a whiskey bottle, and it broke on Sheriff Platner's head. He fell down, and his wife and Mistuh Dotson carried him home bleedin' like a stuck pig. It was awful."

I pull out my pistol and check the loads.

"The crowd hissed like snakes, asking, 'Who are those men? What's their initials? Why won't you tell us? Tell us now!' Captain Ford held up his arms to quiet the crowd. 'Nope, ain't gonna tell you. I'm gonna hunt 'em down with my blood hounds and bring 'em to you. You don't want me to miss out on the fun of the hunt, do you?' The crowd roared in laughter. 'Then, you'll know what to do with these mud suckin' bastards.' The women covered their mouths in embarrassment, and the men shouted even louder. Then I got out of there and came this way quick as I could."

"Stay as long as you need to. What about your folks?"

"They left for my uncle's place in Jackson City for a spell, 'til things simmer down."

"They may be there a while."

He nods. "I'm going to Bankston. Be right back."

Martha yells as he climbs into the saddle, "You get back in time for supper, Tom Poole!"

"Wouldn't miss it for nothin', kind lady."

"Poole. Watch yourself and I—"

Poole winks. "I know."

CHAPTER 20

# IT'S TIME
# TO GO!

## NEAR DARK, APRIL 26, 1868

*Go while the gettin's good, or you might not go at all.*

P OOLE BARRELS DOWN the lane that leads to our house kicking up a fair sized dust cloud. He throws a leg over his mount's neck like he did when we served with the 1st Mississippi Mounted Rifles. He races up the steps as Martha and I step out on the porch.

"You got to go, Lummy, I mean leave, right now!"

Martha shoos the children away as my brothers come out of the barn where they're stirring hay.

Elihu stomps up like he's about to take a swing at somebody. "What's all this, Poole? Ridin' up in here like the Devil himself."

"I ain't the Devil, but I'm here to tell you about him."

Ma steps out the door with a cool cup of water and hands it to Poole. "Sit down, son, tell us."

Poole gulps down the water and takes a couple of deep breaths. "That Tom Ford, he's about to spill the beans on what we did on Grierson's Raid. He didn't tell who the initials belonged to in Greensborough this mornin', but he's hintin' real hard about doin' it in Bankston. Guess he's gatherin' up sympathizers for what he plans to do."

I turn away. "Shit! I wish a thousand times over we hadn't done that now." Martha rubs my back. "Sorry dear." She puts her finger to my lips to cool my temper and curb my cursing.

Poole holds out his cup for more water, but Elihu pours him some muscadine wine. "Captain Tom Ford made another speech in front of the burned down cloth factory about how the Bankston mills were torched by the same Yankees who burned Greensborough. But then he said that the same men whose initials were on the note came back to finish the job back last April. They said we burned the county courthouse, Lummy." Poole sits down rubbing his face in his hands.

I shake with anger. "You and I both know that's a damn lie. We all know it."

Poole accidently burps, having drunk too fast. "Don't matter! We ain't got a leg to stand on if he tells folks whose initials they are. You know I'm right. Folks are still angry as old wet hens about losin' the war, and they want somebody to get back at. Captain Ford aims to make that you and me, brother."

Elihu slaps a porch post. "Did he say whose initials they are?"

"Not yet. He just promised to bring the two men in so they could do with them as they please. He stirred up the crowd sayin' how happy he is to put his blood hounds on somethin' bigger than a coon. He wasn't talking about the four-legged kind either. People were talking about hangin's, stonin's, even skinnin's."

Poole's demeanor changes from a whipped pup to a growling swamp cat. Poole's a happy-go-lucky fellow almost all the time. But when he gets mad, which ain't often, he gets mad all over. He loses his mind, sort of like Pa did when he came after us for a beating. Like me when I slammed Kneehigh on the street. Rage with no recollection.

Jasper shakes his head. "Ain't nothin' you can say or do, Lummy. This ain't goin' away, brother."

"I know that, dammit. But what can I do? I gotta think."

James wipes his hands and scratches his nose. "Problem is, them folks don't want to hear it, not the truth anyway."

Ma whispers, "Truth is, if you don't tell your side of the story, they'll make up their own."

I step down off the porch. "Ain't that the damned truth? People would rather believe a made up story than the truth."

Poole fidgets around like fleas are crawling all over him. "I should write a piece and put it in the paper. Couldn't sign it though. They'd sure enough know who we are then. Damn! I just don't know what to do. Lummy?"

Elihu knows and nods. Jasper steps up as James hobbles over hanging onto a porch post. Ma smiles weakly and walks back into the house.

I look far away into the hills. "Yeah, I know what we have to do, Poole, and it must be now."

Martha kisses me on the cheek. "I'll go pack, dear. We'll leave when you're ready."

# CHAPTER 21

# NIGHT RUNNIN' AGAIN

## CLOSE TO MIDNIGHT, APRIL 26, 1868

*I thought I was done slippin' away into the darkness*
*after the surrender of Vicksburg.*

AFTER A LATE supper, Martha and I sort through what she'll need for an extended visit with Annie Fanny in Vicksburg. I walk outside to get the mules hitched, but Elihu and Jasper have the wagon up to the house ready for the journey. James offers to help carry our belongings out and load them up, but I wave him off. I don't want his wound opening up again.

Elihu rigged up a frame of a sort covered with an oil tarp to keep Martha and the kids out of the wet and cool air. It'll be a long, bumpy ride depending on road conditions. While Ma and Isabel prepare food for our trip, I sit in Pa's old rocking chair in the dogtrot. I can't believe I'm doing this again. Night running.

The last time was back in July of '63 when J.A. and I left the quickly disappearing army of surrendered Confederate soldiers marching to the exchange camp at Enterprise. I couldn't get back home to Winn Parish soon enough. Taking a new oath to the Union, in my mind, freed me to leave an army that was holding on to a cause I didn't believe in any more. That opened the door for me to join the army that still held true to Mississippi being the twentieth star on the flag of the United States of America—the 1st Mississippi Mounted Rifles. Despite what Captain Tom Ford does, who Jason Niles reports as having fought for the Yankees as they return home, or what the newspapers still holding to the Lost Cause write, I made the right choice. The consequences are mine, and I'm not afraid to face them. In fact, I'm running straight at them.

So, slipping away into the darkness ain't new to me. Traveling at night with J.A. through haunted Chickasaw Bayou and taking what we needed from the dead and swimming the Mississippi on a make-shift raft took me back to face the realities of Susannah's death. Escaping a Yankee patrol boat and helping a raccoon get across the river to see Annie Fanny alive again gave me hope that not all was lost. Slipping past Dawg Smith the first time I saw him on the railroad tracks leading to Monroe, and then at the house where his men killed several deserters, I just hope this trip will be much less dramatic.

Funny thing, this time I'm slippin' away into the darkness headed to Vicksburg, not away from it. No matter. Right now I just need to make sure my family is protected. Memories of visiting Susannah's grave, Old Bart recounting Ben and Mr. Gilmore's deaths, killing Dawg Smith in Winn Parish, and Lester here, capture my mind. I don't want to go through that again. I can't.

I stare into the star filled night. "Lord, help me get my family to safety, and protect those who stay here."

Martha puts her arm around my shoulders. "Amen."

It's too much to think about. It'd be easier just to run for good, but really it wouldn't. I couldn't. I wouldn't be able to live with myself.

Poole takes a last walk around the wagon to make sure everything is tied down tight and secure. He starts up on the porch. He and J.A. are the best friends a man could ever have. I wish J.A. was here with me now.

I start for the wagon but stop to shake his hand. "We leave tonight. Should be able to clear the county line before daylight. We'll take the Old Trace. It'll be safer."

Poole lays his hand on my shoulder as we walk inside. "I'm goin' with you, Lummy."

I stop short, bristle up, and shake my head. "No, the hell you ain't. You've got your own worries to tend to. When you boil it down, this is about me and Tom Ford, and you know it. You don't even need to be associated with me in any way, Poole. It'll just get you killed."

Poole furrows his brow like he's about to wade into me with fists flying. "It's about me, too, damn you. They'll figure out my initials as soon as they do yours. You need another gun on this trip. I'm goin', brother, and I ain't askin'."

Ma hands Poole a steaming hot cup of coffee. "Cut out that cussin', or I'll take a switch to both you boys' backsides." She points her finger at us. "I'm still able. Come inside for a couple minutes before you leave."

I slump, sitting on one of the two kitchen table benches where I've eaten many a meal. I rub my eyes and look up at Poole. I'm not sure if he's mad at what I said or just hurt. Probably both.

I scratch at a knot in the pine board tabletop. "I'm sorry, brother. I just don't want you mixed up in all this any more than you are already and get hurt."

"I'm already mixed up in it." I nod staring at the floor. "Your family is my family from as far back as we both can remember, Lummy. You don't have to have the same last name to be blood family."

"Ain't it so. But think about your folks. Ford's damn wicked arm can reach to Jackson."

"I'll check on them when we pass by."

I'm resigned to the fact now. He's going, and I sigh in relief. In my heart, I'm glad he's going. "Okay then, get your gear, and you do know what I mean."

"I'll meet you at French Camp, ready to go." Poole slips out the front door trying not to wake the children.

Martha sits down beside me. "Lummy, I know this won't be good, but somethin' has to be done." She rubs my shoulder and the back of my neck. "All I want is for you to come back, all in one piece, and for this to finally be over."

Tears well up. "I just don't know if it will ever be over, Martha."

She wraps her arms around me and lays her head on my aching shoulder. Like the tree the size of a dragon that rose up when I crossed the Mississippi back in '59 to injure my shoulder, the demon Captain Tom Ford has risen up to hurt the ones I hold dearest. He refuses to let peace rule in the county. Martha lets me go so I can finish last minute tasks. I walk out onto the porch, checking off my mental list.

Ma steps out into the dogtrot. "Son, sit with me for a spell." Jasper and

Isabel, Elihu and James, remain inside to sit with Martha at the table for a few moments.

"There was one other thing your Grandpa Temple sent years ago with the letters I gave you." She hands me a small leather pouch with a new leather string to tie it closed. Inside I find a piece of faded red, white, and blue cloth. I carefully unfold it.

"That's the flag when Mississippi became a state. Your Grandpa Temple was so proud that day he traded a whole jug of shine for it. Said he was finally part of a land where men live free with no lords or church folks tellin' him how and where to live."

I rub the thick cloth.

"Lummy, you've had to become another person to fight for what you believe in, and now I know you have to do that again. Just don't forget why, and come back to yourself when this is over. It can't be about revenge for Chloe's momma, Mistuh Allrice and Momma Sophie, Seth, Susannah, or even James. God's got them in the palm of his hand, and James will be all right. When things get bad, let that little flag and God's good Word remind you of the real reason why you fight. And like your daddy always told you, don't forget whose name you wear."

I stuff the little flag back into its leather pouch and hang it around my neck.

Elihu steps out on the porch. "If you're gonna clear the county line by daylight, you best get goin'. Jasper and me are gonna ride with you 'til then. Poole can take it from there."

"I appreciate it, brother." With the kids loaded in the back of the wagon, Martha and I slip away into the darkness, down the road that leads away from home.

# CHAPTER 22

# SAFE IN THE CITY UPON A HILL THAT CAN'T BE HIDDEN

## MAY 1, 1868

*If a city with no walls can't be safe,*
*an army dressed in blue can.*

THE WAGON TRIP to Vicksburg is a long and hard four days. Once we cleared the county line, we traveled day and night, stopping only to rest the mules, eat, and sleep for a couple of hours. The rains didn't help, except to make the roads worse. The fast pace has been hard on Martha and the children—for Poole and me, too, for that matter. But I figure we'll soon rest safe in Annie's warm café. We stop in Clinton just long enough to send Annie a telegram letting her know we're on our way. Poole detours a bit to check on his folks and meets us soon after.

When Elihu left us at the county line, I was glad he went to get Dan to come stay on the farm. I'm a little uneasy about Elihu, Jasper, and James guarding Ma and the girls while I'm gone. Having Dan there with them helps ease my mind. They're all very capable men, but bullies like Captain Tom Ford don't ride unless they have a gang of men to back up what they can't do for themselves. Still, the Hyenas aren't so stupid as to launch an attack on the Tullos farm. It'd be like Sherman assaulting the 27th Louisiana Lunette when the Yankees first arrived in Vicksburg—a slaughter. Although that wouldn't be all that bad an outcome for Ford.

My brothers are shooters and unafraid to use a weapon. Ma and the girls know how to reload most any weapon, besides being pretty good shots as well. And the Wood boys aren't far away, and they ain't scared. We may not agree with them on all issues that tend to divide good people these days, but our loyalties go beyond politics, even church beliefs. Our ties are strong as the old shade oak down by Phoenix Creek where Seth died. The Wood folk are as good as blood kin. We can depend on them.

We pass Four Mile Bridge where I spent many a night on guard duty in a gray uniform, and then in camp as a base of operations in blue. It's nearly abandoned now, except for the few farmhouses that made it through the war. During the war, it was the picket line for both blue and gray. It was the site where many a prisoner of war was exchanged and returned to the fight.

We rest the mules. "Boys, you're not gonna like this, but we were ordered to throw slaves out of their little cabins here one cold rainy night so we could take our position on the railroad."

John A. asks, "Where'd they go, Pop?"

I have no answer. "Anywhere they could, I'm sorry to say." I'm glad he's growing up not having to wrestle with the white and black issue like I did. He's being raised on the right side of that one.

I pray standing on the spot where I first saw Jasper and James pulling a cannon down the road as I got on the train to go meet the Yankees in Grenada November of '62. Though unbeknownst to me at the time, Amariah died that same dark night. After eating a bite and finishing my story, we take the Jackson Road into town to find Annie and Beau.

We crest the last hill that'll take us down the cobblestone street to the café. Smells of the river waft up between the buildings. I love Big Muddy and have come to love this 'city set upon a hill that can't be hidden.' It surely has been nearly the death of me, but also surely the life of me. On this visit, it will shelter precious lives so dear to me.

Memories flood my mind like watching a school play as mule shoes *clickety-clack* on the cobblestone streets—crossing the river chasing Susannah and getting my shoulder injured, passing through on my way to enlist in the Confederate Army and meeting Annie Fanny for the second time, learning of Susannah's death and losing many a good friend, surviving the siege with my brothers and me taking a new oath to the Union, passing through on my way home to Choctaw County and finding Seth, enlisting in the 1st Mississippi Mounted Rifles just around the corner from Annie's café and meeting Martha, and finally returning here after burning Bankston and marrying Martha when the war ended. So, why should it surprise me that here I am once again?

Vicksburg is a place I can't escape. And now I'm not trying to. The city that once held me captive in one of the worst sieges of the war will now be a safe haven for my family.

We pull up in front of Handerson's Café. The children bounce off the wagon and barrel inside to see their Aunt Annie. They nearly knock Annie down as she steps outside to greet us.

The kids hug her tightly, and Beau calls them from inside the restaurant. "Y'all get on in here! There's a fresh sweet cake for each of you. And something else. It's a big surprise."

The kids gather around him like a pack of yelping puppies, yelling, "What is it, Uncle Beau?"

He kneels and wraps his arms around all of them. "Ice cream!"

They scamper inside, and the door slams behind them, as kids will do. Beau belly laughs and holds his hands up in surrender. "What can I say, I have no discipline when it comes to children. Y'all come on in. Glad to see you."

Poole grabs the reins. "Go on, I'll take care of the wagon and get the mules and horses watered and fed. See you in a bit." He tips his hat. "How do, Annie?"

Annie blows Poole a kiss. "Ain't no woman strapped you down to her bed yet, Tom Poole?"

He blushes, but likes the attention. "Workin' on that very thing, sweet Missus Annie. Too bad you already been hitched or I'd...."

Annie giggles like a young girl getting her first kiss behind the school house. "Oh my, you are the flatterer, my dear man."

I hop off the wagon in one leap to help Martha down. "Go on, Poole, before lose your religion right here in front of everybody."

Annie taps her foot, staring at me. "Um hmm, Martha. You got the finest lookin' man I ever did see, and a gentleman, too. Girl, you better take care of that man. Be glad I was already taken when you laid eyes on him."

Martha slaps the air. "Or you'd do what, big sister?"

Annie laughs. "Get in trouble, that's for sure. C'mon inside, Beau and I been lookin' forward to your comin'." Annie sees the strain in my face. Her face falls flat. "How you doin', brother?"

"Not so good, Annie."

"Things must be pretty bad to bring Martha and the kids this far."

"They are, and I need them to be this far away. I don't know how far this trouble can reach. Just ain't gonna take no chances."

Annie shakes her head. "Lummy Tullos, I love you, boy, always have. From that time when I patched you up on your way through Desoto back in '59 to you marryin' my sweet sister, I felt family with you, brother. Lord knows if anybody ever deserved to have a quiet and peaceful life, it's you. I'll be damned if you're not gonna get it someday." She stands up on her tip toes to grab my shoulders with both hands and shakes me. "You stay alive."

Tears mixed with black eye makeup make dark streaks on her rosy cheeks. Martha wipes Annie's eyes with a flowered handkerchief.

Annie straightens my blue 1st Mississippi Mounted Rifles jacket like a mother readying her child for the first day of school. "That's smart wearin' the Yank coat. It'll get you further down the road around here for whatever it is you gotta do. But be careful in the countryside. My soldier boy customers say there's lots of meanness goin' on not far from town."

"I put it on when we reached Four Mile Bridge. I'll be careful when to put it on and take it off."

She pulls my head down and gives me a peck on the lips. "You better. I don't want to have to patch your ass up again."

I hug her close, and we walk inside the café holding Martha's hand. "You have been an angel in my life, Annie. I won't ever forget it."

It seems like yesterday I enlisted in the Union Army just around the corner and put on the blue suit. It seems like just the day before when I stayed in the Prentiss House Hotel not far in the other direction wearing the gray suit.

Funny thing, this is my third enlistment. But this one requires no papers, no drilling, and no training. I know how to do this. As much as I hate it.

# CHAPTER 23

# A SHORT VISIT BEFORE MY THIRD ENLISTMENT

## EARLY AFTERNOON, MAY 1, 1868

*It ain't easy to eat when somethin's eatin' on you.*

WE SETTLE INTO our chairs as Beau brings coffee and home-made pie. I don't feel much like eating with what's eating on me. The kids have finished their ice cream and are starting to act up. I call them down in a harsher tone than I ever do. Martha looks at me strangely, and I apologize. I call the children over and hug them together and tell them I didn't mean to be so short. Little Margaret smiles up at me like an angel. I do love my children.

John A. shakes my hand, then hugs me and cries. "It's okay, Pop. We know you got a lot on your mind." He remembers a father who went off to war and never came back.

Martha gives me a tearful smile that melts me like butter on the hot fresh bread the cook just brought out. They are no strangers to heartache. I must remember that. Annie tries to change the mood with her terrible off key singing of Camptown Races. We laugh as she pulls apart pieces of steaming bread for us and the boys, keeping time with her singing.

She leans over to Martha. "You'll stay above the café with Beau and me like you did before. I expect you'll want to work while you're here?"

Martha nods, chewing a mouthful of bread.

"Perfect. I got a new contract to supply bread and sweetcakes to the army, so the extra help is right on time, sister."

I stare at Annie until she uncomfortably asks, "What?"

"You, my dear, have become a fine student of the English language. You have really come into your own. You now hold the status of a fine lady in this fair city."

Annie cackles like she did when I first met her. "Honey, the only thing that's fine about me is...." She looks around to make sure the children can't hear. "Is this fine hiney, Lummy honey." She rears back and laughs out loud. "I guess you can call me Finey Hiney instead of Annie Fanny, brother."

Martha blushes, and I shake my head. "Same old Annie Fanny. Please don't ever change."

Martha elbows me in the ribs, and Annie points her finger at her sister. "You can't change everything, my dear sister. It just wouldn't be right. We are who we are. Anything more or less is just being a damn fake."

Martha deepens her voice. "You're right about that, sister."

It's good to laugh, but I stop short when Poole walks in, and I'm reminded of why we're here. He sits down and peels off a piece of bread. Annie signals Beau to bring another cup and more coffee.

Annie leans up. "Just how bad is it, Lummy?"

Martha turns to hide her concern.

I don't want to talk, so Poole starts in a whisper. He explains the situation and about the deaths of Chloe's momma, Seth, Mr. Allrice, and Sophie, and James being beaten nearly to death.

Poole sips his coffee slowly so as not to burn his lips. "It's like the war never ended. It's neighbor against neighbor for sure now. There's some bad stuff goin' on in Choctaw County. All over the state, for that matter. The war's left many a man meaner than a den of copperheads ready to strike at any time. Why them Hyenas...."

I hold my hand up for Poole to stop. "Let's leave it at that, brother, if you don't mind."

Poole nods, and we try to recover the pleasant conversation we were having a few minutes before. Annie still stares at me unsatisfied.

She puts her hand on my arm. "How bad is it, Lummy? And who are these Hyenas?"

Martha goes to sit with the kids while they finish their sweetcakes.

"Dawg Smith and Lester bad."

Annie sits back in her chair hard like she's been slapped in the face. She's not laughing now.

"There's a gang led by Captain Tom Ford who've made themselves protectors of the Lost Cause. They terrorize good folks loyal to the Union and freedmen tryin' to get on with livin' in this new world. They're a force to be reckoned with, and that's what we gotta do. Reckon with them." I tap my spoon on the table. "And I'm hatin' ever' bit of it, Annie."

She bangs her fist on the table, and the café patrons glance over. "Oh Lord God in Heaven, help us."

They quickly return to their meals and conversations, having come to know Annie's unpredictable temperament. But right now, I don't need to deal with her emotions and mine. I sit quiet at she rattles on about the war and what I've had to endure. I don't listen to half of what she says, but one comment strikes clear in my ears.

"You should move to Vicksburg and stay here. Beau and I will help you and Martha get set up. There's plenty of good work for a man like you. You, too, Poole."

I stare into her eyes that plead like a child who badly needs to go to the outhouse during preaching. I understand what she's trying to do.

"I appreciate it, Annie, but Choctaw County is our home, and I'll be damned if...." Martha gently wraps her arms around my shoulders from behind. It's a clear signal that I'm getting too loud. Annie smiles embarrassedly that she's riled me up.

Martha massages the back of my neck and whispers, "Lummy, go see the priest over at Saint Paul's Church. It'll be good for you to talk it out with him."

I look into her eyes, searching.

"Choctaw County is where God put us, husband, and you have to defend your family and our home." She kisses me on the back of the neck. "Go see the priest. We'll be here when you're done."

"This is as good a time as any. He knows I'm comin'."

Martha looks at me questioningly.

"I sent him post a week ago tellin' him we'd be here soon."

Annie gets up to hug me. "I'm sorry, brother, but I had to know. I don't want to add to your troubles, it's just, well, I love you two so much, 'cause you're my only family."

I kiss her on the cheek as she whimpers.

I elbow Poole to stay, and wink at Martha. "Be back in a bit."

CHAPTER 24

# ST. MICHAEL IS NEVER FAR AWAY

## MID-AFTERNOON, MAY 1, 1868

*The thin veil between the seen and unseen is getting thinner.*

I SNEAK INTO the sanctuary like I did so many times before just to sit with the saints for a bit. I still marvel at the beautiful artwork—paintings and statues of people who are in Heaven now but walked through Hell to get there. The western sun beams light through the stained glass windows, bringing their images to life. I meditate on the stories they represent and the one thing common to all—sacrifice.

I whisper a prayer. "Saint Michael, come help us."

A door creaks. "Just like you old friend, the saints trusted God, and he trusted that they would." The priest walks out from behind the altar in his black robe with arms outstretched. He hugs me like a good father should. It felt like God just put his arms around me.

"Still talking out loud, aren't you, boy?"

I laugh and duck my head down, embarrassed like a kid caught picking his nose at school. "Yes, sir, but surely you ain't callin' me no saint?"

"Son, being a saint is what God sees in a person, not what man thinks he is. What's wrong, Lummy? You look worried."

I explain my plight, and he offers sound wisdom. Then he backs away. "You need solitude, my son, to center your soul." He returns to his study. "I'm here when you need me."

I take him up on it. I still my soul and quiet my spirit. I open my mind and chase away unwanted thoughts.

The sounds outside the chapel walls fade, but a voice inside me speaks and sounds very familiar.

It's Pa.

I see a field, the big one in front of our house. Pa plows with my brothers Ben, George Washington, and Amariah. On the porch, Susannah snaps beans in a rocking chair while Saleta churns butter. She and Amariah's wife, Amanda, feed the chickens. Seth and Mr. Allrice unload a couple of hams while Sophie and Chloe's momma tend the kitchen garden. I stand by the barn where we keep our mules and milk cow, enjoying the peaceful family scene. A wagon rumbles up the road to our dogtrot log house. It's Grandpa Temple and Granny Thankful. They wave like they always did arriving for a visit when I was a child. There's a very old wrinkled gray haired gentleman dressed in strange clothes riding in the back. I don't recognize him, but I know his name—Grandpa Cloud Tullos, our ancestor who came from Scotland back in 1661.

Suddenly everything stops. The wind stills, and clouds hover in place. The sun burns brighter than I've ever seen, and I shield my eyes. I look back down, and everyone has gathered in a circle. It's strange, but extremely comforting. A deep peace sinks into my soul that cannot be had living on this earth.

Pa steps closer and takes my hand. "Son, we had our differences, but this time we have none. It's clear who you are and what you must do for the family."

Grandpa Temple puts his hand on my shoulder, "You are a Celt of the moving kind."

Granny Thankful smiles. "And a Pict painted blue of the settling kind. Lean down so I can kiss the back of your neck."

Cloud clears his throat. "It's time to paint yourself blue, my son, and stand and fight for who Creator has made you to be. You are not alone, Lummy."

Flashes of Pict warriors painted blue with all manner of weapons dance naked on the hills that ring the Tullos farm. Then all the men I fought with emerge, gray and blue, white and black, and march into the field. They stare straight ahead with hollow eyes. Not a sound can be heard.

The sailor I killed in Vicksburg points behind me to a sea of red painted men with hyena heads and demon eyes—eyes only haters of all humanity could have. I scan the enemy. The anger I've tried to overcome, but have only suppressed, raises its dragon head within. I thought it was gone. Sorrow fills my soul for what I know it will lead me to do.

Instantly, the roar of a thousand wings sounds with the fury of a tornado and deafens my ears. The earth shakes, and the trees twist and shudder. Thousands of angels follow one great angel, the brightest of all. He carries a fiery sword. He lands in the circle with a great *thud*. He turns to look at me.

"I am here."

All with him stop short in the might of a slammed heavy metal door. The lead angel's eyes burn deep into my soul, and he points at my heart where the anger is taking hold.

"That you cannot use. You must become new for what must be done."

Though I want to ask what must be done, my soul already knows. He and his band of riders, all the men I fought gray and blue, black and white, and the wild blue painted Pict warriors march stiffly down the hill and across the field to form up behind me.

Michael sits high and straight on his mount, half a horse length behind me on my right. We stare at the raging red painted hyenas with flashing demon eyes, screaming taunts and brandishing weapons across the divide.

Michael, the Protector of God's People, commands, "You cannot follow me, Lummy Tullos." His flaming eyes burn into my back. I turn to look with mouth open wide and eyes even wider.

He glares with furrowed brow. "I must follow you. You must lead this fight for the desires of your heart."

I gaze back over the soon to be blood covered hills and vale, knowing what I must do.

"All right, then."

# CHAPTER 25

# BITTERSWEET REUNION

## LATE AFTERNOON, MAY 1, 1868

*Some friends you don't want to see again because of things you did together. And will have to do again.*

THE RECTORY DOOR creaks, and I turn, expecting the priest. In walk J.A., Rainy Mills, and Old Bart. I'm faint with joy. They laugh, and I don't know what to say, so I say something stupid.

"Well hell, if it ain't the Father, Son, and the Holy Ghost." The priest clears his throat. "No harm intended, father."

He laughs, and I grab my old friends for backslapping hugs. "How'd you... why are you...?"

"In Vicksburg?" Rainy Mills laughs.

The priest explains he contacted J.A. by telegram about my troubles through a Methodist circuit rider friend of his.

J.A. looks me over and notices my ring. "Looks like God finally gave you the desires of your heart, huh brother?" I nod. "Well, that's good. That's real good. We're here to make sure you keep 'em."

I nearly burst into tears when I look into my black grandfather's eyes. "Bart, I don't know what to say."

"I told you, Massuh Lummy, God's always had something good for you. I'm here to help, too, son." Old Bart's eyes belie his humor. I bristle at his "Massuh" joke, but laugh it off.

I turn to the well-dressed, neatly trimmed gentleman in perfectly arranged black attire from head to toe. "Rainy Mills, how in the hell are you, old friend?"

"Better than you, I think. But that'll change soon. Long time no see, brother. Had any coyotes snappin' at your ass lately?" The priest clears his throat again. Rainy squints. "Sorry, father."

He waves off Rainy's unnecessary apology.

I laugh. "Only the two-legged kind."

The priest motions for us to all sit down. "What's this about coyotes chasing Lummy?"

I'm eager to tell the story. "You want to tell it, or you want me to?" Rainy shrugs. "Okay, I will. I was on my way to Winn Parish to find Susannah. One night I ran into Rainy's camp like my head was on fire and my ass was catchin'. A pack of hungry coyotes had been chasing me for a quarter-mile. Heck, I didn't even know what a coyote was back then. But I found out. Rainy saved my hide with one just like this when I fell into his camp that night in Louisiana." I pull out the pistol Rainy sent me through Mr. Gilmore just before I left to enlist with the Rebel Army. I hand it to Rainy. "It's scratched up with some of the blue worn and a piece of the wooden handle chipped off. Otherwise, it's in fine working condition."

Rainy looks the weapon over, checking its mechanics. "You must've been in some pretty tight spots." Rainy flips the gun around like a child's toy.

J.A. whispers, "If you only knew. And not far from this very spot."

Old Bart nods. "And not just in the war. Winn Parish, too."

"Yeah, I heard about that scuffle with Dawg Smith." Rainy hands me back the pistol butt first. "Fine weapon."

"I still owe you for it."

"You owe me nothin'. You're alive. That's payment enough. Wish I could say that about my good friend Mistuh Gilmore."

I straighten up as I holster the pistol. "Let's head over to my sister-in-law's café and get caught up. She's got the best food in town and a room in the back where we can talk in private. We've got some plans to make. Join us, Father?"

"No, son, you men in the Lord's army must talk of things I'd rather not know about. I'll be right here praying for you." He makes the sign of the cross and says something in Latin, a blessing I'm sure. Then he raises his arms. "May Saint Michael be with you."

I smile and point to my three friends. "He just arrived, and brought his three toughest angels."

The priest takes my hand. "Come back to see me when this is all over."

"I sure will, father, but I'll be calling on you soon. I need your help with something before we leave."

"Anything, my son."

# CHAPTER 26

# BACK ROOM PLANS

## SUPPERTIME, MAY 1, 1868

*The best laid plans in the Lord often need insight into the Devil.*
*I've got that.*

W E WALK INTO the mostly deserted café, and Annie points to a back room she's prepared for us. The supper rush of mostly Union officers and out of town businessmen will soon crowd in for their evening meal, and we don't want to be noticed.

I introduce her to my friends as we get seated in the room she uses for small private parties and overflow customers. It's a quiet place with a mural of the river landing with steamboats and the Union flag waving proudly over the courthouse. Annie's been criticized for that by some, but she deals with it decisively. She wipes the table off. I stare at the flag on the courthouse in the painting. I notice there is a mix of white and black people milling around on the streets, but no slaves.

She clears her throat. "It's just history. My loyalties lie with my husband, my family, and this café. Anything more than that? Hell, I didn't start no war. And never wanted any part of it. It'll be a long time comin', but folks need to look to the new day. Some won't though. They just don't want to get over it. There's a lot of hurt on both sides, and still a lot of hate around. Why, we don't even celebrate Independence Day anymore. What a shame, treatin' the men of the Revolution that way."

Annie starts to get loud, and I give her a look only a brother-in-law can get away with. She calms down as she straightens the creamer, sugar bowl, and salt and pepper shaker.

I pick up the black pepper shaker and roll it between my fingers, think-ing about ole Miss Lucille. She was the only slave our family had in Choc-taw County, though Pa never treated her as such. Grandpa Willoughby forced Pa to take her when they moved to Choctaw County to buy land after the Treaty of Dancing Rabbit Creek. When she left for her new home with us, Ma wouldn't have her as a slave. Pa and Ma made her family. That was the first best impression made on me about Negroes, and I thank my parents for it. Ma wanted to set Lucille free, but Pa feared folks around wouldn't have it. He worried for her safety. She'd make popcorn in her old black pot, set me up on her lap, and shake ground black pepper on the kernels. I loved that old lady with gray curls dangling and a singing voice as sweet as an angel. She and how my folks cared for her is a big reason I'm here tonight.

Annie nudges me. "Guess I best shut up for now, or I'll be saddlin' up with you boys when it comes time to leave." She turns before shutting the door. "Coffee?" We nod. "How about fresh baked apple pie with ice cream?"

Poole sneaks in, having taken care of my friends' horses. "Ice cream? I'm just in time." He shakes like a kid given his first piece of store bought candy.

Annie winks and pops him on the bottom. "Come on in, sweetheart. I'll keep the area next to this door clear. You boys take as long as you need." She closes the door behind her. We settle into our chairs.

"I sure am glad to see y'all. Thanks for comin'. I wish it were under better circumstance."

Poole clears his throat and elbows me. "I think I know who these good men are, but they may not know me, Lummy."

I put my arm around him. "Sorry. Boys, this is Thomas Poole, my boy-hood friend with whom I chased many a pretty girl, caught a thousand fish, shot hundreds of squirrels, and—"

Poole laughs. "Oh, shut up, Lummy, carryin' on like some schoolgirl."

I pull him closer and lower my voice. "This here man is as brave as any I know. We rode together with the First Mississippi Mounted Rifles, and had the guts to lead the Yanks to burn Wesson's mills in Bankston."

Poole drops his head. "That's our hometown, you know."

Rainy salutes us with a tip of his black hat. "You men are to be commended for going beyond what most men are willing in service of the true flag, the Stars and Stripes."

J.A. lifts his palm. "Here, here, let the truth of these United States of America stand forever, and these good men prosper because of her."

Old Bart sits back, raising his eyebrows. "Dang, J.A., you runnin' for gov'ner or somethin'?"

We all laugh, but the laughter drops off quickly. We all know why we're here and what's coming.

I explain what's happened to bring us together in this room. I lay out my ideas, and the others chime in with ideas to round out a plan that just might work, and hopefully not get us all killed.

J.A. clears his throat. "You know we'll have to kill those boys like we did Dawg Smith and his gang."

I shake my head. "It can't go that way, not this time."

"How you gonna do it and make it stick? It worked in Winn Parish."

"It did, but this ain't Winn Parish." I squirm in my chair because I'm not completely confident of my answer. I'm a little sick to my stomach trying to come up with my best answer. "Whatever we do, it's got be by the law."

Poole speaks up. "We've got that covered with the right people in the right places."

I'm still thinking, but J.A. and the others have come a long way for me to not have this all figured out. Their lives are at stake, and we can make no mistakes.

Poole chimes in to buy me some time. "You know the crazy thing about it is? On one side, Tom Ford of the Lost Cause Hyenas wrote a letter to Governor Sharkey petitioning for a militia. Then, on the other side, our friend William Pollan, who also served with the Rifles, did the same thing for the Unionist Fee Gees, and made himself captain."

Poole explains that situation. "They even listed the names of the men who signed up to serve in their letters."

Rainy whispers, "That helps. We can find out where they live and keep watch on 'em."

Old Bart shakes his head. "Hyenas! We hated them the most in the old country. Damnable animals. Ain't worth the bullet to shoot 'em, except that they kill and gobble up everything."

I'm reminded of Grandpa Temple's story about the Saxons invading Scotland who burned, raped, stole, and killed everything. Captain Tom Ford must've come from good Saxon stock.

Poole rubs his chin. "So, what we got is two opposing militias policing and protecting the good citizens of Choctaw County, both duly authorized by the governor himself."

Rainy snickers. "So, it's the war all over again. Ain't that a kick in the head? So, could we get caught in the middle?"

I put the pepper shaker back in its place. "Don't think so. Ford and his gang are the only ones on my mind. Pollan and his bunch will leave us alone. Actually, I'm countin' on them helpin' us."

Old Bart sits up straight. "That's a helluva situation. So what are you gonna do when you finally run into these Hyenas, if you ain't gonna kill 'em?"

I tap the sugar bowl spoon on the table as I try to find my answer. "Catch 'em and turn them over to the Federal boys. They're huntin' 'em as we speak. But they won't catch 'em. There's just too many hills and hollows to hide in."

"So that's final, we're not going to kill them, right?"

I nod. "Not if we can help it."

Old Bart shakes his head in disbelief and whispers, "They sure as hell will be tryin' to kill us."

J.A. pounds the table. "Lummy, you know them boys will get turned loose and be back at you soon as they get free. Dawg Smith would have, and you know it."

"Not if we set the plan right and catch 'em red-handed."

Rainy and Old Bart shift in their seats. They don't see eye to eye with me so far. J.A. scratches his ear.

"My plan is that we bait 'em in, let the Military Police catch 'em red-handed, and let them arrest them."

Old Bart sits back in his chair. "Damn, if that might not work."

"I'm hopin'." I squirm a bit because it will be the men sitting at this table tonight who might die. "And yes, men could get killed. Like my brother Elihu always says, if you want to kill a copperhead, you go in knowin' you might get bit."

"Dangerous stuff, my friend. We'll have to bait those snakes in," Rainy says under his breath as he looks around the table. "Who's gonna be the mouse?"

I hold up my hand. "We got to come up with victims who won't become victims. I don't want them killed either."

Poole whispers, "And enough witnesses not us, to put them away for good, or even better, hanged."

I nod. "Exactly, we have to do this in a way that—"

Old Bart cuts in. "That it won't look like you were ever involved in it at all, right?"

Rainy taps his empty tobacco pipe on the table. "Because you boys will have to live there long after all of this is done and over with."

It doesn't take long for these men to figure out what's about to happen and why. And what the cost could be.

We sit silent in the warm room knowing the chill of death is not far away. No one is safe from bullets. Old Bart, with eyes gleaming in the sinking sunlight that sneaks through the café window, leans forward in his chair with the look of a kid who just won the prize at a church cake walk.

"I'm good for it."

"To be bait? No way, old man."

"If you call me old man one more time, I'll make you wish you hadn't, boy."

We laugh, and I hold my hands up in surrender. "Okay, okay. I get it. What's your idea?"

Bart rubs his arms, then sets his palms flat on the table. He's serious. "To be an old black niggah mouse with a big mouth they just can't resist shuttin' up."

I'm startled but not surprised. "I don't know, Bart. That might be pushin' it."

"That's exactly what'll draw those bastards in. Bein' pushed. However you plan to do it, I'll be the bait. Ain't no sense gettin' a bunch of innocent folks involved in somethin' they can't get themselves out of."

Rainy brushes a piece of lint from his hat. "Or don't know how to handle it if things go bad."

I sit back hard in my chair. "You're both right." Old Bart certainly knows how to handle himself. Fighting alongside him against Dawg Smith proved that easy enough.

Rainy taps the table with his folding knife. "I don't like it, but havin' our own man on the inside when those devils fall for the trap would give us the advantage. Especially if he's got a couple of good pistols and a certain ten gauge shotgun I'm sure we all know about."

J.A. slaps my chest playfully. "You still got your brother's goose cannon?"

"Yep, and it shoots Hyenas good as geese. When were you there, Rainy?"

"I stopped by Freddy Hawthorne's place. They're still out near Sikes where your brother Ben is buried. Must've been about a year ago. Freddy wanted a new shotgun for his oldest boy. He told me they sent the ten gauge with you."

"Did you see Dorcas and the kids?"

"Sure did. They're doin' fine. Told me if I ever saw you, you better come back for a visit."

I miss them. A lot. Little Elzey's face comes to mind, but I push that away for now.

I turn back to Old Bart. "You good bein' Hyena bait?"

Old Bart, with sad but determined eyes, fakes a grin. "Yeah, the less people in on this the better. You boys'll have to sneak in and out of this thing like a bunch of haints from a graveyard so you get on livin' life when this is over. They don't know me. So when it's all done, I'll slip out in the dead of night back to Texas."

"Only if you promise to take care of yourself, old man, when they go to shootin'."

"This ain't my first hawg killin', son, you know that."

I look around at the others. They nod. "All right then, sounds like we got a plan. We'll figure out what the draw will be to get Ford's men in a tight spot when we get to Choctaw County." It's agreed on with solemn handshakes.

We sit silent, then J.A. laughs. "Seems like I remember somebody set-tin' up a pretty good snare back at Camp Moore for them Flower Boys we taught a lesson."

"I'd forgotten all about that. That I was happy to do."

J.A. leans back in his chair. "Those boys got some pretty rough disciplinary action for cheatin' ignert farm boys out of their few dollars back then." He tells the story. It gives me time to think and relive a good memory. The sound of voices around the table fade, and old feelings come back.

Suddenly, the faces of Pa when he slapped me, Ben when he threatened me, Lester when he cursed me, and Dawg Smith when he laughed about killing Susannah, cloud my eyes. Then the face of Captain Tom Ford threatening me before we burned Bankston chases the others away.

Then Rainy speaks in a dark tone I've never heard from his light hearted way of carrying on. His quiet, deep, yet menacing voice breaks me away from my thoughts. "What's his name again? The snake always has a head."

I rub my brow and look him in the eye. "Captain Tom Ford."

Rainy shifts in his seat to lean forward. He looks each man in the eye. "All right then, you heard him. If none of us make it out of this alive, one thing that has to happen. We get Captain Tom Ford, either delivered or dead. Agreed?"

J.A. growls like a dog protecting his food. "Cut off the snake's head, the rest will slither away."

Old Bart scratches the table with a fingernail. "I did that many times to the slitherin' kind on Mistuh Gilmore's farm, and one time to the two-legged kind for Winn Parish." He glares at the table like a man ready to fight at the drop of a hat.

Tears blur my eyes, hating what I'm asking my good friends to do. "Boys, I've had just about enough of the hate and killin'. When's it gonna stop?"

Old Bart lays his big hand on my shoulder and squeezes. "The Lord will one day make it so, son. You just have to walk it out. But you won't be goin' alone."

I look around at my friends—men who saved my life, and me theirs. Rainy Mills, J.A. Killingsworth, Tom Poole, and Old Bart—ready to give their lives in defense of mine without a blink. I smile at Old Bart, a former slave, who I helped send on his way to a new life. Now he's ready to give his to save mine. A man whose last name I never knew. I don't know if he was ever given one.

So, in the pause of the conversation I ask. "Bart, just what is your last name? For the life of me, I don't know what it is. You never did tell me in all those years we were together."

"You never asked, but wouldn't have done you no good. I didn't have one then. But I do now." We all wait in anticipation.

J.A. breaks the pause. "Well, Bart, what the hell is it?"

"Houston. I took the name of the only man who treated me like a son and who never wanted these United States divided. Sam Houston. He whooped the Mexicans and became President of Texas, then a Senator, and finally Governor of Texas. God rest his soul, he died whilst you and J.A. was runnin' back to Winn Parish from the war. I took it to honor him, but I have to admit that it does offer a bit of protection if I get in a scrape. I've talked my way out of a few tough scrapes tellin' stories about ole Sam."

"Well it fits. Bart Houston from Texas. It's got a good ring to it."

Martha walks in with large pieces of hot apple pie topped with generous scoops of ice cream. "Annie said y'all might be hungry." Everyone immediately stands, and I introduce her all around. As she sets the tray down, each man speaks.

Rainy kisses her hand. "Such beauty is yet to be deserved to be viewed by those privileged to observe your grace while still on this earth, Missus Tullos." Martha blushes like a school girl asked to her first dance.

J.A backhands my chest. "You done good, boy. Not sure how you talked her into marryin' a cuss like you, but I'll be danged if you did catch the prettiest lady this side of the river."

Old Bart rises slowly, his knees popping like an old barn door creaking. "It is my pleasure, Missus Tullos, to meet the one the Lord sent to bless my son, Lummy."

Martha smiles. "You knew Susannah?"

"Yes ma'am, like my own daughter. You would be her first and only choice for my son."

"That's a compliment I won't soon forget, suh."

This is a reunion I never expected. My good friends have come to stand with me in my hour of need and bless my family with the protection of St. Michael's angels. Though saints they may not be, surely angels they are all around. St. Michael's angels, that is. We sit back down as Martha arranges the food on the table.

"Martha, I want our children to know these men. Could we plan a good supper later tonight? We leave in the morning."

She wipes a tear and nods. I wrap my arm around her waist and hold her close as my friends duck their heads. I kiss her lightly. She stiffens up.

"I'll be strong, husband. I understand what you've got to do. Our family cannot live in peace if those bad men have free reign in the hills."

All nod, not wanting to make eye contact with her. Each man knows there's a good possibility none of us will live through what's ahead.

"God bless you men. Come back safe, all of you, you hear? I want my husband back, and my children's father. Will you do that for me?"

They all nod silently, but Poole must say a word. "At the cost of our lives, Missus Martha. Like Lummy's done for all of us."

# CHAPTER 27

# LAST ACT BEFORE
# THE LAST SUPPER

## AFTER SUNSET, MAY 1, 1868

*If a part of your heart remains in a place,*
*then a small piece of you must stay there, too.*

We finish making our plan and eating the pie Martha brought us. Old Bart and Rainy stretch out on cots out back and enjoy the last bit of warm sunshine with full stomachs. Poole has business to attend to, so it's just me and J.A. left in the room, sipping the last of our coffee.

"I've missed you, boy."

I squeeze J.A.'s shoulder. "Missed you, too, brother. It's been too long, and a lot's happened since we parted last."

J.A.'s eyes turn somber. "I'm glad we got a few minutes. There's something I need to tell you about. It ain't good, and it's gettin' worse." He sits quiet.

"Well, you gonna tell me or make me guess?"

J.A. looks up and grins. "Let's get caught up before we get to that, okay?"

"Sure." I tell all that's happened since the Dawg Smith incident, about killing Lester, and joining up with the 1st Mississippi Mounted Rifles. He tells me about his family and farm, how things look really good this year for his crops and growing cattle herd.

J.A. reaches into his pocket. "You know that offer I made you still stands if things don't work out in Choctaw County."

"I appreciate it, but Ma and my brothers are there. It's become home again."

He produces a small bag and lays it on the table. "Sheriff Barnett sends his regards, and the Davises said tell you hello. They want you to come for a visit when you can, too. Winnfield's growing and that property you signed over to the Davises has done them very well." He pushes the small pouch to me.

"What's this?" When I pick it up, it jingles like gold.

"Winnfield's become the center of the county and growing like a weed. Mistuh Davis sent you that."

I count out three hundred dollars gold. "I can't take this, J.A., it wouldn't be right. Mistuh Wiley left me that property when he died, and it was only right I give it to the Davises for helping out so many people during the war."

"Take it, it's yours. Use it any way you want. If it helps get rid of the riff raff in your county like we did Dawg Smith, then Mistuh Davis believes it'll be of good use."

I nod and hand him a double eagle. "To help you get around."

He refuses the gift. "No need, I'm doin' well. What would helpin' out a friend be, if there weren't no sacrifice?" We reminisce a few moments about the sacrifices made during the siege.

"What about Dorcas and Freddie? I bet the kids have grown."

"I don't get up Sikes way much, but the Davises see them when they come for supplies or legal business at the courthouse. They're doing well."

I need to write them a letter. I miss them, the good times we had. We sit, both lost in our own thoughts. Finally, J.A. speaks.

"Lummy, there's trouble brewin' in Winn Parish."

"What kind?"

"The hellish Dawg Smith kind, except this is worse."

"How could it be any worse?"

J.A. lays out the situation of how this gang of outlaws bushwack, rob, and murder migrants going west on the road that leads from Natchez to Texas.

"They're in cahoots with the law. Hell, they are the law. I'm afraid they're gonna take over. There's an election comin' up, and Sheriff Barnett knows he'll be ousted."

I purse my lips. "Damn, he's a good man."

J.A. squints. "That ain't the worst of it, Lummy." He pauses, scratching the table with his fingernail. "You remember that sorry ass John West who fought with us and the 27th Louisiana here in Vicksburg?"

"Yeah, what about him?"

"He's the leader of the West-Kimbrell gang. They have done things to people no man, woman, or child should ever even know about."

I sit up. "Like what?"

"Invitin' travelers into their homes for the night only to murder them and steal their belongings. I've heard worse things that they've done, but no one can prove it just yet. I don't want to talk about all that right now. Damn, Lummy, who does such things?"

"Men possessed of the Devil. What's to be done?"

"Nothin' right now, but a day is comin' when good folks won't put up with such doin's anymore."

"Let's hope it don't come to that."

"Yeah, but hell, West even leads songs and teaches Bible class at the Methodist Church in Atlanta."

"Damn, that is bad."

"Yeah, and his place ain't too far through the woods from mine. He don't bother folks around the parish, just the settlers goin' west." He drains the last of his coffee. "That's about it for now."

I stand up. "C'mon, let's get out of here and leave that behind for a bit. There's somethin' we gotta do."

We step into the kitchen where Martha is making pies for the next day's customers. "Martha, we'll be back for supper." She smiles, and I take J.A. to where Poole parked our wagon in the alley. The mules are still hitched up. I pull the tarp back to reveal twenty-seven flat red sand stones stacked in the wagon bed.

J.A. looks at me and smiles. "We gonna raise an Ebenezer?"

"We are, and right at dark is just the best time to do it."

"You gather the stones on the way?"

"Nope. I brought 'em from the Tullos family cemetery hill back home. They're lying around everywhere. I just wanted a piece of me to be here long after I'm gone." I pop him on the shoulder. "I figure these stones will outlive me, you think?"

"I do, and I'm glad to help you do it."

The ride out Graveyard Road calls for silence. J.A. and I walked and marched this path so many times we can't count them all. Little is left of the destruction and signs of the great siege, except eroding earthworks and our feelings that still remain.

We pull up into the 27th Louisiana Lunette. Palisade timbers have rotted and given way to weather and time. For a moment, we relive the scenes of war and death, sickness and hopelessness. We hop off the wagon and walk to our place on the line in the rifle pit. I run my hand over the failing tree trunks still holding the dirt in place that protected us from cannon shell and minie balls. My hand slides over a few crude letters carved into an oak log about to fall.

## EDROW WAS HERE DEC 1862

J.A. laughs. "That boy never got used to the name Hog Fart, did he?"

I shake my head. I never got used to Edrow dying at such a young age on the march out of Vicksburg.

"Where do you want to do this?"

"I was gonna place them on the parapet overlooking the battlefield in front of us, but I don't think that shows enough respect." He waits. "No, let's place them out front of the parapet down in the pit I fell into when Sherman attacked."

"I remember, but why?"

"To honor our brothers and theirs, gray and blue."

J.A. stands still, hands on hips, studying the pit. "I like that."

We take the stones one by one to the pit after we smooth off a flat spot in the bottom with a broken shovel we found. We place twelve stones for the foundation, nine stacked on top of those, then five, and lastly one. Twenty-seven stones for the 27th Louisiana Volunteer Infantry Regiment.

J.A. kicks the dirt. "I wish it'd only been twenty-seven men who lost their lives those forty-seven days."

"I know, J.A., I know. All that killin', dammit, and most of it for nothin'."

"Yeah, but that Union flag sure looks good on top of the courthouse."

"Don't it though?"

I pull from my pocket the small Confederate flag I'd saved from when we traveled on the train up from Camp Moore along with the small Union flag Sergeant McGugarty gave me when I enlisted in the 1st Mississippi Mounted Rifles. I lay them under the top stone of our shrine and say a prayer—that this will never happen again.

I clutch the small leather pouch hanging from my neck under my shirt with Grandpa Temple's twentieth star flag inside. I'll keep that one.

J.A. pats my shoulder. "Amen, brother, amen. And we're off to make sure it doesn't."

CHAPTER 28

# AND WE SANG
# A HYMN...

## EVENING, MAY 1, 1868

*The Bible says when they had sung a hymn, they went out into the*
*Mount of Olives for what most of 'em didn't know was comin'.*

SUPPER IS EXCELLENT, my friends even better, but the mood is sub-dued, except for playful children. As Martha and Annie pick up the last of the dishes, I'm summoned to the kitchen of the café. All the customers have finished their meals, and the café door is locked for the night. Once in the kitchen, Martha turns to me with eyes that beg me not to go.

"If you must go, Columbus, then you and the men must ride off on the prayers of the women and children who need you to return."

I don't disagree.

Annie shuffles dishes around, placing as many as she can in the double sink for soaking.

"These'll wait," she says. "Prayin' won't."

I send J.A. to get the priest to lead us in our time of worship and prayer. He's back with the father in just a few moments. We gather in the large room of the café and circle our chairs. The children sit on the floor with puzzled looks, not knowing what to expect. I sit up straight as I reach for the small Bible Mary gave me before I left for Winn Parish back in '59. I stare at the wrinkled water stained pages that kept me sane through fierce fighting and hollow starvation.

I start to speak when Rainy, of all people, starts Rock of Ages. We all sing like we're at a funeral. We finish the song, and all eyes are upon me as I look down at the Bible. I have no verse to read.

"Thanks for the song, Rainy. Didn't know you had such a fine voice." He nods. "I do want the Lord to come in amongst us on this night before some of us have to go take care of business."

Little William crawls up into my lap and lays his weary little head against my chest. A lump rises in my throat, but I continue.

"I'll make this short because the children are sleepy, and some of us have an early start. I sent J.A. to ask my friend the priest if he'd be so kind as to join us. Thanks, Father." He nods.

Martha lays her head on my shoulder. I don't want to continue because each moment takes me closer to leaving my family for another foolish but necessary mission.

"Thank you ladies for the fine feast we enjoyed, kind of a last supper for we who go to face the Devil." The men nod.

Martha looks up into my eyes. "Don't tell too much about your plans. Dear, the children." She's right.

"Like in the Scriptures, we've had our last supper, and now we must go to the Garden."

Everyone looks puzzled. I fumble with the tattered pages. I find my place. "The night Jesus was betrayed, they had a supper much like what we had, except it was a special one, to remember when God delivered the Israelites out of Egypt."

John A. speaks up. "I know that one. It's about baby Noah in a boat on the river."

His sister Margaret shakes her head. "No, dummy, it was baby Moses who was in the basket his momma made for him. It saved him from that mean ole Pharaoh."

Martha interrupts, "Hush up children, your father's talkin', and we need to listen."

I open the little Bible to Mark chapter fourteen. "They had their meal, but before they left, they sung a hymn like we just did." My words hang in the air for a moment. "Then they went out to the Mount of Olives. They didn't go to rest. They didn't go climb olive trees." I pat John A. on the head, and he smiles up at me.

"No, they went to pray, and I'll tell you, I've been prayin' a long time before this gatherin' tonight. But don't fret. The Lord will go with us, and this won't be our last supper. No, it'll be the last time we'll have to part."

Rainy stomps his foot twice. "Hear, hear, oh, uh, I mean, amen." The children laugh, and Old Bart pats Rainy on the shoulder.

"So, what this supper tonight means to me is that after we sing another hymn, we go to our garden, where we'll face the betrayers of our families and county. We go to the place where sacrifice is the call, but the strength of the Lord will prevail."

John A. looks up sleepily. "Will y'all have swords like they did in the Bible, Pop?"

Martha lifts her head for my answer.

"Yes, but hopefully we won't have to use them, son."

"I sure hope not, Pop." We sit in silence reflecting on the words I shared.

Poole asks, "I know it ain't Sunday, but can we take the communion?"

I look to the priest. "It ain't Sunday."

He shrugs, saying, "The Bible says that 'for as often as you eat this bread and drink the cup, you proclaim the Lord's death until he comes.' He didn't say it only could be done on Sunday."

Annie gets up. "I've got some wine, and I'll get bread."

I ask, "Father, would you do the honors of sayin' the words? Scripture will do, if that's okay."

He agrees, and as Annie brings in the wine with a few cups and some crackers, the priest shares the communion story explaining what the bread and wine represent. We each take part in hope that the presence of the Lord will fill us and sustain us. The priest finishes with a short prayer, and we stand to sing another hymn.

Old Bart whispers, "Time to go to our places of prayer, wishing the Lord would take the cup of wrath away."

I kick at the floor. "I done asked him three times, Bart, but he said no."

The priest looks up like he's staring into heaven. "Not my will, but yours be done."

CHAPTER 29

# GATHERING FOR THE MARCH

## EARLY MORNING, MAY 2, 1868

*Long goodbyes never ensure a safe return to loved ones.*

THE NIGHT IS short, and dawn breaks early across the streets of Vicksburg. With our horses saddled and waiting in the alley behind the café, Annie and Martha serve a fine breakfast of ham, eggs, grits, and biscuits with gravy in the back room where we make last minute adjustments to our plans.

Poole slurps his coffee from a saucer. "We can be in Choctaw County in three days or less if we stay in the saddle. Lummy and me did that hundred mile march in less than that with the Rifles."

Rainy holds up his hand, finishing off a piece of sugar cured ham. "We need to stop in Clinton. There's a good Baptist professor friend of mine helping the college there get back on its feet. He's got a shipment waitin' for me." He looks up to the ceiling like he's about to start one of his lengthy stories.

Old Bart snickers. "You actually know a preacher, Rainy?"

Rainy straightens up in his chair and throws his hand out like an actor, reminding me of Mr. Gilmore back in Winn Parish. "My father was not a preacher. In fact, my blood father was an outlaw I met just a few years back, just before I met Lummy near the railroad tracks that night. But, as you backwoods illiterates undoubtedly do not know, the old man who raised me in the orphanage was. I do suspect I inherited some of my blood father's traits, how could I not? And as he certainly did, I have on occasion, wandered from the truth to dabble in things that he became proficient in escaping. Except for that once, when I reminded him of the blood of my birth." He laughs, but for the first time I see pain through Rainy's hard, though jovial, exterior.

"But my mother, she was a true angel who had the love to give me away when she knew she was dying." Rainy closes his eyes likes he's trying to dig up a memory. "I never knew my mother. She died not long after I was born."

We say nothing. Quickly, he changes the subject back to the college located in Clinton.

"The good folks at the college built a beautiful new chapel on the school grounds a year before the war started. Cost twenty-five thousand dollars. Provine Chapel they call it, for somebody, I don't know. Beautiful structure. Now that'd be a place to get hitched with a proper preacher, Poole." I duck my head.

Poole mouths, "He didn't have one."

Rainy realizes he must've made a mistake. "Oh, Lummy, I didn't mean you didn't."

I wave off his concern with a swipe of my hand.

Old Bart puts his fork down on his plate with a clink. "Rainy, what you got so important that we have to stop there? You know we ain't got no time for any business but what's at hand. Your gun dealin's will just have to wait."

"Well, you'll want to take time for this. I know a man." Rainy winks at me.

I grin. "Rifles and ammunition?"

Rainy leans back in his chair to stretch his back. "Brand new Henry .44 caliber rim-fire lever-action repeaters made by the New Haven Arms Company, and two thousand rounds of metal cartridges. Those smoke poles can fire all day with one loading. Both sides used them in the war, though not a lot. I bought one a few months back and like how she operates. Keep her oiled and shined up, and she'll never let you down."

Poole asks, "How'd you come by those? They must be at least forty bucks apiece."

"That's exactly how much those seventeen shooters cost. They're mighty hard to come by, but like I said, I know a man. He owed me big for orders he couldn't make good on until now. So he paid me in Henry rifles. It was a good deal, and I can sell 'em after we're done."

Old Bart can't contain himself. "Seventeen shooters, how in the heck?"

Rainy laughs. "You mean, how can a gun shoot so many times?" He stares through Bart like he's looking for an answer, but he has one. "Because men in tall hats make lots of money from dreamin' up new ways to kill a man. That rifle staved off Confederate attacks at the Battle of Franklin. Terrible loss for the Rebs, I heard."

I wonder if my brother George Washington was shot down by one of those same rifles.

Rainy takes out his short knife to pick his teeth. Then his countenance falls a little. "When human beings make money off of war, they figure out the most effective ways to do it, and then cash in on death." We stare at each other, knowing his words are true.

Rainy tries to laugh it off with a joke. "Yeah, should've heard what Colonel John Mosby said when he ran into Yanks usin' Henrys on his men. 'You can load that damn Yankee rifle on Sunday and fire it all week.'"

J.A. asks, "How many you got, Rainy? All I have is my old double barreled shotgun."

"I brought enough for a small army." Rainy turns to me. "How many men do you have?"

"Let's see, besides us five, I can count on my three brothers back home to be a part and Dan Creekwater, my old Choctaw friend. That makes nine. Sheriff Platner will help, but he won't be in the saddle with us or in any fight."

Poole cuts in. "Don't forget the Wood boys, they ain't scared."

I nod. "You thinkin' John and Henry?"

Poole sips his coffee. "Yeah, you know that John, he's a mean one. Henry is becomin' a politician of sorts, but we can count on him. That John, he takes no shit off nobody. After you left chasin' Susannah, one of them uppity Mabus boys, who think they hung the moon, brought his wagonload of corn to be ground at the mill. The line was long, and John took his place like every other considerate man. Not Mabus. He moved to the head of the line thinking he should get special treatment. John Wood was havin' none of that. I don't know what all transpired." Poole elbows Rainy. "That's a good word ain't it, transpired?"

Rainy shrugs.

"I learned that new word readin' the papers. Mary's been helpin' me with my readin' and writin'. Anyway, John and Mabus, they got to arguin' about it all, and then somethin' about John swingin' an axe at Mabus and the law comin'. Long story short, John got fined a hundred dollars, but wouldn't you know it, Mabus went free. You can guess John Wood's still mad as a hornet over that." Poole half chokes on his coffee as he laughs. "And Mabus wears the red shirt like the rest of them damn Lost Causers. Won't take much to get the Wood boys to go Hyena huntin'. And they still make the best moonshine out of that cool clear water from Aaron Wood's Spring."

I tuck that thought away in the back of my mind. Aaron Wood's Spring might be just the place to hide while we do our devilment. Rumor has it there's a huge sandstone rock formation somewhere near Wood Mountain that's hard to get to. A hunter once told us it's got an overhang to keep rain off. Could be a base for our small band.

Rainy smiles. "Perfect, that's eleven men. I've got twelve rifles new in the box waitin' at the College."

Poole taps a spoon on his coffee cup. "There's one more. Wesley Jamison, originally from East Tennessee. He broke with the Rebs like we did, Lummy, and fought with the blue. He's a man we can trust. He works a blacksmith shop in Greensborough and will be useful gettin' word to us on what's happenin' around the county. You know, seen but not seen?"

We all agree, and I close the meeting. We start to rise when Annie eases the door open.

"Somebody wants to see you before you leave."

The priest steps in. "Lummy, I can't let you good men go off to do the Lord's work without a prayer. I've prayed this prayer for you and many men through the years. Please bow. Saint Michael the Archangel, defend us in battle. Be our protection against the wickedness and snares of the devil. May God rebuke him, we humbly pray. And do thou, O Prince of the Heavenly Host, by the power of God, thrust in to hell Satan and all evil spirits who wander through the world for the ruin of souls, Amen."

"Thanks, brother."

He makes the sign of the cross and bows out.

It's later than we realize, so we gather up behind the café checking our saddles and gear. Martha slips out the back door wiping her hands with a wet dish towel. Her face is splattered with flour dust from biscuits she just put in the oven. I look deep into her eyes. She blushes.

"I must look a fright, Mistuh Columbus."

I gently wipe the wet flour from her teary cheeks. "Pretty as ever, Missus Tullos."

"You come back to me, Columbus."

I can't speak.

Poole mounts his horse and yells like Sarge used to, "Boots and saddles men, time to go!"

J.A. leans down to take Martha by the hand. "Don't you fret none. We'll bring him back to you, Martha." Rainy and Old Bart tip their hats as they pass by.

I kiss Martha long and hard, hugging her like I don't want to leave. "I ain't sayin' goodbye because last goodbyes never ensure a return to loved ones. I'm sayin' see you soon, dear wife."

She gently pushes me back. "Like you say, Columbus, the sooner you leave, the sooner you'll get back."

I smile and hop up on my horse without using the stirrups. She waves until we're out of sight.

As we slowly walk our mounts up the alley off of Washington Street, I leave my heart with Martha and give my soul to the Lord. But the rest belongs to Captain Tom Ford.

CHAPTER 30

# GETTIN' SCHOOL EDUCATED WITHOUT GOIN' TO CLASS

### MAY 3, 1868

*Some of the fiercest of warriors*
*are neither seen nor heard.*

WE MAKE CAMP east of Clinton just before dark. Rainy leaves to meet with his contact. He wants us to stay out of sight. There's already enough devilment going on done by unknown men on horseback, and Federal troops are all too happy to jail any they encounter. We build a fire, stretch out our bedding, and eat cold biscuits stuffed with fried pork steak. It's not long that Rainy returns with a fresh-baked blackberry pie.

He holds it high. "Compliments of one of the finest ladies in Clinton. My friend will be along shortly." We divide up the pie, and I savor each bite.

My curiosity gets the best of me. "Bart, how'd you find out about all this?"

He throws a small twig he's been picking his teeth with into the fire. "Rainy over there—"

I hold up my hand. "Don't mean to cut you off, but I was wonderin' how Rainy found out, too."

Bart looks at Rainy, who shrugs. Bart continues. "I was workin' as a cook on an east Texas cotton, corn, and sweet tater ranch near the Looseana line when Rainy came through on his way from out west somewhere." He turns to Rainy. "You was workin' some gun deals out there, weren't you?"

Rainy nods, taking a sip from his flask. "Yeah, I had to go through Carthage, so I stopped to send Mistuh Davis a telegram to see if he had any gun orders. It's amazing how the telegraph lines work so well when nobody's cuttin' 'em down, gray or blue."

Poole laughs. "We sure did a hell of a lot of that with the Rifles, huh Lummy?" I nod.

Bart takes a bite of biscuit and washes it down with coffee. "Yeah, I just happened to be in town gettin' supplies when I ran into Rainy steppin' out of the telegraph office. He told me to get my gear and to tell my boss that I'd be back in a few months. I like Mistuh Milton M. Holland a lot and hated to leave. He's a former slave like me. Most folks don't know he won the Medal of Honor servin' as a sergeant in the Union Army somewhere, but I don't know where."

Poole laments, "That's because he's a black man, right?"

"Yep, folks out there ain't too fond of the idea that first man born in Texas to get that medal was a Negro. Ain't that somethin' though? Anyway, I was gonna lie to him and say my brother died so I could go with Rainy, but I couldn't. So I told him the truth, knowin' if it was you havin' trouble, Lummy, it must be of the Dawg Smith kind. He didn't even bat an eyelid and let me go. He did make me promise that I'd come back. They all like my cookin' out on the ranch, you see."

Rainy pulls out the telegram from his pocket.

Old Bart recites the message from memory. "Mistuh Davis wrote, 'Come quick. Lummy needs your help. Go straight to the Catholic Church in Vicksburg and wait.' I read it myself. So we got to Vicksburg night before last."

Rainy cuts in, "We caught the train in Monroe, which got us here sooner. So, here we are, my fine blue jacketed friend."

A wagon comes rolling up the road like a light artillery company headed to battle. We jump up with guns cocked only to find that it's Rainy's friend driving the buckboard. Rainy gets up from his blanket to introduce his friend as he climbs down from the buckboard. A small, wiry man with a face chiseled like stone with receding hair wearing a small patch of chin whiskers takes his time getting down. Arthritis, I've seen it before. His pain's not only the arthritis.

It's easy to see, if you take notice, that he's a man who's wrestled with the Lord, and himself. Most preachers of any account have. He looks to be a man striving to do the best and right thing, even when the world around him disagrees. He also has the look of a man who's been in a few scrapes, and wise to know when to speak his mind and not.

Rainy throws out his arm. "Meet Reverend Aquila Prewitt, minister of God's Holy Word, and Professor of History and Religion at the fine institution of higher learning, Mississippi College. It's a Baptist school."

"All right, Rainy," Aquila complains, "I see I'm not the only one around here known for long and windy sermons. Good to meet you boys."

We shake hands, and Aquila settles on a log by the fire. "Got anything to eat? And how about a taste of that coffee?" Bart hands him a cup.

Rainy laughs. "Guard your biscuits, boys. This man can eat his weight in good food, even bad for that matter. Why hell, Aquila's got an eight foot leg, and it's hollow as a log from hip to sole."

Old Bart laughs louder than the rest. "Want some fried pork with your biscuits, Reverend?"

"Just call me Aquila, friend. I only allow church members and college folks to call me that because I don't have a choice. It's a title I despise, and surely not the best description of this ole sinner. Heck, there's not a soul in this world worthy of being called reverend unless the Good Lord himself steps back down on his good earth. And with the way things are, I don't think he's a mind to do that anytime soon." He looks around at the trees and up into the sky at the stars. "I do miss this, sleeping outdoors, breathing good fresh air. You know men, the Lord never intended us to be cooped up in big houses with so much stuff that takes on a life of its own. No, had we not messed up in the Garden, we'd all live in the bliss of the light of the Lord, having all our needs met with no death or no disease, no destruction or killing…."

Poole snickers. "And we'd all be wearin' the same thing. Nothin'!"

Rainy whispers, "Damn, now that'd be an ugly sight."

Poole sits up. "Well, I sure as hell wouldn't be lookin' at you, Rainy Mills." Aquila clears his throat. "Sorry, Reverend."

He waves off Poole's apology. "I'm still a man, you know. And this I know, too. A Creator big enough to make all of this was never meant to be boxed up on Sunday morning with preachers saying the only way Creator can be found is in a church house. Now look at me, done gone to preaching."

I pitch my coffee dregs into the fire. "That's all right, I heard another man say the same thing years ago up in the hills."

"Well, I don't know the man, but I like him already."

"He's a Choctaw." I watch Aquila closely. I like him already, too.

Aquila finishes his biscuit. "The best of God's children, I say. Well, enough lecturing for today, but I will leave you with this. I was created to walk in the cool of the day with my Creator in a beautiful garden easily recognizing his voice when he calls my name." Aquila falls silent.

Poole grins. "Thanks for the lesson, Aquila. I just got a church school education without even goin' to class."

I've dreamed of such peace and ask, "When, O Lord?"

Aquila looks back up into the stars. "When he calls our name to leave this earth, I'm afraid."

He's talking about his wife. And though he says she's dying, Mrs. Prewitt mustered up the strength to bake the pie we just finished off. We thank him. I can see Aquila carries peace in every part of him, but sadness creeps up on him like shadows overtaking the forest when the sun goes down behind a ridge.

Bart asks timidly to lighten the mood, "So where does all that food go, Mistuh Aquila, suh? You ain't big as nothin'."

Aquila shrugs. Poole hands him a couple more salt pork biscuits and says matter-of-factly, "Tapeworm."

Old Bart stops chewing. "Tape wha-a-a-t?"

"Yep, that's right. A long ole worm that latches onto your insides somewhere, I don't where, and feeds on what you eat somehow."

Bart closes his eyes, cringing as he spits out what's left in his mouth. "Close your mouth before you catch a fly. Enough of that."

Poole takes advantage of the situation. "Yep, saw my daddy pull one out of a young fellow's backside once. Must've been ten foot long. Honest to God's truth, it was an ugly thing."

Old Bart puts down his biscuit. Poole starts to say more, but now I've had enough.

"Shut the hell up, Poole, before we puke all over you. If he had one of them worms, I'm sure the doctor would've found out by now. Let the man eat."

Aquila looks a little worried.

Poole ducks his head in shame, realizing he went too far. "Didn't mean no harm, Aquila."

"None taken, son. But I think I'll go see the Doc tomorrow." He lays his tin plate down. "I best go now. Thanks, Rainy—and the rest of you men, for your hospitality."

Rainy stands to help him up, but he's slow to move. "Ain't nothin', Aquila, and I do appreciate your help. But don't run off so soon. As you could imagine, the conversation might just get taken up a notch or two if you'd stay a little longer."

"Wish you men could stay a few days. I'm sure you need to listen to a good preacher."

Rainy laughs. "Do you know any, Aquila?"

Aquila laughs and throws a stick that Rainy dodges. "Sure as hell do. My wife!"

Rainy takes a knee. "Let me say this before you go, Reverend. Boys, Aquila brought the weapons and cartridges I told you about in his wagon, and I'm grateful. It's not uncommon for him to take his wagon out, but if he doesn't take it back soon, well, that will be noticed. So, we'll take our new rifles and as many bullets as we can carry, then put the rest on the mule we brought along. We'll cover it with a tarp, and nobody will be the wiser."

Reverend Aquila gets up. "Men, I need to get back to the missus."

I reach into my shirt for the pouch of money I've hidden there. As Poole and J.A. unload the wagon, Old Bart and Rainy distribute the guns and ammunition and load the mule.

"Hold up, Aquila. Here, take this." I hand him two double eagles. "Ain't much, but maybe it'll help with the chapel repairs or somethin'."

"Keep your money, son, we'll figure it out."

Rainy takes the gold coins from my hand and places them in Aquila's with another twenty dollar gold piece. "I ain't never whooped a preacher's ass, but I'm about to if you don't take this money." Aquila drops his head. "I know how hard it's been on you and the missus, Reverend, so take it, and don't be givin' it to the school. Consider it our contribution to your salary."

Aquila nods. "Thank you, men. I don't like what you're doin', but I know it has to be done, if the twentieth star truly ever gets put back on the true flag."

I grab his shoulder. "What did you just say about the twentieth star?"

"I never wanted Mississippi's star taken off the Union flag, and had a heck of a time not showing my hand these past few years. Three faculty members, most of the college students, and some men from town formed the Mississippi College Rifles in April of '61. I used my wife's illness as an excuse not to enlist. I feel bad about that, but if I'd told the truth, I wouldn't be standing here with you men tonight. I'd been jailed or hanged. There was strong sentiment for the Bonnie Blue Flag in those days. Those men fought with the 18th Mississippi, mostly in Northern Virginia." The glisten of a tear forms in his eye. "One hundred and four men marched off to battlefields unknown. Only eight returned. Good men and boys, that bunch." He shakes his head. "What a damn waste. Some of those boys would have made fine educated leaders in their communities."

Rainy motions for Aquila to sit down.

"So you see, I never could really speak my mind about slavery and staying with the Union. Too risky, especially after Grant used the chapel for a hospital, which wasn't a bad thing at the time. But stabling his horses on the first floor of the building was. And besides, the hatred for Negroes around here, oh my, I just don't know what to say about that except that if it wasn't for blacks, most white men would be the lowest rung on the ladder. No harm intended, Bart."

Bart waves off the comment and motions for Aquila to continue. "Go 'head on with your talkin'."

"That all started way before the war, but when Sherman passed out rations when he came through in '63, he required the men distributing them to share food with former slaves only and pass by Confederate soldiers. That didn't help matters none." Aquila sits like a man defeated.

We stand in silence.

Aquila gets up and moves to his wagon. "I best get going. God be with you men, and don't let the devil take your soul while you do his kind of work against him. Sometimes you got to be a devil to fight the Devil." Aquila stops before climbing aboard the wagon and reaches for Rainy's hand. "Don't be a stranger. You know you're always welcome at my table. All of you men are."

Rainy steps back. "I'd like to see that chapel sometime."

"You come by anytime, even if you don't have business pending. Wait a spell though, they're still makin' repairs from the war, and it's taking a while. Not enough money just yet."

Rainy rubs his chin. "I'll see what I can do about that, Reverend."

"I'd appreciate it." Aquila slowly climbs into the wagon, groaning with every arthritic ache. "So long, take care of yourselves."

We wave as Aquila disappears into the night.

Rainy watches until sounds of the wagon fade into the shadows. He whispers, "Some of the fiercest of warriors are neither seen nor heard."

# CHAPTER 31

# AN OLD STAND ON
# AN OLD ROAD

## AT DARK, MAY 4, 1868

*Finding a new friend in an old place can't replace an old friend now lost.*

DARK CLOUDS DRIFT in from the west. We follow the Old Trace to a familiar spot where we can get in out of the rain.

"Let's duck in here, boys."

I look around old Brashear's Stand sitting just off the Old Trace. J.A. and Poole make a wide circle to check for anyone or tracks. I poke my head in the doorway, half expecting an owl to fly out like it did when I found Seth hiding here five years ago.

"All clear." I wave the others in. "Let's get some wood before it rains. Poole, there's a good place for the horses and that mule in that thicket over there."

Rainy leads the mule to the door. "We can't leave this equipment out in the open. Horses we can replace, but not these Henry Rifles. Besides, I don't want them out in this drizzle."

I help him get them inside. I step inside, and something moves in the darkness. I pull my pistol in a flash and point it at a shadowy figure in the corner. "Who's that? Speak up quick, or I'll let go with this pistol."

Poole pokes his head in the broken down door. "Hold on, that's George Wesley Jamison. I told him to meet us here. I wanted him in on this from the beginning."

A gruff voice speaks with no emotion. "Just call me George."

I lower my pistol and offer my hand, apologizing for the quick response. George grins. "Ain't nothin'. In these times, a man's got to be ready."

Rainy walks in, extending his hand. "Ain't that the truth? Rainy Mills is my name, and my good friend here is Bart Houston."

George offers his hand to Old Bart as eagerly as he did Rainy.

J.A. walks in with a sack, meets George, and announces, "Time to eat. It won't hurt to build a fire, will it?"

I shake my head, and he breaks out coffee and food. Rainy hands George a Henry repeater. He looks it over like a fine woman, then sits down on the hard dirt floor covered in old leaves to get acquainted with his new weapon.

Rainy tosses George a box of cartridges. "Tell us about yourself, George. If you're as good a man as Poole, then I like you already. And as Lummy over there knows, I love a good story." He elbows me. "Seems like I told you one time that I suspected there was more to your story than you let on at the time."

"Yeah, just after you almost shot my ass off runnin' into your camp with those coyotes about to have me for supper."

Rainy starts to tell it, but I hold up my hands. "Let George tell his. We'll have plenty of time to tell ours." Rainy laughs and takes a sip from his flask.

George begins. "I was born in Jefferson County, Tennessee, oldest son of Eli and Jane Jamison. We came to Choctaw County when I was five, bought and worked the land like everybody else. When the war started, I joined up to protect family and farm, we all did. Long story short, I got captured at Fort Donelson and did some decidin' on my own."

Poole cuts in. "He enlisted with the Union like we done, Lummy."

George clears his throat, and Poole apologizes for interrupting. "So, I finished out the war with the Yanks, and glad of it."

I nod, and he holds up his hand.

"One other thing. You'll like this, Rainy, since you enjoy stories. After I got cut loose from the prison camp up in Indiana, I didn't return to my company. I sneaked off home to steal my bride."

Old Bart gasps, "You didn't."

"Yep, took her plain as day, right out from underneath her mean old daddy Amos Wisner."

Old Bart sits up. "Tell the truth and shame the devil. You stole her and didn't even get shot?"

"He-e-e-ell, no. I was too slick. Boy, oh, boy, how I wanted that girl Dar-lene Wisner from my earliest church goin' days. She's a couple years older than me, but that didn't bother her none. I slipped off from the Army after the exchange. She had her bag ready the night I came to get her."

Poole, eyes glued on George, asks, "Da-a-amn, son, ain't you the bold one?"

"Don't know about that, but that's what I did."

Rainy leans up on his elbow. "They call it eloping."

Poole asks, "Say what?"

Rainy sits up and reaches for the cup of coffee Old Bart hands him. "It's when two people sneak off and get married by themselves, usually by the Justice of the Peace, or a willing minister, but most often without the consent, or the blessing, of the bride's family."

George kicks the floor. "That's about it. So I took her to my folks, who welcomed her right into the family. Then, rather than gettin' caught as a deserter, I joined up with the Yanks. The cause was right, and the pay even better. I finished out my time wearin' the blue suit."

Coffee is passed around, then bread, hoop cheese, and cold ham. George gives us news of what's happened in Choctaw County since Poole and I took the family to Vicksburg.

It ain't good.

I lay back, having heard enough bad news. I laugh at how big Seth's eyes got when he saw the big shotgun and pistol I carried into this rotting stand. He was shivering in the corner, cold and afraid. I thought he was going to squeal like a pig when I showed him a picture of Susannah and told him she was my wife. But my greatest pleasure was bringing him home to become part of the Tullos family. That was my first true act living in the new world the Lord opened up to me.

I like George already. He'll be a good friend like the others here with me. But I guess you just can't compare friends, like Poole and J.A, or Rainy and Old Bart. They bring a different kind of friendship to the table that makes my life so much better. And safer.

So, when I think about Seth in this place where we first met, finding a new friend in an old place still can't replace an old friend now lost. I can still see Seth hanging from the great old shade oak down Phoenix Creek that borders our farm. It's a sight I'll never forget.

CHAPTER 32

# AN OLD FRIEND FOR A NEW CAUSE

## EVENING, MAY 5, 1868

*Strength lies not in what a man's capable of doing,*
*but in what he chooses not to do.*

WE RIDE HARD and steady until we reach the outskirts of French Camp. We surely don't want to be seen by anyone there, so we give the town a wide berth. George leads us now and takes us to a farm outside Greensborough, far off the Starkville Road. My mind goes in a thousand different directions now that we're back in Choctaw County, the place where my life began—and could end.

Never in a thousand years would I have believed this quiet kid who loved wandering the streams and hills of this land would be forced to deal with bullies and eventually kill men to survive. I don't want that anger in me anymore, and I plan to keep the promise to myself not to kill another man ever again. I made it through the 1st Mississippi Mounted Rifles days without doing it. I'm not so sure it'll be as easy to avoid with Captain Tom Ford wanting my head on a pike.

The easy thing would be to sneak up on him and his gang and kill them outright, like we did Dawg Smith. I can't do that. No, if I'm going to live in a new world, then I must restrain myself and follow the rules as best I can. Mr. Gilmore told me once that the strength of a man lies not in what he's capable of doing, but in what he chooses not to do. Restraint is harder than giving in.

We ride up to an old house with most of the paint peeled off. An old familiar man peers out his front door, squinting. He waves us in. It's Sheriff Platner, no longer sheriff, standing solid as a rock on his front porch.

We gather around his warm rock chimney fireplace to dry our clothes from the rain shower. His wife Rhoda brings out a big pot of ham and purple speckled butterbean soup with corn pone. We express our thanks and sit down to a fine meal. Poole starts to take a bite when Rhoda clears her throat. Poole nods and sets his spoon back down.

Sheriff Platner lowers his head. "Lord, for this blessed meal we are truly thankful. Thanks for Ma who made it. Bless these boys who now have to fight once more for the ones dear to them. Keep them safe and help 'em defeat the enemy, and Lord, the quicker the better, Amen."

We amen and dig in like men who haven't eaten a decent meal in days. I guess we haven't.

As we eat, Sheriff Platner talks. "Boys I appreciate you callin' me sheriff, but that ain't my business no more. It was a good long run, but the other man got the votes. Just call me S.C."

J.A. nods between bites. "Yes, sir, Mistuh S.C., and thank you ma'am for havin' us. The food is truly the best."

Mrs. Rhoda smiles and finally takes the soup ladle in hand to fill her bowl now that we've finished our first and are ready for a second helping.

S.C. lays down his spoon, pushing back his bowl. "Ma, I'm not too hungry. I'll eat this later."

"You all right, Mistuh S.C.?" I ask.

"Not really," he says as Rhoda wipes away a tear. "I got the cancer in my lungs all of a sudden, and Doc says I ain't got too long. A year or two, maybe, if that."

I drop my head. "I'm sorry to hear that, old friend."

"Ain't nothin' to be sad about, son. I've had a good life, the best wife a man could ever have, and good men tryin' to do what's right with their feet under my table tonight eatin' from the blessin's only the Lord can give." This man never ceases to amaze me.

"I'm not sure how much I can help you besides what I'm doin' right now. I can't ride, and I'd be no good in a fight, but there is one thing I can do. I can sit in Greensborough and keep my ears open. Captain Tom Ford is the problem. He all but called out yours and Poole's names the other day."

I set my soup spoon down. "I heard. But you gotta be careful, Mistuh S.C., bein' sick and all."

"Don't worry, son, it's your own skin you need to be concerned about. And they'll come for it soon."

Rainy leans up. "Sir, you are a good old soldier, and there's always a place for men who want righteousness. Reconnaissance is as important as the men out front."

"You're right. I am too old to be totin' a rifle, but the law, which is no law these days, won't suspect a thing if I sit up near the sheriff's office playin' dominoes and drinking coffee with the worn out old jack legs every mornin'. I'll keep my eyes peeled and ear to the ground and send someone when I need to get word to you."

George clears his throat. "That'll be me, Mistuh S.C. I'll keep up my blacksmith work until Lummy calls for me. How's that?"

S.C. nods. "That'll work."

We finish supper with a cup of fine moonshine, and S.C. invites us into the front room of their small house to continue talking.

"You boys got a plan?"

I shake my head. "Not exactly, not yet"

"Well, while you're strategizin', you'll need a place to hide and rest. I know just the place."

Poole starts nodding his head. He knows what S.C. has in mind.

"You boys know Wood Mountain and Aaron Wood's Spring?"

Poole laughs. "The Wood boys make the best damned shine in the county out of that sweet spring water."

S.C. pulls out his clay pipe. "That's for sure." He lights the sweet tobacco. "There's a big sandstone rock near there." S.C. looks at me as he lights his pipe. "It lays due east from your farm, but it ain't easy to find. There's hollows so deep a man could get turned around in there for days."

I rub my chin. "Yeah, I've heard, but never have been there. They say you can see for miles from its perch."

S.C. blows smoke through his nostrils and looks at his pipe. "Rousted a couple of ruffians out of there years ago. Thought I'd never find the place.

Heck, I stayed lost two days before I found them boys. If you find it, it's got a long overhang good for gettin' out of the rain. Somebody dug a good sized hole underneath that can house several men and their stuff if you don't mind cramped quarters."

J.A. rubs the back of his neck. "Can't be no tighter than the bombproofs we hunkered down in durin' the siege at Vicksburg."

S.C. blows out a nice round smoke ring. "It'd be about the same, but at least you'll be warm if we have a cool spell, and cool if it heats up. Big Sand Rock will work well for men who ain't strangers to hardship and war. And you men ain't."

# CHAPTER 33

# HE LEADS ME IN THE PATHS OF RIGHTEOUNESS

## EARLY MORNING, MAY 6, 1868

*I need no one to lead me to this fight.*

EVEN WITH THE directions Sheriff Platner gave us, Poole doesn't trust his memory to get us to Big Sand Rock. We stop by McCurtain Swamp to get Dan Creekwater. He's ready, bow and arrow quiver strapped across his back. He mounts the horse we brought for him and he leads us straight to our new home. We split up to circle the hideout that's only a mile from Aaron Wood's Spring. The ancient stone, a hundred feet long and forty wide, sits on a high ridge near Wood Mountain on a pine covered knoll out of sight of the most seasoned hunter.

Satisfied no one's around, we dismount and walk our horses to the rock formation. Hidden next to Big Sand Rock, two horses snort, having smelling better than ours. Guns are pulled in a flash. We hear faint laughing coming from the hole under the rock overhang.

I yell, "You in the cave, come out."

The first thing that emerges is a hand welding a gallon stone jug with a corn cob stopper.

"Glad you boys could make it. Saw you comin' a mile away."

It's John and Henry Wood. We relax and tie off our horses. I scan the area and realize how safe this position is. John hands me the jug, and I take a swig.

I wipe my mouth. "Best damn moonshine around."

John takes the jug and hands it to Rainy. "Made from the sweet waters of Aaron Wood's Spring."

Rainy hands the two brothers each a Henry rifle. "I'm Rainy Mills, gun dealer and savior of your friend Lummy's ass." He takes a long draw from the jug. He coughs and chokes a little. "Hellfire and damnation, that's good stuff."

Henry laughs. "Burns the hair right off your tongue."

I chuckle. "Ain't that the truth?"

John brushes dust from his britches. "You boys take a look around and get your bearings. Henry and me know every nook and cranny in these hills. Truth be told, we use this hideout on occasion to escape our wives. But we'll deny it if ever you meet 'em. We'd sure enough have to move here for good if you told on us." We laugh.

"Hey!" Rainy pats the air for us to get down. "Three men coming up the west ridge."

I shade my eyes from the sun. "Relax, freinds. It's my brothers, Elihu, Jasper, and James." I wave them in and they wave back. "Y'all come on, glad you came."

I ask as they sit and catch their breath, "You get Ma and the girls to Sheriff Platner's place. I know he'll be glad to watch over them." They nod.

Rainy hands them each a brand new Henry and they look them over like eyeing a shapely woman.

Jasper takes in a deep breath and lets it out. "I can take care of a bunch of trouble with this."

I ask, "James, how's the head?"

He touches the wound. "Healin' up all right. Good enough to be here."

"Well, rest when you need to and we'll keep an eye on that wound."

Elihu unloads two jugs. "You boys will be wantin' to sample this."

John Wood laughs. "I hope that's what I think it is."

Elihu grins. "It is. Sweetest and tastiest muscadine wine in whole county."

Rainy smiles. "Wood brothers' moonshine and Elihu's fine wine. What a joy to behold."

Dan Creekwater, who's been quietly taking it all in, laughs. "Ain't none of you boys right in the head."

I make sure everyone is introduced.

Jasper and James walk around the huge stone like they're inspecting a fortification. Jasper smiles. "Not bad. We should've come up here a long time ago." Both would know a good one when they see it.

Rainy and Old Bart trot a wide circle, checking approaches and escape routes. George ducks into the cave to see where he'll be sleeping tonight.

I take the jug back from John. "You boys make the best shine in the county, but let's keep that jug open only when we come back to rest after giving Captain Tom Ford hell."

John nods. "Good idea. We can't face that rascal drunk as a skunk."

"That goes for you, too, Elihu." He sticks his tongue out at me.

Poole looks around and sighs from exhaustion. "Looks just like Pa told me. You don't come out here for a Sunday picnic. A man's gotta want to be here to find this place."

"Why didn't you ever show me this place?" I'm aggravated that he didn't when we were kids, but I guess he had good reason.

"I should have, but my daddy made me swear that I'd tell no one. It's a place where outlaws and murderers hid out for years, and if I'd spilled the milk on that one, he said them outlaws would come slit my throat. Bein' a kid, I was too scared to tell you. I forgot about it after that."

"Good enough."

Big Sand Rock ain't four miles from our farm as the crow flies. Sandstone rocks and boulders lie all around everywhere in these hills, but I've never seen anything like this one. It sits atop a flat ridge facing west. The almost undetectable roadbed swerves from the flat top ridge to drop around in the front where the ledge hangs over roughly ten feet and twenty feet long. Old crates, cooking utensils, a few busted moonshine jugs, and some canning jars are scattered about. This has been a well-used camp from time to time.

I walk along the sandstone wall rubbing my hand on the grainy rock. I like this place. Big Sand Rock runs north and south, as does the ridge, and the ground in front gently rolls into a deep drop-off that falls into a hollow I can't see the bottom of.

Rainy has his hands cupped over his ears, listening. "Two deer just over that hill there. That's a good sign." He bends over to look inside the hand dug cave. "I've heard about places like this. I once took a load of guns and powder to a party led by some fellow named West in the Devil's Punchbowl near Natchez on the river."

J.A. and I look at each other at the same time. He says, "Surely not the same John West we know?"

I squint. "Wouldn't surprise me

J.A. asks, "What happened?"

Old Bart snickers. "I've heard this story too many times." He grabs an old bucket he found near the hand dug cave entrance and walks down the hill to find water in the deep hollow.

Rainy continues scanning the countryside as he speaks. "I made a fair deal with them, but I wasn't sure I'd make it back out when I slipped into that wicked lookin' place. Snakes were everywhere. Even so, they were gentlemen when it came to honest business. I gave them the guns and powder, and they handed over the gold. Guess they didn't want to bite the hand that was feeding them. Surprised the hell out of me. In fact, one of those riff raff lives in Winn Parish. J.A., Lummy, you should know—"

I cut in, knowing Rainy gets longwinded telling his stories and I don't want to talk about John West right now. We got things that need tending to. "Let's unload the gear and get camp set up. We'll sleep inside with a guard at the entrance to the cave at all times. No night fires unless inside, and no day fires at all. You can smell fire smoke in the daytime as easy as seein' its light at night." All agree.

Rainy laughs. "Good thinkin'."

Poole complains. "So, cold food most of the time, but we'll cook when we can?"

"That's the deal."

Old Bart brings a bucket of spring water up the hill, breathing hard. "Dang, that's a hill for a stepper right there. Sheriff's right, a man will be lost for days if he gets turned around out here. I looked back up the hill I just came down, and all them ridges look the same. Had I not eyed me a tree to mark my path comin' down, I'd still be wanderin' around down there."

Old Bart sets the bucket down, drops to his knees, and rolls over, stretching his legs out. He pats himself on the chest and takes a deep long breath.

Poole asks, "You gonna be all right?"

"I think I'm dyin'."

I kick dirt at him. "You ain't dyin', old man. You're too ornery for the Lord to take you yet."

 Old Bart sits up. "Hope not. Lord knows this is pretty country. I see why you always wanted to come back. I'd like to visit the farm you grew up on sometime. Bet it's a sight."

"Some of the best bottomland in the county," Poole says, "and grows the prettiest cotton you ever saw."

Bart takes a long deep breath. "I like the smell of these woods, old leaves and dirt. Reminds me of Alabamy when I was a child. I could stay a spell in a place like this."

I nod. "You'd be welcome as any family member I got, Bart Houston."

"Oh, Lummy, I would, but you know I made a promise to my boss. Besides, these hands are gettin' too old to start up new again. It's a good thought though."

We stare into each other's eyes, remembering all the good times we had working and laughing, hunting and fishing, becoming the best of friends.

My head drops. I'm a little sad. "Ain't it so."

# CHAPTER 34

# OUR FIRST PATROL

## MAY 8, 1868

*At some point you gotta step out. When you do, it's on.*

CAMP IS SECURE, our weapons are ready, and the men are mounted, waiting in silence for my order to start out. I look into the eyes of seasoned men who fear little. I call each by name before the Lord so that it will be clear who it is St. Michael needs to watch over and protect.

"Thomas Poole, Dan Creekwater, Elihu, Jasper, and James Tullos, George Wesley Jamison, John and Henry Wood, we're here because we must defend our homes from men who not only call themselves Hyenas, but according to Old Bart who once lived in Africa, act like 'em, too. Rainy Mills, J.A. Killingsworth, and Bart Houston, a man could have no better friends than you. Thank you for coming in our time of need. Boys, I wrote no letter to Governor Sharkey asking permission to form you men into a militia. That means we're probably more outlaw than the bastards we're gonna hunt down."

I look at my brothers. "We won't make the dumb mistake Sherman did when he thought he'd just waltz into Vicksburg and attack. No, we're gonna catch 'em the way Dan coon hunts."

Dan leans up in the saddle. "Bait 'em and let 'em fall into a pit trap they can't resist."

"Exactly. I got some ideas about how to bait 'em up as they say, but the first thing to do is make them so uncomfortable, they lose their edge."

J.A., looking like a dog with his ears pinned back ready for a fight, asks, "What's first?"

"Prayin'." We remove hats, and I say a short prayer for protection and strength. I pray like I did when the big blue Yankee snake slithered up to Vicksburg and several thousand men attacked the 27th Louisiana Lunette in a tornado fury. With that done, I hesitate, knowing once I take this first step, there'll be no turning back. The battle will begin, and the dying will commence.

I've told these men over and over that I want Captain Tom Ford captured alive. But in the heat of battle, I know there ain't no guarantees. Even for me. For what I might have to do. I finish praying.

Rainy reins up his mount, smiling, but with fire in his eyes. "Let's go get into some mischief."

We venture out on paths less traveled and parallel at a distance more common roads, avoiding detection at all costs. A party of twelve men is neither easily hidden nor always quiet. I drew a crude map of the countryside, but nothing replaces traipsing up and down these hills through bottoms and hollows and wading swamps and creeks.

Poole breaks off to mail some money to his folks, who left on a weekend when the bank was closed in Greensborough. He rides away yelling, "Gotta surprise when I see you next. I'll meet you at Little Mountain on the Old Trace side in four days."

I yell back, "Surprise? What?" But he's already out of earshot.

Dan leads as scout, and we wander the land for a couple days, letting the men get their bearings. It's not long that each man learns a number of ways to safely return to base, which will also serve as escape routes in case our camp is found. Fortunately, no one comes near the Big Sand Rock hideout. Most folks are too scared to venture out that far, even the old and experienced hunters and trappers. It's just too dangerous with men lurking about who claim to be protectors of good citizens but rape, pillage, murder, and steal.

On the third afternoon of our patrol, Dan locates the Hyena's position near French Camp. We move up the Old Trace to meet back up with Poole.

We ride west to Little Mountain where Sergeant McGugarty and I sat the evening I left to join the 1st Mississippi Mounted Rifles. It was there he reminded me why I was going off to fight—to do my part to get the twentieth star for Mississippi back on the Union flag. I want to go there again to be reminded of why I'm fighting now—to get Choctaw County fully back into the Union fold. We top the highest point in the county.

I scan the woods as we make our way to the slope facing the Old Trace. "It's a good thing we're camped at the Big Sand Rock. Josiah told us the Hyenas made theirs near French Camp. It gives plenty of space between us."

George is waiting for us at the top. "Yeah, two of 'em came to get their horses re-shoed at my shop in Greensborough day before yesterday."

I turn. "They say anything?"

"Naw, except they'd heard that a group of armed men passed through not long ago. But then the bastard himself, Captain Tom Ford, asked if I'd seen any strangers. I made up a story about a couple of men who dropped by to get their knives sharpened but kept goin' on to Starkville. That satisfied him for the moment."

J.A. grins. "Guess he thinks he can trust you since you're feedin' him news."

"My thoughts exactly." George throws his leg over the saddle and stretches. "I saw Mistuh S.C. for a minute, but he had nothin' to report. He did say the only way to get this thing goin' is to start somethin'. Raidin' their camp when they're gone would start the fire, he said to tell you."

Rainy pulls off his hat and brushes away a bug. "What do you think, General Lummy? It might be a good start."

I laugh. "It seems we have a pretty good general in Greensborough, playin' dominoes with big ears, hearin' the strategy of the enemy. Ain't nothin' like stirrin' up a good hornets nest."

J.A. snickers. "I bet ole red-haired Sherman and cigar smokin' Grant wished they'd had Sheriff Platner at Vicksburg."

I dismount and feed Cloud a handful of corn. "Damn straight."

# CHAPTER 35

# AN OLD FRIEND FOR A NEW FIGHT

### DARK, MAY 9, 1868

*Havin' the law on your side don't always make you right,*
*but it does make it legal.*

I T'S LIKE I can see the whole world sitting on top of this small mountain. A gentle, late spring breeze whispers melodies through the leaves at a time when the peace in my soul will soon be broken. I breathe it all in knowing what's ahead.

Suddenly, the sound of two horses walking in the shadows brings me back. Pistols are cocked, and rifle levers send rounds into barrel chambers.

"Hold on. It's me, Poole." Everyone relaxes. He walks his horse over, and then I recognize a familiar shape I've not seen since he and I mustered out of the Rifles in June of '65.

"Sergeant McGugarty! What—*How?*" We jump off our mounts and back-slap for a moment. "How in the hell are you?"

Elihu slides off his horse and says to the rest. "Might as well stretch your legs a bit, this may take a while."

Sarge turns me loose and shakes Elihu's hand. "Damn, if you ain't a sight to see, Lummy boy, and few more pounds to boot."

"Yeah, a beautiful wife who can cook good will do that for a man."

"So you married that pretty gal in the blue skirt?

Poole sticks his hand out. "The same lady who ran to the landing the day we steamed away from Vicksburg with the Rifles."

In crisp military form, I snap a salute. "Yes, sir, Sergeant McGugarty. And I report for my husbandly duty every chance I get."

Dan whispers under his breath, "You ain't right in the head, Lummy."

Sarge straightens like when he called us to parade drill. "You're a good man, Lummy Tullos. I'm here to help, so I'll make this quick. When I mustered out of the Rifles, the Army offered me a chance to serve as a provost, like you did in Vicksburg with the Rebs. It's the same military type police authorized to keep the peace, but my territory covers a wide area. When they said trouble was brewing in this part of the state, I volunteered, hopin' I'd run into you boys."

Poole cuts in. "Yeah, I saw Sarge in Jackson City when I took the folks down there. I asked if he'd come help us."

I scowl at Poole. "Why in the hell didn't you tell me?"

Sarge barks like he used to giving us orders. "Because I wanted it to be a surprise, Private Ignert Ass Tullos."

"I guess he told you, Lummy," Dan snickers.

I backhand Poole's chest. "Good enough, shit face." I shake Sarge's hand. "So glad you're here, but why?"

Sarge scratches his ear. "Well, the government wants to catch that damned Captain Tom Ford they should've hanged when we came through to burn Bankston. Come to find out, a spy in the ranks helped him escape. Anyway, I'm here to make sure you boys do everything legal, you know, by the book as they say. I'm deputizin' you men here and now, but lettin' you run the show because I know you'll catch that bastard." The men look around at each other.

Sarge raises his right hand. "Get 'em up, boys."

We swear an oath of allegiance to uphold the law of the true United States, and with a few other promises we all say, "So help me God."

Poole has the look of a child getting a beautiful big cake on his birthday. "Ain't never been a deputy before. Do I get a badge, Sarge?"

"Private Poole, you will refrain from askin' ignert ass questions that have little to do with the mission at hand, do you understand?"

Poole drops his head, grinning. "Well... once a private always a private, I reckon."

Sarge slaps Poole on the shoulder. "If I had any badges, you'd be the first to get one, brother."

WE TRAIL DOWN a hill near French Camp at midnight. In the distance, the lights of the Drane house Pa supplied lumber for, and our family helped build, flicker in the darkness. I was only fourteen, but that's when I learned how to carpenter a house. I'm not sure the Colonel would claim us as friends tonight. Pa once taught him a valuable lesson about the evils of gambling when they were young men. I'm guessing it steered him back on the right path at the right time.

Poole slips up beside me as Sarge glasses the area for any movement.

Poole asks, "Remember Colonel Drane?" I nod. "Well, he sure made a name for himself." I nod for him to continue.

Even though I'd rather enjoy the quiet in times like this, I let Poole talk because it calms his nerves. "James Drane has been an active member of the Choctaw County community for years, servin' in Mississippi politics since 1839, and helped incorporate the Masonic and Odd Fellows High School in Bankston back in 1852. Fancy place, and only the richest could get in. I ain't never thought much of societies like the Masons. It seems like a cover up for deeds done in secret by men more loyal to each other than what's right. I guess I can't say that about Mistuh H.P. Petty's Union Society though, huh? He just wanted Mississippi to stay with the Stars and Stripes. But it didn't stay secret long, and he had to hightail it out of the county during the war."

"You talk like you're readin' a history book, boy."

He laughs, and we sit silent for a moment, but then Poole soon continues. "You know Drane didn't vote for Jefferson Davis when he ran for governor back in '51 and lost the election to the Unionist Henry S. Foote by less than a hundred votes. Even at the great State's Rights barbeque in Greensborough that my family attended, I was proud that Mississippi still held its place as the twentieth star on the Union flag. That didn't last long though."

Poole shifts in his saddle and scratches his knee. "Colonel Drane went on to serve as president of the state senate, which would have put him in next in line for governor had something befallen the man serving. Soon after, he was put up by many county conventions as their choice for governor, but unfortunately his wife Matilda took sick. He gave up the nomination, which would've secured him bein' elected back in those days. Said his first duty was to his wife, and he proved that true until she passed."

Sergeant McGugarty sits up quickly in his saddle to focus on a particular spot in the trees not four hundred yards away.

Poole whispers, "I'm sure we would've disagreed with Drane's views on state's rights and slavery. You know he and other delegates demanded that slavery be the main issue in the presidential election at the 1860 Democratic Convention in Charleston, South Carolina. When things didn't go their way, they just walked out. Even so, I do honor a man whose family priorities are clear."

I wish I'd thought that way when I left Susannah behind for the war. Oh how my life would be different now had I stayed home and not enlisted then. But then, Martha.....

J.A., who's been listening to our conversation, snickers. "They would've conscripted you quicker'n a duck on a June bug, Lummy." I start to say something, but he beats me to it. "Ain't changed a bit. Still talkin' out loud."

I look at Poole, grinning. "Where'd you hear all that?"

"Didn't hear it. I read it. I may not know the meanings of some big words, but I'm learnin'."

We sit for moment, and though a few of the men have the itch, no one dares light up a smoke.

"Lummy, I read in the Greensborough paper that Colonel Drane is in bad health and not expected to live much longer."

I rub my rough beard that's sprouted and itches. "I should go see him. We did a lot of work for that man, and he always treated our family well. He might have words of wisdom for a man like me who's still searching."

Sarge sits up high in his saddle again, straining to see something in the far distance.

"What is it?" I ask.

"They're movin' out."

Dan Creekwater eases his mount up. "Yeah, they've been doin' their devil work in the wee hours of the night, when good folks least expect trouble. Their camp should have only one guard, two at best."

We spread out around the smoky camp, junked up by men who have little discipline and far less sanitary concerns. Two men sit near the fire, sipping tin cups and laughing at each other's crude jokes. Little do they know twelve Henry repeaters are aimed at their heads by men who rarely miss.

Elihu slides off his horse. He pats me on the leg and whispers, "I'll do it." Before I can say anything, he stumbles into their camp like a drunk. The two guards stand up in a flash and pull their pistols. Elihu switches one leg in front of the other and falls down sprawling like a newborn calf. The guards laugh.

"Got anythin' to drank? I done plum run out of shine. Broke my damn jug down the road a piece."

The tallest one, who wears a deep scar on his neck, takes a few steps forward and points his pistol at Elihu's head. "Which way did you come from, mister?"

Elihu gets up clumsily. The younger one, only a boy, lifts his pistol up with shaky hands.

"How the hell do I know? I've been wanderin' around out here all night like a coon huntin' frogs." Elihu steps forward. "I need a drink. What'cha got?"

They give him a cup of whiskey, and he turns it up. Elihu stumbles into the older of the two, our signal to rush them. Elihu makes quick work of the scarred man with the pistol, nearly lifting the man off his feet as he drives his fist upwards into his chest. The boy just throws his gun down when he sees several rifle barrels bearing down on him and feels the point of Old Bart's Arkansas Toothpick in his back.

The tall scarred man asks, choking and coughing from the blow that knocked the wind out of him, "What y'all want?"

Rainy steps up in the coolness of a riverboat gambler at a poker table. "Everything, damn you—including your lives if you don't cooperate."

# CHAPTER 36

# TRUTH IS HARD TO HEAR

## JUST AFTER MIDNIGHT, MAY 9, 1868

*Confession's good for the soul.*
*And the body, too, sometimes.*

GEORGE TIES THE two men up tighter than a lid on a hogshead barrel. Firelight dances in their fearful eyes.

The younger of the two recognizes him. "I know you. You're the blacksmith in Greensborough, ain't you?"

George says nothing, but Elihu kicks dirt on the boy. "Yeah, he is, and I don't live far from him, either. If you want to ever see your folks again, you best shut the hell up, boy."

The kid cowers like a dog that's been whipped one too many times. He starts to cry. "I don't want to be here. I promise I won't tell nobody."

The tall, neck scarred man, kicks at him. "Shut up, boy, or I'll tell the Captain you folded like a damn bird shot out of the sky."

"I can't help it, Herod, my uncle knows I don't want to be here. He made me come. Said it'd make a man out of me."

Rainy steps up. "Yeah, and a dead man at that." The boy drops his head and sobs into his coat. Rainy turns to the tall scarred man. "Herod, huh? Sure livin' up to your name, ain't you?"

The tall scarred man sneers and spits on Rainy's shiny black boots.

"That's all right, I needed to spit shine these cow hides, and I'll be using your shirt to make 'em glow in the dark here in just a bit."

Listening to him talk, seeing the scowl of defiance in the tall scarred one's eyes, my face burns hot, and my throat thickens, making it hard to swallow.

I have flashbacks of Seth dangling from the old shade oak in the firelight of the new cabin these men burned. I toss my head this way and that to shake it off. It doesn't work.

I snatch the knife Pa made me years ago from my belt—the one that saved me more than once fighting in Vicksburg. The knife I took Dawg Smith's head off with. I start toward the tall, neck scarred man, gripping the knife, thinking about what happened to Mr. Allrice. As I raise my blade, a dark hand reaches out to stop me.

"This ain't the way, son." My fiery eyes turn to look in the soft dark eyes of my black grandfather. "You're better'n this." I jerk to get free, but Old Bart softly says, "Son, get ahold of yourself. Don't let that old demon you chased away come back into your soul."

He's right, and I calm myself. Just a little.

Poole slaps the tall scarred man's head. "Did you help burn the Negro boy's place on our farm?"

He winces but says nothing. He just grins with a gleam in his eyes. "If I had, I would've enjoyed every minute of it, heh."

I can barely contain my anger.

Rainy kicks the young boy's foot. "What about the old man with hams, were you there?"

He hesitates. Rainy kicks his foot harder, and the boy squeals like a young pig. "Yes, sir, I was there. I helped take his hams and turkeys. That's all. I didn't shoot nobody!"

I have to ask, "Who shot the old man?"

The boy looks at the tall scarred one, who shakes his head, hoping the boy won't say. The boy turns away frightened. With either courage or fear, or maybe both, he motions with his elbow. "He did it."

The tall scarred man snickers, "And I thoroughly enjoyed putting a noose around your black boy's neck. It gave me great pleasure."

I lunge at the scarred man, but Jasper and James catch me before I can drive my knife deep into his chest.

The man rolls over laughing, believing he's safe. He rubs his neck scar with his tied hands. "You ain't doin' shit, niggah lover, 'cause you can't prove nothin'. Besides, if you hurt me? Captain Tom Ford will come after you like a bobcat on a rabbit. He won't let up until he's done skinnin' your hide and feedin' you to his hounds!"

Sergeant McGugarty steps up. "I'm countin' on that very fact, son. Best get your heart right with Jesus, because now your ass is mine."

The scarred man looks up in surprise at Sarge in his Military Police uniform with three stripes.

Sarge points to his badge. "See this? There's a new sheriff, and he needs no county badge. He's got one given by the President himself. I'm duly authorized to hang any man found in violation of the new laws that govern this land. You clearly have done so based on the testimony of this young man. You have been found guilty, and I sentence you to hang by the neck until dead."

The tall scarred man says nothing. What can he say? He played the wrong game with the wrong men.

Sarge snaps, "Get him up on his horse." The men don't move. Sarge barks out like he did in the war. "I said now, damn you deputies!"

The Wood brothers jerk the tall scarred man up and set him on his horse with a noose around his neck.

Sarge asks, "Any last words?"

The scarred man blinks through his tears and spits. "If this is what the new niggah lovin' Yankee world has come to, I want no part of it. Damn you, your uniform, and your fake badge. In fact, damn you *all* to hell."

"You first." Rainy slaps the horse on the hip, and the deed is done.

I cringe at the man dangling with his eyes bulging and feet kicking. Old Bart puts his arm around my shoulder. Even though I don't want to hear it, I know he'll have the right words.

"I sure wish I could've met your young friend Seth. Sounds like a good man with a promisin' future."

They are just the right words—words to remind me of the righteousness of what we're doing.

"Me, too, Bart. You would've liked him."

# CHAPTER 37

# NO TURNING
# BACK NOW

## LATE AFTERNOON, SEPTEMBER 2, 1866

*If a fire needs to be set, then start a blaze
somebody else will have to put out.*

WE LEAVE THE camp in ruins with nothing of any use to Captain Tom Ford. We ride away with the tall scarred man still hanging with a message tied to his shirt.

*This is what happens to bastards
who follow their own law.
The Twentieth Stars*

Nothing is said as we take a trail that parallels the Old Trace, except to warn the young boy to say nothing of what he saw or who it was that destroyed Captain Tom Ford's camp.

He cries as he pleads, "I promise I won't. I just want to go home."

Rainy points his pistol at the boy's head. "I want you to leave the county for a while. If we hear that you said anything to anybody, no matter what else happens, capturing Tom Ford or not, I will personally come after you and kill you myself. Do you understand?"

Old Bart shakes his head. "You'll want none of that, son, I'm tellin' you. He takes his time."

The boy brightens a bit. "You know, what my uncle is doin' ain't right, and I want no part of it. My Grandpa lives over in Winona. I'll go there first thing in the mornin', God willin'."

I cut a glance his way. "Son, the Lord always lends a hand to a man decidin' to do right. Ain't no turnin' back now, not for you or us. You will do better in Winona."

He gives me a faint grin.

Sarge slaps the boy's mount on the rump. "Get goin', and we don't want to see you ever again. Do you understand?"

"Thank you, sir. You won't." He peels off on the road that leads to Bankston. He waves and sets his horse to a trot.

George pulls up beside me. "I know that boy's folks. He doesn't remember me, except that I shod his daddy's horses once. They're good people, and I believe he'll do what he says. I'll keep an eye on him 'til he leaves for Winona."

"Good enough. But watch him, George. That boy could turn whichever way the slightest wind blows."

We pass an overgrown wagon trail leading into a pine thicket. "Sarge, I'll meet you boys at the Big Sand Rock later. I need to see somebody. Poole, you wanna come?"

"Nope, got somethin' I need to do."

"J.A.?" He nods.

We tie our mounts to a peach tree in the front yard of a one room shack.

I call out in a hoarse whisper, "Old man, you got any fish for sale?"

We hear a chuckle from behind the cracked front door, and the rabbit ears of a double barrel shotgun click back to their safe position. "Only if you got some good Yankee gold." Josiah steps out onto his small porch, happy to see us. He leans the shotgun against the doorframe. "It's been a spell, Lummy. Get your family away safe?" I nod as I walk to the porch. "Elihu told me you took 'em to Vicksburg. Good thinkin'. Y'all come on in out this cool mornin'. I ain't got no fish for sale, but I got some left from supper with a good chunk of corn pone on the stove, if you're hungry."

"Now, Josiah, you know boys like us. When did you ever know us not to be hungry?"

"Get on in here then, and catch me up. Who you got there with you?"

J.A. sticks out his hand. "J.A. Killingsworth, from Winn Parish, Looseana. Lummy and me fought at Vicksburg together."

"Glad to have you, son. Y'all make yourselves at home, now. I'll get some plates."

We wade into the pan of fried bream and catfish like nobody's business. I have many a good memory fishing with this old man who once ran the great machines that powered Wesson's mills when no one else could. I still marvel at the that idiot *. Wesson naming his best engineer, "Chat," to remind him not to get high minded because he was still just a Negro. I always knew who the high-minded one was.

Josiah sits back to smoke his clay pipe. "Yeah, ole Mistuh Wesson, he thought he had them Yankees tricked when he switched from makin' army goods to civilian. It worked the first time Sherman came through in '63, but not when you boys sneaked up on him with General Grierson that cold rainy winter night. You boys caught them bastards red-handed with their britches down."

Josiah reaches to pour us more coffee. "Anyway, first time around, you should've seen all them broke down worn out ole white men tryin' to play soldier, workin' them cannons they got from General Pemberton at Vicksburg. Colonel James Drane was one of the captains. He commanded a forty man bunch of horse soldiers who weren't worth spit. Your man Lester was one of 'em. They called themselves the Choctaw Reserves. The only reserves about them boys was how they reserved the best of what good honest folks tried to live on for themselves. Colonel Drane quit because of their devilment. You know the rest. That rascal Captain Tom Ford took over and still claims his useless authority from havin' been in the group."

I stop chewing, and through a mouthful of fish and corn pone I offer, "You know Ford sent a letter to Governor Sharkey and got permission to raise a militia."

Josiah points his crooked finger at me. "And he's lookin' for you, boy, real hard." I shrug. "But yeah, early December of '64, Wesson was gettin' wagon loads of supplies ready to send to General Hood, but you boys took care of it. Things won't never be the same, no matter how hard he tries to get his factories goin' again. There's talk he might be movin' to a new location."

We finish up our meal and sit by the fireplace sipping coffee.

Josiah brings out two blankets. "This is all I got, but it's enough if you want to stay."

We stand up. "Temptin', but we best get goin', young man, before Captain Tom Ford finds his cozy little camp a wreck."

Josiah covers his mouth. "Oh, hell no, you didn't!" J.A. and I grin. "Well, ain't that the best thing done happened around here in months. You boys have declared war on the Ford Gang."

I hadn't thought about it that way. I guess this is my fourth war—fighting for the gray, against Dawg Smith's gang, then for the blue, and now against Captain Tom Ford and his Hyenas.

I sit back down for a moment. "Josiah, could you get into town and keep your ears open? I want to know how Ford responds to what we did, and maybe you can get wind of his plan."

"Sho' will, Lummy. Who else you got with you?"

"My brothers Elihu, Jasper, and James. Poole, John and Henry Wood."

Josiah cuts in. "Them Wood boys be the ones who make that good moonshine whiskey, ain't they?"

I nod. "J.A. here, of course. You don't know Rainy Mills. He gave me this Colt Dragoon pistol before I enlisted. Or my other black grandpa, Bart Houston, from my Winn Parish days. You two could be brothers. Oh yeah, and George Jamison. You know, the blacksmith in Greensborough. You can pass any messages along to him, if you get over that way."

"I'll make it a point to get there, and I know that boy, George. We did some dealin's together when I ran Wesson's machinery. He a real good man."

"Old Sheriff Platner is with us, too but only as a lookout. He's doin' poorly, but pass any messages you got to him if George ain't around, and he'll do the same."

I slip a ten dollar gold piece under my plate. He'll find it later.

"Thanks for the supper, old man. This'll all be over soon, and we'll go fishin' down where Bywy Creek runs into the Big Black River. What do you say?"

"Best catfishin' in the county. You boys be careful, and I'll let you know what I find out."

I make for the door after giving the old man a hug. J.A. and I slip out into the darkness. We have to get back to Big Sand Rock before daylight. By then, men will be scouring the county for the Twentieth Stars.

J.A leans over. "You know a man like your Captain Ford might be dumb, but he ain't stupid. He'll know who did this to his camp."

"I'm countin' on it."

"There ain't no turnin' back now, is there?"

"Nope. We've started a fire he's gonna have to come put out."

CHAPTER 38

# WHEN VIOLENCE TAKES ON A LIFE OF ITS OWN

### EARLY MORNING, MAY 17, 1868

*There's no killin' the killin'.*

WE TAKE A week off from our patrolling to get our crops in. With the help of the Twentieth Stars, we make short work of planting corn and cotton in the hours after dark. Ma and the girls manage the farm without much trouble during daylight hours. After one long Saturday night in the fields, Ma and I relax on the porch after feasting on a fine breakfast Isabel and the girls prepared. We'll leave a couple hours before sunup to get back to Big Sand Rock before good folks start out for morning church service.

To quiet suspicions, Ma had Pastor Dobbs announce that the family and I went to Vicksburg for an extended stay with Martha's family. I don't like that we told where they are, but if anyone passes through and asks, Martha can tell them I took a trip to Winn Parish. Rainy left Martha a small pepperbox pistol to hide in her skirt, and Annie and Beau aren't afraid of a fight should it come to that. I can't think on that now or I'll worry too much. The hundred miles to Vicksburg is no distance for evil men to travel if they go after my family.

"Men have become exasperated beyond repair," Rainy whispers as he steps out onto the porch. He shivers. The wind is cool and damp this early morning.

Old Bart clears his throat. "We'll get a rain in a day or so."

Dan Creekwater raises his hand to feel the air. "Yeah, a soft one, I believe."

Elihu stirs sugar in his tin coffee cup. "The best kind to get the crops up and growin' right."

Poole lies back on the dogtrot floor with his arm folded under his head for a pillow. "That's a good piece of work. You'll probably have the prettiest chest high cotton in the county."

Jasper squats at the bottom of the porch steps, his butt on his heels. How he does that, I do not know. My knees couldn't take it, and I'd never get back up if I tried. Jasper just stands up without any help. It hurts just watching him.

I ask, "Boy, how can you sit on your haunches like a hound dawg and then stand straight up without holdin' on to nothin'?"

"Hell, I don't know, but Uncle Silas could do it, too."

James slaps Jasper on his chest. "Do that other thing, too."

Jasper takes a couple of steps and suddenly flips over to walk on his hands like a kid. He keeps going as long as he wants and sticks his tongue out at us when he passes the steps. He finally falls back to land on his feet and squats back down with his butt squarely on his heels.

I shake my head. "If I did that, I'd done broke my neck by now."

Ma walks out with her straw broom. "You boys put them cups away and get on out of here before somebody sees you." She starts sweeping, making sure to hit each of us with the broom. It's one of the joys of motherhood I guess, still telling her sons what to do. I wouldn't have it any other way.

James complains, "All right, Ma, we're goin', just give us a minute."

Ma wraps her arms around him and kisses him on the cheek. He melts like butter on a biscuit from her caring touch.

We mount our horses to make Big Sand Rock before daylight. We slip through deep hollows and cross steep ridges the size of small mountains. Dan scouts ahead, and Jasper trails a quarter mile behind to watch our backs.

Big Sand Rock is as we left it with no signs that anyone has disturbed anything. We care for the horses and hunker down inside the Big Sand Rock Cave, trying to stay warm. Old Bart builds a small fire to break the chill and makes coffee in the pit near the entrance of the cave. The small hole at the top of the tarp J.A. laid across the opening lets the smoke out fine. We're all worn out from the week long nights of farm work and hiding in the woods in the daytime.

Poole stretches out on his bedroll. "This is the safest place in the county, I do believe."

Rainy polishes his pistol. "Yeah, and we gotta keep it this way."

Old Bart asks, "Is it always this cold here in May?"

I laugh. "It's been known to be—"

James lifts the tarp covering the cave entrance. "Somebody's comin'."

The sun blinds me for a moment, but by the time my eyes adjust, the Wood boys come into camp from the direction of Aaron Wood's Spring. They must've finished their farm work, too. Fortunately, they have a number of young men and boys to get their crop in. They bring four gallon jugs tied to their mounts. They catch us up on their family business as we sip a little moonshine. We sleep the rest of the day and wait for nightfall to venture out of the cave.

At twilight, Dan suddenly grabs his Henry rifle and dashes into the woods. The rest of us grab ours, but we're relieved to see George Jamison returning from Greensborough. He went to catch up on his blacksmith work and spend time with his family after we destroyed Captain Tom Ford's camp.

He dismounts and takes the cup of corn liquor John Wood offers. "Men are desperate. Now they're killin' their own and blamin' others for it." We gather around.

I ask, "What do you mean, George?"

"Ran into Sarge yesterday. He's been pretty busy while you boys have been farmin'." He drains the rest of his cup. John offers him more, but he waves him off. "Got any water? I need some water." George sounds like a goat drinking as he swallows at least a quart of the cool liquid. "You ain't gonna believe it, Lummy, nor the rest of you boys."

We sit down on crates and empty hogshead barrels.

"It seems Tom Ford and his Hyenas assassinated Brigadier General W.F. Whitley, lately of the Confederate States Army. You might remember him. He started off as a captain of the Wigfall Rifles in the same regiment as your brother George Washington that formed up in Greensborough. Whitely was a true Lost Cause patriot, but who also wanted peace, too. Poole, remember that pretty young sweetheart Miss Mary E. Gore all the boys drooled over?"

"Yeah, didn't she present the company flag to Whitley just before they left out for the war?"

George winks. "I confess I was one of them boys drooling like a pig waitin' on slop."

I'm getting impatient. "What happened, dang it?"

"General Whitley, as you know, stepped in to keep your friend William Pollan from shootin' up Greensborough. Ford didn't like that because he wanted Pollan to fire on the town to give him good reason to start a war. In the meantime, General Whitley's brother A.J., the mayor of Winona, was assassinated. They shot Mistuh A.J. in a crowd of men and women attending a play just like Booth killed Lincoln in Ford's Theatre. General Whitley had gone to Winona to catch the men who killed his brother and get justice. Ford and his Hyenas shot him dead in broad daylight on the Greensborough Road just this side of Lodi. They say the General didn't even twitch."

I rub my chin a bit, worried. "That ain't good, dammit. That just ain't good."

Poole grimaces. "The General was a brave man who wanted what we want. Peace."

George throws a stick away he'd been peeling the bark from. "That ain't all. Ford came to Greensborough tellin' everybody it was the Twentieth Stars who burned his camp and hanged his man Herod. People gritted their teeth like they were set on fire. They want you and Poole real bad."

Poole looks up, his hands shaking a little. "Did he mention our names?"

"Not yet, but he gives them just enough to get them thinkin' that way. Ford wants to make an example of you two. He'll be callin' for a public hangin', you can bet on that."

I slam a sandstone rock down hard on the ground. "There's enough evil in this county to make the Lord come back sooner than he planned."

George reaches for the coffee pot. "I hope not. I know I ain't ready just yet."

I shake my head. "When's all this gonna stop?"

Old Bart lays his hand on my shoulder. "Reminds me of Winn Parish, son. The sun won't shine 'til the storm passes."

CHAPTER 39

# WRONGLY ACCUSED

## JUNE 1, 1868

*Being wrongly accused can provide the opportunity*
*to create the proper amount of fear.*

S ERGEANT MCGUGARTY MAKES his way up the steep ridge that drops into the hollow below the Big Sand Rock. I'm not sure which is sweating more, him or his mount. James takes his horse, and Sarge dips a cool dipper of spring water, draining it with one gulp.

"Got somethin' for you." He hands me a copy of the *Southern Motive*, Greensborough's only remaining newspaper after the war. "You're not gonna like what you read, son."

The headline article reads like a bad novel.

### GENERAL WHITLEY ASSASSINATED IN BROAD DAYLIGHT!

*Just outside Greensborough near Lodi, as General W.F. Whitley returned from Winona June 6, he was assassinated. He went seeking justice for his slain brother A.J., the mayor of that fair city, recently assassinated at a public event. An ongoing feud has finally brought bloodshed to our county like nothing since the war. The General's attempt to catch the perpetrators of his brother's murderers failed, and to this date they remain unknown. The General was no stranger to danger and served admirably during the recent War of Northern Aggression. Wounded twice and escaping capture, the general faced the singing of bullets on the battlefield, never allowing the risk of danger to sway him from his course. It is said that, though he sought*

*peace on all occasions, he deserved honor from both enemies and devoted*
*friends. He will be remembered as a man who cared deeply for our county*
*and her people. His slayers remain at large.*

When I finish reading the article aloud, Sarge points to another on the
front page entitled, *Men of No Account Free to Roam the County!*

*It has come to the attention of the good and loyal citizens of Choctaw Coun-*
*ty that we now coexist with men of low moral character, even less of saintly*
*soul, who perpetrated the murder of one of our most beloved citizens, Gener-*
*al W.F. Whitley, former lawyer and family man. It has been given on good*
*authority that these men of carpetbagger persuasions perform deeds of the*
*secretive kind, lying in wait to do harm to good men of the community and*
*the Old South. These men of misguided loyalties and commitments for-*
*sook the cause of freedom for which our founding fathers died in exchange*
*for those of northern oppressors. They terrorize those striving to maintain*
*order in this our upturned world, seeking an ill-informed glory. The so-*
*called "Twentieth Stars" can only be called so having been cast down from*
*heaven like the Devil and his angels! They deserve the same fate reserved*
*for that old serpent in the abyss of fire, with no hope of release. Two of*
*these men were responsible for the destruction of public and private proper-*
*ty during the war. They may believe their present mission is righteous, but*
*they are men who ride low in the saddle, hiding their faces with scraggily*
*beards and long hair so as not to be recognizable. But our honorable and de-*
*voted Sheriff Lindsey, and his men who wear the red shirt, will eventually*
*catch these men of no account. We must take back what the invader tried*
*to take away in the previous, though unsuccessful, War for Southern Inde-*
*pendence. The Sheriff offers reward for information leading to the arrest,*
*conviction, and hanging of these men who ride low in the saddle.*

Poole yells like a wasp stung him, "That's a damn lie, we didn't kill the
General! That son of a bitch Ford would rather climb a tree to tell a lie than
stand on the ground and tell the truth."

I motion for Poole to sit down. "It's all right, boy. They're just trying to get your goat, don't you see? They want us to get into a rage and make a mistake. Won't work. Ford thinks that by holding off tellin' our names, he'll be the big hero." I take a long drink of my coffee. "Mistuh Ford will hang for doin' that very thing."

Sarge takes back the paper. "I'll have other uses for this in just a minute." We laugh. "But seriously, whatever you have planned, do it soon. This thing's about to blow wide open. If we do it just right, nobody'll know who the Twentieth Stars are. Excuse me while I visit the latrine."

George snickers. "I guess we can only go up in the world's eyes from here."

Poole pours himself another cup of coffee and yells after Sarge, "Who wrote that article? Not the one about the General—the one about us?"

"Jason Niles, your friend who rats out anybody who held onto the Union during the war."

"He ain't *my* friend." Poole shakes his head and calms himself. "That son of a bitch said some pretty nasty stuff about us. I'm comin' to hate that bastard a little too much."

I'm only half listening, but speak in a calm voice, "I know what you mean, brother."

Poole spits his coffee back into his cup. "Too hot. But that's it."

"That's what?"

"Our name. We need to be called something."

"We got a name. Twentieth Stars."

Poole scratches his head. "But that's it, don't you see? We take the name Niles gave us and use it against him. When we set our trap and Sarge takes them in, he'll call us by this new name, and Ford's gang will be done in."

"So, what is it?"

"Well, that there paper said that we're men of no account, who ride low in the saddle."

"And?" I can see the wheels turning in Poole's head.

"Low Riders."

I give him a look like I'm fixing to slap him. "Hell, I don't know."

"Well, dammit, it is us, ain't it?"

Rainy pours himself another cup of coffee. "I like it."

Poole grins. "Thank you. Better to be called something when you stand for something, I say."

I kick his foot. "You talk too much sometimes, Poole, you know that?"

"Yeah, and I'm about to say more when I write my own article for the *Southern Motive*."

"I guess you'll sign it, The Low Riders?"

"Why not? Hyenas wearin' red shirts ain't shit for a name, either."

"I guess you're right about that."

"So what do you say?"

"About what?" I'm too tired for this and need sleep.

"Me writing an article and puttin' it in the *Southern Motive*. What do you say?"

I'm getting irritated. "I say I don't give a rat's ass. Write the damn article and call us whatever you want because when this is all over, I'm going home. For good."

Poole stretches. "I better go check on the folk's house. Hope I don't find it in ashes."

"Be careful, boy. You almost got caught the other day after we tore up Ford's camp."

He salutes stiffly. "Yassuh, General Lummy, suh."

I throw a rock at him. "Ain't kiddin', neither."

# CHAPTER 40

# CHAP THEIR HIDES AND THEY'LL COME RUNNIN'

## JUNE 12, 1868

*If you want a house burned down,*
*don't spare the coal oil.*

W E HAVEN'T SEEN Poole for several days now, and I'm getting concerned. Hanging out at Big Sand Rock doing nothing doesn't help, either. I've about done all the chess playing I can stand and listening to the same ole stories told by restless men with idle hands. Rainy is a story teller almost by trade. I'm sure his talent for spinning tales has sealed a gun deal on more than one occasion. We sit outside the cave soaking in the warm sunshine.

I ask, "Rainy, I know you grew up in Natchez, but where's home now?"

"Anywhere, everywhere, I guess. I don't have a place I call home right now. If I go somewhere to take a break from selling guns, it's usually Memphis. Lots of pretty girls and good places to eat there. I guess you could say I can live everywhere, but I don't belong anywhere."

I mull that thought over. Rainy takes the opportunity to pass the time with another one of his jokes. I'm glad, if nothing else, to get a chuckle out of the boys and break the boredom of waiting.

"Lummy, you and J.A. will appreciate this. I don't think you've heard this one. It happened in the restaurant in that Vicksburg hotel where you boys stayed during the war. The Prentiss House, I believe it was called?" I nod.

"Anyway, a couple in their early sixties or so came in one evening while I was dining. She wore a plain but neatly starched dress, and he looked to be a farmer wearin' his best Sunday go to meetin' clothes and brogans. It was obvious this was the first time they'd ever been in a fine eating establishment. The man stared at the various plates and silverware, uncomfortable about what do next as his meal was served in courses. With help from the waiter, the old man finally figured out the proper eating etiquette, which eating utensil to use at each turn, and so on. He actually smiled at his accomplishment and seemed to enjoy himself. About halfway through the meal, the old man leans over and passes gas rather loudly. I mean, he rattled the window panes. The other guests are appalled. He just keeps eating like nothing's happened."

Old Bart rolls his eyes. "Oh, my, here it comes. Get ready."

Rainy holds up one finger. "Hold on a second. A couple of minutes later, when all is quiet, except for the sounds of people eating and holding polite conversation, the old man leans over again and passes gas even louder. Fed up with the rude behavior, one guest throws down his napkin and says to the old man, 'How dare you pass gas before my wife!' The old man, embarrassed at his mistake, apologizes. 'I'm sorry, mister, I didn't know it was her turn.'"

The Wood boys roll around on the ground roaring, while the rest of us wipe tears from our eyes as we howl like Tom Ford's hounds.

Rainy holds up his hands. "True story, I swear."

Dan shakes his head. "White boys, ummph. Y'all are somethin' else."

"Amen to that, brother." Old Bart snickers.

We finally settle down, when suddenly Rainy stops to cup an ear with his hand. There's a faint rustling down in the deepest part of the hollow in front of us. A deer maybe?

Elihu and I grab our Henrys and get behind a fallen tree with a broad view of the hollow. A whistle shrills sharply, and I know it's Poole coming up. Sarge is with him.

Poole hops off his horse all smiles, and Sarge chuckles. "Your boy Poole here did the deed that'll push ol' Tom Ford right over the edge."

"What'd you do now, boy?"

"What I should've done already, boy—but I believe it came at just the right time."

Sarge takes the cup of coffee Old Bart offers. "Talk about stirrin' up a yellowjacket's nest. Whew, he's done it now."

Elihu leans his Henry repeater against a tree. "Well, spit it out, boy. What'd you do?"

"I took a can of blue paint to the newspaper office and wrote some choice things about our adversary, ol' Tom Ford."

Sarge shakes his head. "Words a good man wouldn't repeat in public, I do say."

Poole snaps back, "I ain't ashamed of what I did."

Sarge backs up, holding his hands up like he's surrendering. "Just sayin'."

"Well, you're right, I wouldn't want my momma to know what I wrote."

"That bad?" I ask.

He grins. "Somebody had to throw coal oil on the smolderin' embers, those words were so hot."

Elihu squats, leaning his back against the rock wall. "Go on then, tell it."

"I won't use the exact words I wrote on that big picture window at the office of the *Southern Motive*. I'll just give you the short of it."

In as few words as possible, Poole wrote about Tom Ford and his Hyenas bedding Negro women, murdering Chloe's momma, hanging Seth and burning down his cabin, killing Mistuh Allrice and Momma Sophie, and General Whitley.

Elihu claps his hands. "Chap their hides, and they'll come runnin'. Watch what I say."

Sarge cuts in. "Exactly, but the thing that'll send the Hyenas our way in a hurry is what Poole wrote about Ford's mating his with black and tan hound dog. Nasty, but effective all the same."

Rainy scratches his head. "Dang, that's a story I'll be proud to tell."

I hand Poole a cup of coffee. "And I guess you had to sign your work?"

"Damn straight, I did. *Compliments of the Low Riders.*"

CHAPTER 41

# SETTING
# THE SNARE

## JUST BEFORE DAWN, JUNE 21, 1868

*To catch a fox, you have to use his own scent to do it.*

IT'S AN HOUR before sunrise, and mosquitoes buzz in our ears. It'll be a hot one today. In more ways than one. I sip my coffee, but I don't want to eat. The ham biscuits Old Bart cooked up smell good, but nervousness makes my stomach queasy. I step out to the edge of the two hundred yard drop off into the hollow below. I wish I could just keep walking and disappear. Won't happen. Can't happen. St. Michael already told me if I lead, he will follow. I have no choice. At least we'll have the army of the Lord behind us. And a few blue painted Picts and gray and blue soldiers in the unseen, too.

The day has come, and the plan is in motion. It's taken a few days, but the trap to catch Captain Tom Ford is set exactly how Dan and I caught raccoons in a pit in McCurtain Creek Swamp. Captain Tom Ford thinks he has the low down on the Low Riders. But he's wrong. Poole wrote his newspaper article, a letter to the editor, better said, and had Josiah slip it under the door of the *Southern Motive* office in Greensborough. Captain Tom Ford appears to have taken the bait. Sneaky, but I like his idea.

I throw the remaining cold coffee in my cup into the smoldering fire and gather the men to discuss final preparations for this day of reckoning. Josiah spread the word that an educated Negro has been sent down by Washington to encourage parents to get their children in school and strengthen their church communities in anticipation of Congress working to get Negroes the right to vote someday. We set the time so Captain Tom Ford will come for him at our farm this early Sunday morning before good folks get their breakfasts cooked and head to church. We figure Ford won't leave any witnesses this time, so Elihu and Poole went to Sheriff Platner's place and took Ma and the girls to Mary Wood's cabin at Aaron Wood's Spring. They'll be safe there.

Josiah makes sure the postmaster in Bankston, the one who'd hidden Seth's school books, hears every word about the educated Negro from up north. He "accidentally" let it slip that he's staying at our farm and will make a speech at Mt. Pisgah Baptist Church today during services. He also casually mentioned that Mr. H.P. Dotson, who ran the Unionist Society back during the war, would pick him up at our place on his way to the church. Josiah said the two red shirt Hyenas couldn't help but show their excitement for having information Captain Tom Ford would delight in knowing.

"They laughed, and one of them said, 'We'll send 'em all straight to Jesus, and on a Sunday morning to boot. At least they won't have to go to church and hear that niggah lovin' Pastor Dobbs rail on for an hour.'" So, we wait for Poole and Elihu to return.

We load our Henry repeaters and check our pistols. Dan smiles at me as he steadily strokes his long knife blade on a whetstone to make it razor sharp. I hear a familiar whistle, and two horses enter our camp. Elihu and Poole hop off their mounts and help themselves to coffee and ham biscuits. Poole pulls a newspaper from inside his shirt.

"They printed it. Right on the front page of the *Southern Motive.* I guess Jason Niles just couldn't stand it." This is an important moment for Poole.

I push his shoulder. "Well, go on and read it before you explode like the thunder barrels Jasper and James rolled down on the Yankees at Vicksburg."

Pride oozes from Poole as he reads the article aloud.

*Most Respectively To All Concerned,*

*Good and honest men of Choctaw County learned early that lies spread by the Devil himself will only lead a man to the lake of fire. Captain Tom Ford and his band of red-shirted Hyenas operate from values that can only stem from a failure to heed their Heavenly Father's instruction. His reign of destruction, rape, and thievery will soon come to an end because so-called "men of no account who ride low in the saddle" will bring about his demise along with his mongrel gang. May the Lord come quickly to finish him and restore what faithful and loyal men and women believe life should be in these United States of America.*

*Unafraid, The Low Riders*

Poole stuffs the newspaper back in his shirt.

Old Bart rubs a little oil on his Henry repeater. "That ought'a stir up a hornet's nest, all right."

Rainy laughs, polishing his short sword. "Well, at least they got the name right, if nothin' else."

Poole proudly squawks like a jaybird, "Damn straight. We're the Low Riders, and it'll be the Low Riders who take down Ford and the damned red shirt Hyenas."

I turn away, knowing Poole is just trying to keep our spirits up and minds off the fact that there's a good chance some of us will be dead this time tomorrow.

We plan to leave an hour before dawn to get set, before Ford and his men get close to the farm. We can make no mistakes. Mistakes bring death. I think on that for a minute. I pour my last cup of coffee and write Martha a letter. I haven't written her since I left, but she deserves to at least have a last word from me, should I fall today.

*Big Sand Rock, near Aaron Wood's Spring*
*June 21, 1868*

*Dearest Martha, light of my heart and keeper of my soul. Today we face the enemy, and by God's hand and mercy we will prevail over Captain Tom Ford and his demon gang. You must believe that I will return to Vicksburg and bring you and the children back to a safe and secure*

*Choctaw County, where we will live in peace in the shade of God's loving hand. Martha, I love you and will soon hold you in my arms. I look to the day when we have our first child. You must know that I will take special care not get hurt in the battle today. I will come for you soon, my loving wife. I know you pray for me every day. Hug and kiss the children, and give Annie and Beau my many thanks and love for caring for you and the children in this difficult time. Should I fall today, my dear Martha, please know that I will see you soon on the other side.*

*Your loving and affectionate husband always,*
*Columbus Tullos*

I give the letter to J.A., who for some reason I believe won't die in the coming battle.

# CHAPTER 42

# RIDERS TO THE EAST!

## DAYBREAK, JUNE 21, 1868

*The Devil walks the same paths the Lord takes,*
*sometimes a step ahead of Him.*

WE WAIT FOR the trap to spring and snap shut. Old Bart is in place by the barn on our farm. The farm is the only logical place Ford will suspect me hiding or returning to get food and supplies. He'd love to catch me, Mr. H.P. Dotson, and the "highly educated niggah," as he'd call Old Bart, and kill us all together. I wait and watch for Dotson's wagon to peel off Null Road and onto the path that leads to our dogtrot home. There's no dust just yet. I'm antsy with Bart out in the open by himself.

He's working on a piece of furniture like he's always belonged there. It won't be long before Captain Tom Ford shows his demon face. Even with twelve Henry lever action rifles in the hands of good trained men, I still need to calm my spirit. Bart finishes the piece of furniture, holds it up to the house like he's showing it to Ma inside, then goes to chopping kindling. I suspect one or two of Ford's men are lurking about, checking for an ambush. We're hidden away like rabbits in a briar patch.

I sit on top of Tullos cemetery hill with my back to my Pa's grave marker. I wonder what he'd say about all of this. I pray, "Help us Pa," and I recite the 23rd Psalm. I want to feel the cool grass of green pastures and the peace of still waters in my soul for just a moment. Not to be had.

Sarge eases his horse over without a sound. "This is a place of decision for you, ain't it?"

"Yeah, fancy meetin' you here again."

"That's what I'm sayin'. Last time I was here, I thought you'd shoot my head off when I came to get you to enlist in the First Mississippi Mounted Rifles. Funny thing, H.P.'s in on this little shenanigan, just like last time."

I stare at the small dust cloud billowing behind a wagon that's turning onto our farm road. "There's Mistuh Dotson. This won't be like last time, Sarge. This'll be the last time."

Poole whispers loudly, "Riders to the east!"

Elihu asks, "How many?"

Poole shivers, from fear or excitement, probably both. But that's a good thing. "Twelve to fifteen, best I can count."

Sergeant McGugarty whispers an order he gave many times. "Boots and saddles, men."

Easing into their saddles, they move into position, careful not to draw any attention. The summer time brush hides us like a herd of deer traveling from bed to feeding.

I get up from my pine straw seat and take a last look at the graves of the people I hold dear, who wait just across the thin veil in the unseen. "It might be I'll be joining you all today."

I walk to my horse. I pause. I need no Union sergeant—or even H.P. Dotson of the Union Secret Society—to prod me this time. I don't need Ma to tell me that I could be killed. She and the family will be if I don't. My anger rears its ugly head like it did at Vicksburg, with Dawg Smith, and Lester.

No, this time I lead the fight, and it's easy to find. When you seek out the Devil, you have to think like him. It's not hard to do. I've done it before.

Sarge whispers, "Yes you have, son."

We watch H.P. turn his wagon sideways to block the dogtrot porch like we showed him, and he climbs down to greet Old Bart. They put on a show like two actors in a play. I'm nervous.

A second dust cloud stops short at the head of the road leading to our farm. Two men step out of the woods. They must be the spies who hopefully haven't seen us but will lead Captain Tom Ford's gang of demons into our snare. I recite the Psalm again.

I'll just have to wait a little longer for the table to be set before me in the presence of my enemies. Right now, I have to walk through the valley of the shadow of death, one more time. I must let the shepherd lead me in the paths of righteousness—for his name's sake, and not for my own.

Without thinking, I bark, "I thought only the Son of Man would be comin' from the east."

Rainy tugs the reins of his horse our way, rifle in hand. "Well, he must not be far behind, because those men ride like the Devil himself. Let's go."

J.A. shields his eyes from the sun. "Looks to be fifteen men, for sure."

About the time we start to our assigned positions, a man in a blue jacket rides up in a fury. We all instinctively turn our Henrys on the rider.

Poole yells in a loud whisper, "Hold it boys, he's with me."

"Private Lummy Tullos," the rider asks, "How the hell are you?"

"Better'n buttered biscuits slathered with blackberry jam, Will Pollan. Wasn't expectin' you."

He reaches to shake my hand, then Sarge's.

Poole reins over with his hand out. "Good to see you, old friend, and thanks for coming. Men, this here's Captain William Pollan, formerly of Company A, First Mississippi Mounted Rifles, but now serving as captain of the Choctaw County militia, loyal to the true United States of America, and protector of the freedom of all men. He's not only our witness to what's about to transpire, but he'll also take Captain Tom Ford and his gang in for trial so we don't have to."

Poole winks at me. "Sergeant McGugarty and I worked this part of the plan out a week ago."

Pollan laughs. "We're here to prove to Governor Sharkey that Choctaw County is serious about its loyalty to the Union, looking for the day when Mississippi is readmitted to the Union for good."

Rainy nods at Pollan and tugs on my jacket. "Excuse me, General Tullos, they're gettin' pretty close."

I backhand Rainy lightly on the chest. "Let's go get into some mischief."

Except for Captain Pollan and his twenty riders, who will remain hidden in the Tullos cemetery, the men pair off, moving stealthily through pine thickets to assigned positions surrounding the house. Sergeant McGugarty and Poole are with me, we three who rode together on Grierson's Winter Raid and know each other's every thought and move in times of battle. We'll lead the attack, and Pollan will follow after Sarge arrests the gang. Those who are still alive.

Hoof beats of galloping mounts thunder as the dust from Captain Tom Ford's gang billows into the air like a summer storm roaring toward the dogtrot cabin.

I still don't want to do this, but it has to be done. I close my eyes, and Martha's face comes to me as clear as if she was standing right in front of me. The last words she gave me before I rode away from Vicksburg give me the courage I need. "Never say it's too hard if it's what you've chosen. If it's right, keep choosing it."

I choose it now.

# CHAPTER 43

# THE FINAL
# BATTLE

## 8 A.M., JUNE 21, 1868

*And at that time shall Michael stand up, the great prince which standeth for the children of thy people: and there shall be a time of trouble....*

FORD'S MEN LOOK like they just came off an all-night drunk at Bucksnort as they send the chickens running in our front yard.

Poole whispers, "Talk about no accounts ridin' low in the saddle. Bet they smell worse than the south end of a north-bound mule."

Sarge warns, "Don't let the lack of personal hygiene lead you to believe they can't fight. They don't know how to do anything else. Stayin' alive, drinkin' whiskey, and deflowerin' women is all they care about."

"I need it quiet," I snap.

The twelve of us slip down the hill shielded by pine thickets to surround the cabin, leaving no room for escape except the road Ford came in on. That's where Captain Pollan will station his riders when and if the shooting starts. I have no doubt it will. Ford won't give up without a fight. We're in position.

Ford yells as the red shirt Hyenas train their weapons on our cabin. "In the house! Come out! Come peaceably, and no harm will come to you."

That's the second lie Ford will tell today. The first was when he told his men they'd win the day when they left their camp.

H.P. cracks open the door. "What's your business here, Ford? You up to no good like always?"

Ford's men laugh, and he looks around like a wolf with a rabbit already in his mouth. "Not if you and that high-minded educated niggah come out with your hands where I can see 'em."

H.P. is no fool. "Now why would we want to do that, Captain? You got a warrant?"

Ford raises his pistol, aiming it at H.P. "I sure do, and it spits lead!" Nobody moves. Ford yells again, "Where's Tullos?"

H.P. lies, "In the bed, sick with a fever. I guess you want him outside, too?"

Ford grins, thinking he has the three men he came for hogtied, and me worthless in a fight. "An old uppity niggah, a Yankee lovin' turncoat, and a sick ass niggah lovin' deserter, all caught in the same trap together. Now don't that make for a good hunt this mornin', boys?" His men laugh. "Wish I had more time. I'd turn you bastards loose on foot and then track you with my hounds like the coons you are." Ford looks around at his men. "Now dang it, why didn't I think of that?"

They all laugh louder.

I'm getting antsy. "I've had about enough of this," I whisper.

Sarge leans over. "Ford ain't broke no laws yet. I need him to do more than make threats."

Suddenly H.P. is pushed to the side. Old Bart walks out onto the porch, planting his feet firmly like a man entering a fisticuff contest.

"You rotten, sorry, no account, weak-ass white boy. Ain't nobody here afraid except you. The world has changed, and it's fixin' to leave you behind."

Tom Ford shivers with anger being talked to like that by a Negro. He cocks his pistol and aims it at Bart's chest. Ford looks around at his men, who wait for him to do something.

Old Bart knows his part, but I fear for his life. "You sucked your bitch dawg momma's teat too long and figure somebody owes you somethin'. No, I bet you probably hung onto the teat of a black mammie, and you're ashamed that a niggah helped bring you into this world. They should've slapped you sideways and thrown you to the dogs like a ham bone."

Ford is shaking with anger, but Bart pours it on. He steps to the edge of the porch and taunts the taunter.

I start to charge, but Sarge holds me back. "Hold still just a minute. I know what he's fixin' to do, and when he does it, we'll go after 'em like robins pluckin' worms out the soft dirt after a rain. I just need to hear the words."

Ford starts to speak, but Old Bart's voice booms like thunder. "I know what you've done, sister boy. I know you killed Chloe's momma, that good boy Seth, and them fine folks, Mistuh Allrice and Missus Sophie. Hell, I heard it took all of you damn Hyenas to take James Tullos down in a fight. Worthless sacks of dawg shit! Ain't much to you mule-faced boys, is it? One Tullos is worth ten of you sorry sons of bitches."

That did it.

"Yeah, I did it, damn you, and I loved every minute of it! Just like what I'm gonna do to you, you old gray-haired, slave-ass bastard!"

Old Bart smiles like the Devil himself. "We're about to see, aren't we?"

Sarge whispers, "Got him! That's a confession if I ever heard one."

Ford walks his horse closer to the porch. "So go ahead, have your fun. Ain't gonna make a hill of beans no how, 'cause I'm gonna send you to the gates of hell with this here pistol."

"Oh, hell no, you ain't! I'll be watchin' you beg for a drop of water from Abraham's bosom."

I almost laugh out loud listening to Old Bart give Ford hell.

"Here's what's gonna happen. You're gonna lay down those guns, go home, and start gatherin' up little black children for school every day so they can learn to read and write. And when they do, you'll be the first in line to support Congress approving an amendment that gives us niggahs the right to vote."

Bart's getting louder, and Ford is at his wits end. I'm surprised he hasn't pulled the trigger already.

I look at Sarge, wanting to rescue Bart, but he puts his arm across my chest. "He knows what he's doin'."

In the voice of a preacher pleading for lost souls to return to the fold, Bart cries out, "But first, you're gonna get on your knees and beg the Lord to forgive your devilment. Then you'll make plans on how you're gonna pay back all those you've hurt, startin' right here on the Tullos farm."

I've never heard Old Bart speak this way. Its years of being beaten down and watching his people get degraded coming out. I want him to have his say, but I also see fifteen men ready to shoot him down like a dog. Ford can barely restrain himself.

"Niggah, you best shut the hell up, or I'll—"

Old Bart seals the deal when he interrupts in a quiet but firm voice, "I know an old black mammie if you need one, while you're prayin'. If that don't suit you, you can always go back to your black and tan bitch dog."

Tom Ford can restrain himself no longer. "That's all, niggah! Time for you to meet Jesus."

Old Bart dives for cover. "I've already met him, and he's on my side!"

Ford fires, and the bullet looks to hit Old Bart. Shots ring out all around the house.

Sarge spurs his horse and screams, "Take 'em!"

A shotgun blasts the rider closest to the house right out of his saddle. He flops to the ground lifeless like one of little Margaret's corn silk dolls. I know that sound. It's Ben's old ten gauge shotgun, and H.P. knows how to use it.

Sarge, Poole, and I ride in fighting from horseback like we did with the 1st Mississippi Mounted Rifles. Bart drags himself into the dogtrot out of the line of fire with H.P.'s help.

The look on Ford's face when the Low Riders step out of the woods with their Henry repeaters in hand couldn't be bought in any store. It's that way with bullies. Their only power is in what you give them, and Ford just got what little he has taken away.

The Low Riders fire rapidly, spooking the Hyena's horses, and in the confusion Ford's men try to find targets. A Hyena goes after Dan with a knife, but when the old Choctaw brandishes his own, the man drops to his knees and throws up his hands. Ford yells for his men to fight, firing his pistol in all directions.

Poole and I wade into close combat, and Sarge yells, "You're all under arrest by the authority of the United States government!"

Ford's mount is grazed by one of his own men's bullets, nearly throwing him off. His pistol explodes several times as we move in to capture him. Something slaps the side of my head but not enough to stop me. Poole doubles over as he rams his horse into Ford's, knocking him off his mount.

Sarge quickly dismounts and starts scrapping with Ford. He takes the stand of a boxer and proceeds to wear Ford out like he's beating dust out of an old quilt. Ford can't even get a lick in as his head snaps right to left with each blow. Finally, Sarge delivers an uppercut that smacks the outlaw squarely under the jaw and lifts him a foot off the ground. Ford folds like a damp dishcloth and sits down hard in the ground. Gunfire slackens, as do the shouts of men fighting.

Sarge sticks his pistol barrel into Ford's mouth. "Say somethin'! *Please* say somethin' smart, so I can stretch your dead ass across a saddle and be done with you."

Ford drops his empty pistol.

"Tell 'em it's over."

Ford curses under his breath, knowing he's beaten.

Sarge screams in his ear, "I said, tell 'em it's over, dammit!"

"All right! Give it up, boys. Lay down your weapons."

The fighting ceases, and Ford is put in chains by Captain Pollan's men. I rub my aching head and pull back a little blood, but not enough to worry with.

Rainy smiles. "And I thought I made it through without fighting in the War Between the States."

I rub my head again and feel a little faint. "I'm glad you were here, all of you. I'm alive because of you men. Thank you." My head starts pounding like someone took a ball peen hammer to it. Then it goes dark.

A familiar voice tells me to get up, that my time isn't done yet. It's Pa.

I sit up quickly. "Where's Bart?"

James holds me down. "Lummy, you've been shot. Lay still for a minute. I'll check on Bart."

"I can't, he took a bullet." James helps me to the dogtrot where Bart lies with blood everywhere.

H.P. has tears in his eyes. "Bravest man I ever saw."

I fall to my knees with a *thud* from the dizziness, but more so from the pain I see in my grandfather's eyes. "Bart? You're gonna be okay."

"I'm all right, son. Don't worry your head over me now. You got your own wound to think about." He coughs, and blood bubbles out of the wound in his chest. H.P. shakes his head. Bart is dying.

I cry. "I want more time with you, old man. Why did you have to be so damn brave?"

Rainy steps up on the porch. "He was like Jesus givin' himself up for us." Rainy's never talked about God before, but he's speaking truth today.

I try to hold back the tears. "You saved us all today, old man. And that bastard Ford will get his due. I just wish you could stay around and get your reward, grandfather."

"It's a new world, my son, and you made it so. Don't cry for me, my reward's comin' for me right now." He stares into space for a moment but returns. "Oh, Lummy, you just ain't gonna believe how beautiful it is." Bart listens for a moment. "It's Susannah, my son. She says she's proud of you."

With those words, Old Bart closes his eyes for the last time.

I pass out.

# CHAPTER 44

# IN THE PRESENCE
# OF MY ENEMIES

## JUNE 26, 1868

*Thou preparest a table before me and mine, in the presence of mine enemies,*
*but with a few empty chairs.*

IWAKE TO Ma wiping my fevered forehead with a cool damp cloth.

"Lummy, there's something you need to know."

I cringe. "Poole?"

Ma nods and whimpers. "He was shot, too. The bullet nicked an artery in is thigh that won't stop bleeding. The Doc's done all he knows to do."

I turn my head to cry, but snap back, "What about his folks?"

"The folks hurried back up from Jackson. They took him home and have been watchin' over him day and night. We're all prayin' he'll heal up."

"I need to go see him."

"Lummy, you're not—"

I bark, "I'm goin'. That's final."

"Yes, dear. Can I send Dan with you?"

"I'm sorry, Ma, I just—"

"No need, son, I know how dear that man is to you."

"Will you help me up, please? I need to go see Bart."

I hobble off to find Old Bart laid out on the back porch, covered with ice. I need to see him off and tell him I look forward to seeing him again. I wail at the loss of my black grandfather. I can feel Ma and the others watching. I don't care. Losing this man takes a huge chunk of my spirit away. I calm down.

Ma whispers to everyone, "He's all right now. Y'all give him some room."

I quiet my spirit and still my soul. I open my eyes to see green hills surrounded by tall trees and small mountains. I hear singing. It's Susannah, Seth, Momma Sophie, and Mr. Allrice sitting under a great shade oak. On a far hill, Pa, Ben, Amariah and Amanda, George and Saleta, and Mr. Gilmore and Grandpa Temple stroll in the warm sunshine. Granny Thankful offers her palm that's filled with all the colors of the rainbow. I feel for the agate she gave me in Vicksburg in my pocket and clench it tight. Then, she points to something behind me.

Bart whispers through the thin veil like the sound of water trickling over smooth stones in an easy flowing creek, "It's all right, Lummy. Susannah and everybody is here with me. I am where I'm supposed to be, my son." A door slams, and I'm awakened from my vision. My soul finds peace.

We bury Old Bart in our cemetery up on the hill above the farm in the shade of tall pines. Pastor Dobbs came and gave a fine service. I couldn't do it. Ma and J.A. plant flowers around his grave marked only with a flat sandstone rock. I'll carve a head marker out of cypress for him like Pa's soon. I send a letter to his boss in Texas, letting him know of Bart's bravery—and his death.

Ma and the girls doctor me well and keep us all in good food. My head constantly aches and at times my anger flares up at the least little thing. Then in the same moment I feel low, like I want to hide in a corner and not be seen. Strange.

It's been five days since the battle on our farm. Dan and Rainy keep us in fresh meat while J.A. stays busy with chores. I know he's ready to get back home to his family in Winn Parish. George returned to his blacksmith shop to keep an ear open to what's being said about Captain Tom Ford's capture.

My brothers and the Wood boys keep watch in case anyone else tries to make a move on us while they keep the farm going. Sarge assures us that with the snake's head severed, the rest of the Hyenas will fade into the shadows, at least for now. I want to ride patrol with Sarge and Pollan's men, but I can't seem to shake the dizziness out of my head or control my outbursts. I need to go see Poole.

Doctor Lamb from Bankston drives his buggy up just as I sit down in

Pa's rocking chair on the front porch. He's been a friend of the family since James was born.

"How do, Doc?"

"That's my question to you, son."

"I'm doin' fine, but how's Poole?"

He drops his head. My tears splatter lightly like a warm summer sprinkle shower on my shirt.

"That's why I came to see you. Let's get in the buggy. Poole's dying. The bleeding won't stop. If I operate, well, it'll do no good. He doesn't have long."

Elihu points. "There's some good homegrown shine in the house, if you need a taste, Doc."

"Believe I'll take a swig to clear the throat and bolster my courage, thanks."

Ma brings two cups, one for Doc, and the other for me. "Doc, drive easy, Lummy's head ain't right just yet."

"Yes, ma'am, I will. Thank you for the drink. I needed it. Before I go, Mary, how's Martha's little one coming along?"

"Oh, she'll be a good'n when she decides to come into the world."

Doc grins, "A girl, you say?"

"You know I have a way of knowin' such things. Neither of us have said anything, you know, so folks don't get their hearts set on what the baby will be."

"I see."

Ma points her finger at Doc. "You know I do, you old coot. I ain't never guessed wrong on callin' out babies before they're born."

Doc laughs. "I know, Mary, you should've been a doctor."

"What do you think I've been doin' for this bunch all these years?"

WE PARK THE buggy in Poole's front yard. Doc squeezes my arm. "Wait here for a bit until I see how things are."

I nod and pray.

Doc is back out to see me in less than five minutes, shaking his head.

"Ain't no good way to say this, son. He's dying as we speak." I can see the tears well up in this old man's eyes.

"I was afraid of that."

"I told him you're here. He wants to see you."

"How long, Doc?"

Doc Lamb shifts from one foot to the other. "Today." Doc sees my pain and tries to change the subject. "Let me look at your head before you go in. You might have jostled my stitches on the road here." Doc peels back the bandage.

"Ain't it interesting that I made it all the way through Vicksburg fightin' Yankees, killin' outlaws like Dawg Smith and Lester, survived the raid on Bankston, only to get shot by that rascal Captain Tom Ford."

"Well, it's getting better, but she's a beaut. A perfect crease like you took a straight razor and shaved a line from just above your ear down the side of your noggin'. You're lucky he didn't take your head off."

"Or blessed, wouldn't you say?" I chuckle to myself. I guess that old scamp Mistuh Wiley and me got one more thing in common besides lovin' lemon drops now. Watching him die back in Winn Parish makes going in to see Poole harder. I put it off for a moment, asking questions that could be answered later.

"Doc, I got to ask. My head's feelin' better, but how long before the dizziness quits?"

"Should go away in a week or so. Anything else?"

I don't want to tell him, but I need to know. "These past couple of days, one minute I'm happier than a honey bee on a flower feelin' like I'm half lit up with moonshine, but in the next, I'm so low I can't seem to find me nowhere inside myself."

"Hmmm, that bullet could've affected your brain."

"What do you mean?"

"The force of a bullet creasing your head like that can pull your brain over with it as it passes. It usually does no permanent damage, but it could trigger something you already have and make it worse. I've seen that happen to some folks who get cancer. They'll have a real bad fall or something, and next thing you know, cancer shows up. Just gets triggered, I guess."

He stops looking at my head and notices my questioning eyes. "Oh now, I'm not saying you got the cancer. But I do suspect the bullet messed up your thinking, you know, how your brain works. Time will only tell. That's all I can say right now, I'm sorry. Just keep the wound clean and take it easy for a while."

"I will, Doc, thanks. I'd like to keep this between us, if you don't mind."

He nods and goes back into the cabin to check on Poole again. Doc pokes his head back out the door. "You better get in here."

I walk to the bed I slept on many nights staying over with Poole when we were growing up. Poole's Ma cries as his Pa wipes sweat from his son's clammy forehead.

Doc gives Poole another spoonful of medicine to ease his pain. "Any minute now." He backs away.

I kneel down beside the man who's been my friend since before I can remember. I cup my palm on his cheek and talk of old times, the fun we had as kids, fishing and hunting, chasing pretty girls, and getting into trouble together. He can barely muster a grin, but smiles just the same.

"We did the right thing, didn't we, Lummy?"

I nod, tears dripping on his chest. "We did, brother, and you're the hero."

At that moment, Sarge walks in, having delivered Ford and his gang to the county jail, where they're guarded by Captain Pollan's militia.

Sarge kneels down beside Poole. "You're a very brave man, Thomas Poole. I never fought with any better." He pulls a small case from his blue jacket pocket and opens it.

"In recognition for bravery under fire and in defense of your fellow soldiers in the heat of combat, I duly award this medal to Private Thomas Poole, defender of the true United States of America and servant of the twentieth state, Mississippi." He pins the medal to Poole's nightshirt.

Tears trickle from the corners of Poole's eyes. "You see, Lummy? I wasn't afraid, after all"

"No. No, you weren't, and you have no reason to be afraid now, my good friend."

"I'll tell Susannah hello for you."

"You tell her I'll be along soon enough."

Poole closes his eyes and breathes his last.

I cry like a newborn baby.

I walk outside to find the Low Riders gathered in the yard.

Rainy, J.A., Dan Creekwater, John and Henry Wood, my brothers, and I lay Poole's body into his folk's wagon. They want to bury him in the Greensborough Cemetery next to his little sister, Viola, who died as an infant. Sarge will escort Poole's parents with a couple of his men and dig the grave. They prepare to leave, but not before we have a brief service. I want to say a few things. The words come hard.

"Poole was the best childhood friend any boy would be proud to have." I look around at the forest and into the hills. "We roamed this land like good Choctaws, thanking Creator for such a fine place to become men. And when we did become men, Poole came to my side when I needed a good man to help me do the right thing. He and Bart both offered the greatest sacrifice so we could have better lives. Poole has that better life now. I will never forget you my friend, Thomas Poole, friend of friends. Amen."

I watch the road long after the wagon has disappeared. As the dust cloud hovers, a young boy skips my way, switch cane fishing pole in hand, with a big grin on his face. I wave. He waves back. And then Poole fades away as the last bit of dust settles on the road.

Jasper puts his arm around me. "Poole will always be here, tryin' to steal you away for some boyish adventure."

"Yeah, and I have one more adventure planned before I go get Martha and the kids."

# CHAPTER 45

# WHEN A HANGING NEEDS TO BE PUBLIC

## NOON, JULY 4, 1868

*Let judgment run down as waters,*
*and righteousness as a mighty stream.*

I SIT BY Poole's grave in the Greensborough Cemetery, not far from where General Whitley lies buried under a tall obelisk tombstone with a likeness of his face carved into it. A Confederate flag is draped over it today. More flags, Union and Rebel, are scattered around the cemetery.

Captain William Pollan puts his hand on my shoulder and whispers, "Lummy, it's time."

Captain Tom Ford was captured, delivered to the county jail, and with a quick trial, was judged guilty without protest from anyone. The sentence is harsh, but Ford's deeds demand retribution. Hanging Captain Tom Ford won't balance the reckoning needed in this county, but it's a start.

Pollan leads me to a spot out of the line of sight. He wants no trouble, and there's been talk that Ford has an escape plan. "Sergeant McGugarty gave me the details of Ford's escape from Captain Beckwith's men after the Bankston raid. We're taking no chances." Fifty troops and militia surround the gallows.

Sarge walks Captain Tom Ford up the steps where a Union flag tops the wooden structure. Ford is chained hand to foot. Sarge holds it like a lease on a hound dog. How fitting. I guess if Ford tries to escapes, he'll have to take Sarge with him. That won't happen, not today.

A large crowd fills the street that still shows reminders of when Poole and I helped fire the town. Sarge stationed his men at strategic points near the gallows with Captain Pollan's men scattered throughout the crowd.

I look around at our worn crew. They're weary but glad to put this deed to rest. J.A. brought two extra horses, saddled and ready to ride, in honor of the two men we lost, Old Bart and Poole. Boyhood memories of Poole flood my mind. The warmth of good moments wraps around my soul as I remember Old Bart's kind and wise spirit. Those two will be sorely missed.

Dan Creekwater lays his hand on my shoulder as my horse shifts to move closer to his. "They'll walk these hills and hollows from now on." I nod. "They'll always be with you."

"I do believe that. It's just a loss I hadn't counted on. I'm havin' a hard time acceptin' it."

"Time, my son. She's the great healer of the soul. Find ways to honor their memory in the little things you do every day and look for them in your dreams. Hear Poole the talker in the happy squawk of a blue jay and Old Bart in the wise hoot of an old owl. They will come to you, and you must listen, for they walked the path with you. Watch for the visit of the redbird. He will bring you their words, and you may send a message to them. It is the redbird's purpose given by Creator." Granny Thankful used to speak of such things.

A wagon full of spectators passes by, laughing and talking. One shouts above the rest, "Hot damn, we better hurry! They got his hands shackled, and that Yankee sergeant is holdin' on tight. Ole Captain Tom Ford's escaped the bluecoats once before. But they got him hawg-tied this time, for sure. Boy, oh boy! Greensborough ain't seen nothin' like this in years, if ever. Hand me another one of them chicken legs, Ma." They rumble past like children on their way to the county fair.

J.A. looks at me with sad eyes. "What's this world comin' to when good folks bring their wives and children to see a man executed like they was goin' to a church social or somethin'?"

"I don't know. I just don't know."

Rainy spits a long stream of tobacco juice that lands on a rock in front of our horses. "I know you boys have to live here now that this is done. But the good folks will come to know, already have, that a man like Captain Tom Ford is just a bad reminder of a wicked past. Killin' your own kind to set yourself up in this world for profit and worthless ideals, heck, a hangin' is what it leads to. Let the kids see, I say, and then let their folks calm the little ones down when the nightmares come."

I squint to see Ford's eyes as they turn him around to face the crowd. He has the look of a defiant demon—eyes flashing red, eyebrows furrowed, jaw protruding forward, teeth gritted, and a stiffness of body not unlike what he'll soon experience once they take him down from the gallows. I really don't want to watch, but I must see this through.

J.A. whispers, "If I didn't know better, I'd say that man has horns on his head."

I push his shoulder, trying to jest. "If he don't have them now, he will soon." I find no humor in my own joke.

An old man in a Confederate officers jacket, riding a very expensive horse, eases up beside me. I tip my hat.

"Colonel Drane, suh, I do believe?"

He salutes. "Yes, it is. Archibald Tullos's boy, Lummy, right?" I nod. "Thought I recognized you from when you men built that house for me."

"Hope it's holding up all right. You know I was just barely old enough to tote boards and tools, carry water and such, to the men doin' the heavy work."

"It's in good shape, but don't sell yourself short, Lummy Tullos. You were there, and it's been a good house all these years. And you've been here, son, doing what you think is right, protecting your family and the rest of this county. While I'll be a Lost Cause fool 'til I die, I do not agree with the likes of Captain Tom Ford."

"I appreciate you sayin' that, Colonel, suh."

"Still bein' the good soldier. That's good, son. I appreciate the lesson your daddy taught me when I challenged him to billiards and lost that bet years ago. Don't know if he ever told you that story. I never forgot it."

"He did and always had the highest respect for you. That story kept me from ever wantin' to lose my money gamblin'."

"Here, son, I want you to have this." He presses a fifty dollar gold piece into my hand before I know what it is. "Been carryin' it around hopin' I'd run into one of you Tullos boys."

"I can't take this, Colonel. It ain't right."

"What's right, son, is that I wouldn't be where I am, have done what I've done, or enjoy the good life I have with my wife and family, had it not been for the lesson your daddy taught me. Call me payin' off an old gamblin' debt with interest. I've made a lot more money than this because I listened to Archibald Tullos that day."

"Thank you, sir. I'll tell Ma and my brothers what you said today."

"Good enough. Now, let's watch Captain Tom Ford get his due."

The crowd grows quiet, and Sergeant McGugarty reads off the charges and sentence. "Do you have any last words, Tom Ford?"

He looks up at the Union flag and spits. "Hell, no! Not for any of you sons of bitches!"

Mothers cover their children's ears, men either laugh or hurl insults, and young boys climb higher to make sure they can see better and hear every word. Soldiers move about in the crowd to keep the peace. Pastor Dobbs starts toward him for a last prayer, but Ford stomps his feet.

"Don't want no niggah lovin' pastor prayin' over me. I'm meetin' my Maker with a clean conscience."

Pastor Dobbs prays anyway. "Lord, forgive this man, for he does know what he did, but not what he's saying now."

Ford screams, "Shut up, preacher! Don't worry, I'll be back. I'll haunt every last one of you bastards. My work ain't never gonna be done. There's people you don't know about who'll come for you. And when they do, I'll be right there with 'em, and my blood hounds will be with me. So look for me in the shadows, in your nightmares, under your warm and comfortable beds, and in your mirrors. I'll catch every last one of you. And especially you, Lummy Tullos. For burnin' Bankston and Greensborough, and killin' Lester. That's all right, everybody knows now. We killed two of yours in the fight, and my boys will get all you Yankee lovin' heathens. And when it's all done, my hounds will feast on your carcasses until they're fat and happy. Ha, ha, ha!"

I hold tight the little pouch with the small American flag Grandpa Temple once had.

The hangman tries to put a hood over Ford's head, but he jerks away. "Oh, hell no, I want you all to see my eyes when I die. Remember 'em, because they'll always be watchin' you."

Sergeant McGugarty nods, and the hangman jerks the lever. Captain Tom Ford's body drops like a rock, and his neck snaps like a chicken bone. His feet don't even kick.

Captain Tom Ford is dead.

And I kept my promise not to kill another man.

## CHAPTER 46

# IT'S DONE...
# AT LEAST FOR NOW

### LATE EVENING, JULY 4, 1868

*The sun always shine brightest after the darkest storm.*

J.A. AND I sit on the front porch, watching two deer amble across the road leading to our farm. We sip a tin cup of Elihu's muscadine wine as the sun fades behind Tullos Cemetery Hill.

"I can see why you protect this place, Lummy, and never want to leave. Beautiful farm and good people. It's a little bit of heaven in the middle of a whole lot of hell. I do hope things settle down now."

"Me, too, brother."

We sit still with neither of us wanting to bring it up, so I do.

"When you leavin'?"

"I figure in the morning."

"I know you're ready to get back to Winn Parish and that pretty wife. Bet that boy of yours watches day and night for your return. What's he, eight, nine now?"

"Just turned ten, growin' like a weed, and eatin' everything in sight. I swear that boy can't ever get enough vittles."

"Sounds just like us when we were boys."

In my mind, I can see Poole sitting at Ma's table eating like there's no tomorrow right next to me when we were only ten.

J.A. sits up in his seat to watch the deer pass out of sight. "Guess I'll be followin' them come dawn. I want to get an early start to Vicksburg."

"I'll ride to the county line with you."

"I'd like that." We both know with demands of family and farm, this may be our last visit. I savor every moment. Elihu brings another jug of wine. We drink into the night.

WITH HEADS ACHY from too much wine, we still make the Old Trace by midmorning, and I turn my horse back toward our farm.

"I ain't got the words, J.A."

"Me neither, Lummy."

A rider appears down the road. It's Sarge.

"Thought I'd ride with you to Jackson, J.A. I need to report what happened here."

I give J.A. a firm hand shake and a shoulder hug. "Watch out for them haints in Chickasaw Bayou, boy. Them dead soldiers are probably still huntin' us for takin' their silver and pistol loads when we slipped away into darkness after the surrender."

J.A. reflects a moment. "That darkness sure brought the brightest light, wouldn't you say?"

"The sun always shines brightest after the storm."

J.A. wanders out of the shadows of the great oaks standing over us into the bright sunshine, turns, and waves. "Be seein' you, Columbus Nathan Tullos."

"Not before I see you, James Aaron Killingsworth."

Sarge waves. "I'll be checkin' in on you, Lummy."

I salute. "I'm countin' on it, Sarge."

My heart aches all the way home.

# CHAPTER 47

# VICKSBURG NEVER NEVER LOOKED SO GOOD

## DAWN, JULY 7, 1868

*A city set upon a hill cannot be hidden.*
*This one never will be.*

LIGHT BREAKS OVER the hill, and Elihu leads two horses to the front porch. Ma hugs me and hands me a sack of food for my journey. Two days rest is long enough. I want to kiss my wife and hug my children. And come back home to stay.

"What's the second horse for?" I ask.

"I'm goin' with you. You, Jasper, and James have all been to Vicksburg. I never have, so I'll go today."

Ma yells, "Take him with you. We got the farm." Jasper and James shrug their shoulders. Ma orders us, "You boys stay out of trouble and get back soon. We'll pull corn when you get back."

Elihu elbows me. "I love it when she plays general with us."

"She sure deserves a medal for puttin' up with us boys."

"The Lord's got a big shiny gold one waitin' on her."

We laugh as we head down the road that leads away from our farm. Vicksburg can't get here soon enough.

Elihu snickers. "Never been to a big city before. Who knows, I might just find me a pretty girl in Vicksburg like you did."

"Hell, boy, she'd have to be blind."

We joke and laugh all the way to the county line. Elihu has been a rock in my life these past few years. For a brother I hardly knew growing up, he's become the good big brother I always wanted Ben to be.

THE FOUR DAY trip to Vicksburg is uneventful, and Elihu marvels, "So, this is the city set upon a hill that can't be hidden." The beautiful architecture of the Warren County Courthouse nearly overwhelms him. "That's bigger and prettier than the capitol building we saw passing through Jackson City."

I tell him my Vicksburg stories as fast as I can. I have one for every street corner, every back alley, and every spot by the river as we travel down Crawford Street to Handerson's Café, where Martha and the kids are waiting for my return.

"That's a big damn river, Lummy."

"Ain't it so."

We pull up in front of Handerson's, and Martha rushes out like the building's on fire. I leap from my seat to catch her just as she makes it to the street. I hug her like there's no tomorrow, and she kisses me without reserve. The younger children grab my legs, hanging on like raccoons on the side of a tree. I try to walk, but they hang on for dear life.

"What are these varmints doin'? Somebody get my scattergun!"

We all laugh.

John A. peeks out from behind his mother's back and steps up to shake my hand. I ain't havin' it. Though eleven now and nearly five feet tall, I pick him up so we can see eye to eye. He carefully touches the bandage on the side of my head.

"Does it hurt, Pop?"

"A little, but not so bad."

"You could've been killed?"

I laugh and pull him close. "Oh, heck no. Don't you know my head's so hard that bullet bounced right off this pine knot like you shootin' watermelon seeds at your brother? I'm fine, son. Don't worry yourself none."

Annie and Beau step out to welcome us back. Annie gawks at Elihu, and in true Fanny fashion, says, "Ooo-*wee!* I didn't know there was an older, more distinguished lookin' Tullos gentleman runnin' around loose." Elihu turns five shades of red.

Martha takes the opportunity. "Why, Mister Elihu Tullos, I do believe you're blushin'."

He tries to get away. "Where do I take these horses? Can't leave 'em in the street."

Beau laughs. "Just around the corner. Take the first alley... aww, come on, I'll show you."

As Elihu walks the horses away, I can't help myself. "You can come in the back door, pretty boy."

Elihu sticks his tongue out at me so that the children can see. They laugh and hurry into the café to get freshly baked cookies.

I never thought of my brother as having good looks, but, hey, he *is* a Tullos. That counts for something. Martha smiles, and that's all that matters to me.

Annie turns to follow the children, but stops like a train hit her. "Jasper, James, and the rest, they all right?"

"The family is okay, but Old Bart, and Poole—" I shake my head.

"I loved that boy, Poole. Sweetest kid I've ever known. I'll miss him. Bart, he sure was a kind old man. I'm so sorry, Lummy. What about Rainy and J.A.?"

"J.A.'s probably close to bein' back home in Winn Parish by now, and Rainy's visitin' a professor friend at Mississippi College at Clinton. Somethin' about helpin' restore a church house for the students, called Provine Chapel."

Annie presses down her skirt that's fluttering in the breeze. "Well, come on in and stay awhile. You give any thought to what I proposed, about stayin' here in Vicksburg?"

I hold the door open for the ladies, eyeing Martha, who shakes her head.

"Annie, we leave in the morning for Choctaw County. Home is where the heart's at peace, and I think we have that now."

"Then I'll just have to come for a visit. To liven things up a bit."

Martha and I burst out laughing.

Annie slaps me on the shoulder. "What?"

I hug her close and whisper, "We've about had all the excitement we want for a lifetime. I'm not sure folks in Choctaw County are ready for An-nie Fanny." I give her a peck on the lips. "If you come, you'll have to behave."

"I'm comin', but I won't behave. Folks in Choctaw County will just have to learn like everybody around here did, won't they?"

"I reckon so."

Annie laughs and keeps talking, but all I hear is the sweet voice of my Martha whispering thanks to the Lord that I'm alive as she wraps her arm around my waist.

CHAPTER 48

# THE BEST FRIENDSHIPS
# LIVE LONG BEYOND THE GRAVE

## JULY 13, 1868

*No tribute is worthy of men who gave their lives for others.*
*Except not to forget them.*

AFTER A LONG two day wagon ride, we stop in Clinton, just this side of Jackson City, to visit Rainy and the Prewitts. I want see the Provine Chapel. Reverend Aquila Prewitt and his sweet wife, who is doing much better these days, put us up for the night. Resting in a bed rather than on the ground is a welcome pleasure after our many days and nights at Big Sand Rock sleeping in the smoky and musty hand dug cave. I'm not complaining—just happy for the simple comfort.

The children sleep on pallets next to the fireplace after feasting on a fine meal Martha and Mrs. Prewitt prepared. Elihu sneaks out to the wagon to bring in a jug of muscadine wine.

Aquila settles into his chair like he's ready to deliver a sermon from the chapel pulpit. Rainy slips in quietly, so as not to break Aquila's concentration. He's just returned from a short business trip to Jackson and is all smiles. He must've made a good deal on some guns.

Martha walks out of the kitchen. "Got a plate warm on the stove for you, Rainy."

"Thank you kindly, ma'am."

Taking advantage of a captive audience with full bellies, Aquila speaks up in good professor fashion to school us on the finer points of religion. "Church has become more of a ritualistic social club resembling a community meeting with more business and idle talk than you might find in your local bar."

He laments that true worship has taken a back seat in church services to the fashion shows every time the door opens. "You should see the way folks make their way to their self-assigned special seats in strategic places making sure they'll be seen. Why, it's ridiculous."

Mrs. Prewitt brings Rainy his food. "Downright shameful, if you ask me."

I sip a taste of wine. "That's too bad."

Aquila barks, "Ain't got a single damn thing to do with worshipping the Good Lord."

Mrs. Prewitt peeks out from the kitchen where she and Martha are finishing the dishes. "Aquila, a reverend shouldn't be cussing, dear."

"I don't feel much like a reverend when I think about all that. But all right, dear, I apologize."

Rainy turns to me and Elihu. "That's what I like about Aquila. He can preach the Devil right back into Hell, but can cuss up a storm and sip good wine with the best of them."

Aquila throws his handkerchief at Rainy. "Shut the hell up, boy, before I—"

Mrs. Prewitt peeks around the corner again. "I heard that, Aquila." She glares at all four of us. "You know the elders want you fired for all the good you did in the war. Those men have done much worse than curse, you can bet on that. It's all about image for them. No tellin' what they do when no one's lookin'. When a man turns a lantern light back on himself, there's a whole lot of darkness behind him. You boys'll do well to remember that," she says, shaking her finger.

I throw up my hands. "I'm out. I don't want the real head talkin' preacher in this family bringin' down the wrath of God on my head."

Mrs. Prewitt laughs, and we with her. Elihu starts snorting like a hog and falls out of his chair and mumbles a string of curse words without thinking.

Mrs. Prewitt points her finger at Elihu, snickering. "We keep our hogs outside in the pen, and that's where all of you will be staying tonight if you keep on cursing."

Elihu ducks his head. "I'm sorry, ma'am. It's just the wine."

Martha peeks around the corner to point her finger at me, smiling, and mouths, "Stop." She's so beautiful. I can't take my eyes off of her.

Martha steps out and takes up the lesson from where Acquila left off. "I know that if a man wants to be honest and true before God and man, he must be what he is, cussin' and all. Presenting an image that covers up who a man truly is ain't of God. It's too bad that church has come to that, like Aquila says. I'm glad Mount Pisgah Baptist Church is better than that. Pastor Dobbs has been known to curse a little, sip wine in one moment, and preach a fine sermon in the next. There, I've spoken my mind." Martha and Mrs. Prewitt return to the kitchen.

Rainy changes the subject. "I found a buyer for those Henry repeaters in Jackson today, unless you boys want to keep yours. J.A. took his and will send the money by post. Sarge, the Wood boys, and George Jamison left theirs with me. And, of course, I have Poole's and Old Bart's. I let Dan Creekwater keep his and several boxes of shells. That old Choctaw deserves to keep it."

I take the Henry rifle I set against the wall next to my chair. "Thanks, that was the right thing to do."

"I thought so. If you two want to keep yours, I'll make you a better deal than I offered the man in Jackson."

Elihu blows on the cup of coffee Martha brought him. "That gun is built for only one thing."

Rainy reaches out. "Yeah, I know, killing."

Elihu hands his over.

I'd like to keep the rifle, but that's the war in me talking. And maybe a little fear things might heat up again.

"Sell it to you for half price, Lummy, how about that?"

Martha peeks out and nods her approval.

I'm surprised. "I think I will, Rainy. Thanks."

"Sounds good."

I toss him a double eagle, and he proceeds to pull two boxes of shells from his saddlebags.

"Just a little gift just because I like you, Lummy Tullos. Besides, you never know when you'll run into those coyotes again."

"Or Hyenas."

He snickers. "Well, good, all the Henrys are accounted for." Rainy pulls a small bag from inside his shirt and stuffs the twenty-dollar gold piece I gave him in. He tosses it to Aquila.

"What's this?"

"Making good on my promise, brother. I got more for them than I'd hoped, and made several other good sales besides. There's two hundred in gold there. A hundred of it is yours, and the rest is for the chapel." Aquila starts to speak, but Rainy holds up his hand. "Like I told you not long ago, Aquila, I ain't never whooped no preacher's ass, but I'm fixin' to if you don't—"

Mrs. Prewitt steps out of the kitchen, drying her hands on a dish cloth. "You can whip his ass anytime you've a mind to, Rainy Mills. Won't bother me one bit." She points at her husband. "Now then, Aquila, you're not the only one capable of speaking colorful metaphors with a silver tongue at the right time."

We howl like hound dogs baying a coon up a tree. Martha tries to quiet us down for the sake of the sleeping children. Elihu wipes his laughing tears.

Rainy finishes his coffee and stares at the dark red color of the muscadine wine Elihu pours into his cup. "You boys have seen too much of the color in this cup. I understand you want no more of it." He takes a sip. "Here's to you good men. I'm the better man for knowin' you."

We lift our cups and join in the toast. We enjoy the quiet of the evening, listening to the wood crackle and pop in the fireplace. I hate to break the sweet silence, but I have a question for Aquila.

"I need a favor, Aquila, if you're willin' to help me."

"I will if I can, son."

"I want our story put in a newspaper. There needs to be a record of what we did, but mostly to not let Poole and Old Bart be forgotten. I read and write fine, but I know you can make my words sound better, if you don't mind."

"I can do that. Rainy told me all about you losing Old Bart and Poole in the fight."

"Good, then I don't have to relive that part. I want the story told, but so that it pays tribute to them. I want it put in the Greensborough newspaper, the *Southern Motive,* if they'll publish it."

"Oh, they'll have to. I've got a friend working for the Jackson newspaper who'd be happy to put it in his as soon as I get it to him. Then, the Choctaw County paper will have to pick it up, or be embarrassed that they didn't."

Aquila gets up to find pen and paper and brings back a portable writing desk he levels on his lap. He settles back into his reading chair and puts on his spectacles.

I make for the kitchen. "Martha, could Mistuh Prewitt and I have a cup of coffee?"

She brings in steaming cups of coffee for all and pie to go all around. "Missus Prewitt and I want to hear this."

"Good. Rainy, Elihu, chime in if there's somethin' I forget or get wrong."

They nod.

The Reverend smiles. "Consider me your amanuensis, my apostle of justice and good will."

Elihu sits up. "Aman-yoo-who?"

I look to Rainy, holding out his cup for another taste of wine, as the ladies pass coffee and pie around. "That means he'll only write what Lummy says, like men did for Paul in the Bible. You do read your Bible, don't you, Elihu?"

Elihu playfully pulls back the jug like he might not fill Rainy's cup. "Only on Sundays when I ain't drinkin'."

Rainy laughs as Elihu fills his cup.

I scratch my ear. "It's kind of hard to know where to start."

"Start with a title, if you think that'll help."

I ponder that for a moment.

Martha squeezes my arm. "What is the main thing you want said in the fewest words?"

"That helps, thanks. I'm thinking maybe, Two Men Give Their Lives for the Twentieth Star."

Aquila smiles. "That sounds good."

"Here goes then. Two men, who shall remain nameless, were killed recently in Choctaw County by the lawless red shirt Hyenas who refuse to rejoin the Union. The fight resulted in the capture and hanging of that misguided rascal, Captain Tom Ford. The first to die, an aging Negro, sacrificed his life in a trap that caught Ford and his gang red-handed in the act of perpetrating murder and mayhem on innocent folks who want the recent conflict between the states behind them. The other, a patriot who grew up in Choctaw County, gave his young and promising life to restore Mississippi as the twentieth star on the true flag that flies over these United States of America. These two men of good account, who rode high in the saddle, are to be honored for their service to this country and Choctaw County. These good men, and others who will remain nameless, deserve the greatest recognition. They will not be forgotten by all who know their deeds. More importantly, the Lord knows their names. CNT, Leader of the Low Riders."

Aquila looks up. "That'll make a fine piece of writing, son. Couldn't have said it better myself. No tribute is ever enough for men who lay down their lives for others. I'll check for any errors and sharpen up the grammar, but it's pretty much done."

"Thank you, Aquila. Would you send it in to the papers for me?"

Elihu interrupts. "Mark it for Jason Niles of the *Southern Motive*, that butt sniffin', no good, school house tattle tell, porch hound."

I hold up my hand. "Don't have that part printed, Aquila, please."

Rainy sits up. "Sounded like a pretty good description to me, and I don't even know the man."

Mrs. Prewitt covers her mouth and laughs, then looks to Martha, who's shaking her head.

Rainy shakes his head. "Sorry, Missus Prewitt, I think I've gotten used to these Tullos boys."

She chuckles. "They *are* something." Mrs. Prewitt shakes her finger at Elihu. "I warned you, Elihu. Keep on, and you'll sleep with hawgs tonight."

Elihu covers his mouth.

Rainy whispers, "Those were as good of men as I've ever known. I guess it's true. The best of friendships live long past the grave."

# CHAPTER 49

# AN UNEXPECTED BLESSING

## LATE AFTERNOON, DECEMBER 2, 1868

*Nothin' like hope heard in the cry of a newborn baby.*

THE FARMING YEAR ended with a good crop, despite all the nonsense. Working alongside my brothers has been nothing but a pleasure. Cotton prices were good, and the corn came in full and sweet. Hogs have been butchered, and vegetables and fruits have been canned. There's not a lot of money to be had, but that's most folks' situation nowadays.

Sarge drops in for a visit, having heard about the expected birth of my and Martha's first child together. He holds out a newspaper. "The Jackson paper put your article right in, but it took a while for Captain William Pollan to convince the editor of the *Southern Motive* that to be fair and honest, he'd better put it in—or else. Good men, they deserve to be remembered."

Although we've had peace these past months, Greensborough is becoming more lawless. Gunfights and drunken brawls are all too common. Living in the hills, we have little reason to be concerned. I'm happy to stay close to the farm, teaching John A. and his brother how to fish and hunt. Jasper's wife Isabel announced not long ago she's expecting a child. But today, I have the honor of telling the whole world that we have a new baby girl.

Sarge smiles. "Now that's news worth putting in the newspaper."

The sun warms the porch of our dogtrot cabin this lazy afternoon in December. Martha brings our first child outside just a few hours after she was born to breathe in air filled with smells of pine and farm. Only her tiny face can be seen for being wrapped up like a Christmas gift. The family gathers around Martha holding the small bundle as she slowly rocks the child. After everyone has a look, Martha covers the baby's face, taking no chances of her getting sick. Naming the child will be a memorable moment.

"I want to hold her here in a minute, Martha," I say.

She smiles and keeps rocking.

Sarge quiets everyone to read the newspaper article. "Lummy asked me to read his tribute to Old Bart and Poole published in the *Southern Motive*. It's my honor, as well as my privilege, to do so."

Tears form in my eyes as I listen quietly. I cough and clear my throat as Sarge finishes. "I just felt it fitting we should honor the two men who gave their lives so Martha and I could see this child into the world together. Their sacrifice will make a difference in this county for a long time. May the Tullos family never forget them. This article will ensure that for a while."

Elihu, in his characteristic uncouth fashion, blurts out, "What's that baby's name?"

Martha and I smile at each other.

His impatience gets the best of him. "Well, that baby's got to have a name, don't she?"

I pat the air for him to settle down. "We've got one. A name that Martha's always liked. We chose a name neither our family nor hers has ever used. If it was born a boy, we were goin' to name him Archy, for Pa. But, it's a girl, and we couldn't be happier."

John A. steps up to his mother. "What is it, Momma, what's my little sister's name?"

Martha nods, giving me the signal.

I gently take the infant wrapped in a soft blanket. I hold her high above my head, thanking Creator for the greatest blessing he's given thus far.

"Delaware. Her name is Delaware."

Elihu has a puzzled look. "Ain't that the name of a state or somethin'?"

"That's right. Martha's people went there first when they came to America and settled on the Delaware River. She liked the sound of it. The name honors her people's first home in the New World. I like it, too." I let that sink in for a moment. "Bein' the scholar that he is, I had asked Rainy to do some checking on his way to Natchez, just in case it was a girl. He found several meanings that make the name Delaware fit. He wrote 'em down and sent them to me. John A., why don't you read what your Uncle Rainy wrote?"

John A. excitedly takes the paper. "Okay, Pop."

John A. clears his throat and smiles at Mary, who taught him to read better under her tutelage. "Uncle Rainy writes that this information wasn't easy to find, but he got help from some folks in Jackson City. Here's what they found, and he said, 'Y'all gonna like it.'" John A. looks over the folded piece of paper with scribbling front and back, gathering his thoughts.

Elihu becomes impatient. "Lord, boy, Jesus'll come back before we know what her name means." We all laugh, and John A. is ready.

Mary cuts in to defend her student. "It's just a bunch of notes scribbled, Uncle Elihu. He's doing what I taught him to do—collect his thoughts to make a good presentation."

Elihu sticks his tongue out at Mary, and the kids laugh.

John A. looks up from his reading. "All right, there's somethin' here for everybody, I do believe. It may not be in the order Uncle Rainy would have wanted it read, but I'll read all he wrote on this paper."

Martha's face glows as John A. reads about our new baby's name.

"For you, Uncle Elihu, there's a grape some fella discovered in Delaware, Ohio a few years back. It's become a favorite for the sweet wine they make from it."

Elihu grins. "They call it a Delaware grape?" John A. nods. Elihu pats his foot. "I'll have to get a jug of that sometime."

"This next line is for you, Uncles Jasper and James, your two brothers who died in the war, and you, too, Uncle Sarge. The word was once used to mean a soldier ready to confront any enemy—the warrior who runs toward trouble, not away from it."

Jasper and James elbow each other like two schoolboys waiting for the girl in the seat in front of them to find the frog they put in her lunch pail.

Sarge whispers, "Fitting."

"For you, Uncle Dan and Uncle Josiah, and Aunt Chloe, Grandma Mary, and all the rest of us, it's the name the early settlers gave the Indians who lived along the river named Delaware. It simply means pure and genuine. That fits us and all who came before."

Dan nods as Josiah rubs his chin smiling.

Ma snickers. "Pure and genuine, maybe, but for dang sure, original." She throws her head back, laughing at her own joke. It's good to hear her laugh.

I take little Delaware into my arms and kiss her small forehead.

John A. steps closer to Martha. "Ma, for you, it's the name of a beautiful river, ever flowing to bring new life around every new bend of the journey in this world."

She grabs my hand.

John A. lays his hand on my shoulder. "And for you, Columbus Nathan Tullos. Delaware was one of the first and original thirteen colonies to become a state. It was the first state to ratify the Constitution. Though Delaware was a slave state when the war broke out, she stayed with the Union. The governor said at the beginning of the war, 'We were first to embrace the Union and will be the last to leave it.' They still have a long ways to go on how they treat black folks, but it's not anything Choctaw County still don't wrestle with."

Mary whispers, "Doesn't, not don't."

John A. corrects himself. "Doesn't wrestle with, either."

I rub John A.'s head. "It's been worth the struggle, I'd say." Whispers of agreement come from those who've lived it as we remember those who died for it.

I lift tiny Delaware up high again. "Lord, I ask you bless this child to be sweet and strong as good wine, a powerful soldier unafraid to stand against the wiles of the Devil even to the point of sacrifice, and to be pure and always genuine. But as Ma just said, 'For damn sure, original.'"

Everyone laughs.

"Sorry about the cussin', Lord. Lastly, please keep your hand of healin' on Choctaw County and the State of Mississippi. We got a long ways to go, in Jesus Name, let us all say, amen."

The small crowd belts out a resounding amen so that those buried up on Tullos Cemetery Hill can hear. The family cheers, and the girls want to hold little Delaware in their arms. But Ma gets the first honor, as it should be.

"My sweet little Delaware. Good to meet you."

Up the road, I spy a cloud of dust trailing a sutler's wagon, with clanking pots and pans and tools of every sort swinging back and forth. The wagon rolls up in the yard.

Martha leans over and whispers, "See if they got a heavy stone milk pitcher. I broke mine the other day."

Before I can get down the porch steps, an old woman climbs down the side of the wagon with difficulty. Hobbling with stick in hand, she beelines straight for Martha.

Ma hands little Delaware back to Martha. I stand close to my wife and child as the old woman struggles up the steps. A man who must be her son and wears a funny little round black hat, helps her up each step.

He bows and asks. "May I ask, what is the child's name?"

"Delaware, why?"

He whispers the baby's name to the old woman, who falls to her knees and carefully lays her wrinkled hand on Delaware's small forehead. Delaware looks up with a tiny grin, and the old woman chants in a language I've never heard, repeating Delaware's name several times. I have no idea who these people are or what she's doing, but it seems right. The family gathers around, the children especially curious. The old woman finishes, and her son helps her to her feet. I look at him curiously, expecting an explanation.

"I'm so sorry if we have caused you any alarm. My mother travels with me as we sell our wares to good folks such as you. I had suggested that we keep going to the next town to find a place for the night, but suddenly she pointed down your road. My mother, who speaks no English, said that the Lord told her we must come to your home, and right now."

I pick up Delaware again. "So, what was she doing?"

"Blessing your child in the name of the Lord so that she may have long life and bring peace and happiness to your home."

"I appreciate it. Thanks for coming, and for the blessing on our daughter. I appreciate those who listen to the voice of Creator and obey."

Martha smiles up at me as I gently lay Delaware in her arms. "Don't forget the stone pitcher."

The old woman's son brings out a heavy stone pitcher with blue flowers dancing around its base and asks, "The sun is going down. May we stay the night? We will cause no problem."

Elihu chimes in. "It's a free country."

The son shakes his head. "Not everywhere yet my friend, I think."

I take in a deep breath. "It is here on Tullos land. Supper will ready soon, and you're welcome."

"Thank you, brother."

CHAPTER 50

# BACK IN THE FOLD, FINALLY

## FEBRUARY 23, 1870

*Comin' back into the family ain't always pleasant.*

W E KEEP OUR heads down as the battles continue around the county through 1869 right up to this day of days. Fortunately, we developed a reputation few miscreants want to challenge, especially with the Wood boys not far away. John and Henry have families of their own and know we're just a yell away from coming to their aid when needed.

Word got out that it was us who took Captain Tom Ford down with the help of the Military Provost. No one wants to go against government troops, or us, being connected with them. Thankfully, we've lived in peace without incident.

Greensborough has gotten so violent that all day courts have been moved to Pensacola, where Amariah died. When court went into session, the town offered free whiskey and allowed what goes with it, especially knockdown, drag out fights. Things got worse around the state after Tom Ford's hanging. A new gang, calling themselves the Ku Klux Klan, vows to live only under a white man's government and stay armed at all times. They ride around wearing hoods, acting like ghosts, terrorizing Negroes through torture and murder. President Grant was quoted in the newspapers as saying, "If Civil government fails to protect the Citizen, Military government should supply its place."

I guess Captain William Pollan gets to witness his prophecy come true— make enough noise, and the boys in blue will come.

For doing nothing about the growing violence, Governor Humphries was finally removed from his post June of 1868, and replaced by former Union General and new Military Governor Adelbert Ames. He's a fair man who wants to restore peace and has done much to help former slaves secure their new rights. He's even appointed Negroes to a number of political offices, the first time in Mississippi's history. He's hoping, with Grant as President, Congress will do something to end the terror of the night riders.

I sit on the front porch of the new cabin my brothers and I built for my family. It looks just like the dogtrot house I grew up in. The world around us might still be on fire, but the sweetness of the sugar in my coffee reminds me that on this farm, we get a little taste of what this county and country should and could be one day.

I think about the day we marched into Vicksburg after the surrender and eating good Yankee rations across the street from General Pemberton's headquarters on Crawford Street. We witnessed Pemberton treat Grant rudely when he asked for a simple glass of water, saying, "You know where to find it."

That didn't deter the blue suited general from treating us well. His compliment, that if he'd had men like us on his side he would've taken Vicksburg sooner, caused me to see him and the Yankees much differently that day. His words and wanting the twentieth star for Mississippi returned to its rightful place on the Union flag flying over the Warren County courthouse changed me that day.

I wonder, what would President Grant think now knowing his words that day led me to join the 1st Mississippi Mounted Rifles and fight to make Choctaw County safer from the red shirt Lost Cause Hyenas?

Jasper rides fast up the new trail leading to our new home nestled in a hollow not far from Tullos Cemetery Hill. He jumps off his horse and unrolls a newspaper he bought in Bankston. He holds up the Jackson City paper, and the headline reads, *Mississippi is Back in the Fold!* I ask him to read the article out loud for the family.

He looks up from scanning the words, smiling. "Jackson City. Our beloved state has come through much these last few years. Despite continued

violence, Mississippi is officially the twentieth state in the Union again. Today will be the first time since 1861 senators and representatives from our
beloved state will take their seats in the United States Congress.'"

I sit back. "Well, ain't that somethin'?" I want to jump and yell, but I wait
for the rest.

Jasper reads a little more. "Says here Mississippi drafted a new constitution and adopted the Thirteenth Amendment. That means slavery is done
for good."

"But that ain't the same as ratifying an amendment, is it?"

"Hell, I don't know, but it's a step in the right direction."

A step in the right direction doesn't mean others will go along with it.
Just because a man is set free doesn't mean he'll be treated as free. "Yeah,
that's good news, anything else?"

Jasper pulls the paper closer, straining his eyes. "Well, Mississippi rati-
fied, as you say, the Fourteenth and Fifteenth Amendments in a new state
constitution, meaning Negroes are now citizens, and black men have the
right to vote."

"I wish Old Bart and Seth could've seen this day. Now that is somethin'."

"Listen to this. 'Military rule has ended, and soon Federal soldiers will
return home. It's a glorious day for Mississippi. Loyalists, both former gray
and blue, can reunite to make Mississippi a prosperous land again, offering
great opportunity and reward for hard work and good living.' It's what
you dreamed of, brother. The Year of Jubilee when slaves are set free has
finally come."

Jasper reads more, but my mind trails off to what it's cost to get to where
we are. It's official. The folks up in Washington finally did it. I wasn't sure I'd
ever see it. Mississippi is readmitted back into the Union. Today.

I pull the little pouch from my jacket pocket. I hand John A. Grandpa
Temple's twenty star flag. "Tack this to that porch post, would you, son?
Today we fly the right flag over this farm."

Jasper continues reading silently. He asks, "I wonder how it can be that
southern states are being readmitted to the Union when they never were
recognized as having left in the first place?"

Ma speaks up. "When southern congressmen walked out, it meant we left the fold."

I stare at the old flag. "Now we can start the process of ruling ourselves again. Don't know how that'll go, but with the Military Police being relieved, Sergeant McGugarty will finally get to go home to his family. It's been a long time comin' for him. I'll surely miss that man."

I still fret for my Negro family and friends who've had at least some protection with the soldiers being around. I fear there'll always be a Captain Tom Ford, Lester, or a Dawg Smith around, too. If so, I guess there will always be a Tullos around to deal with them. Bullies don't fare well with folks born with hills in their souls and a wild loyalty to things colored blue. What was that old Scottish word Grandpa Temple said our name came from in Scotland? Tulach, that's it. And the color blue, well, I still want to paint myself like a Pict and dance naked around a woodland fire some early spring night. That is, if Martha lets me.

CHAPTER 51

# A PERMANENT TWENTIETH STAR

## MARCH 2, 1870

*What's worth dyin' for is worth livin' for.*

I SCAN THE fields close to the farm, nursing a cup of good coffee. We gather at Ma's to lay out the day's work. James repairs a harness in the barn. Martha's oldest, John A., pedals a sharpening wheel as he slides a blade back and forth across the stone. John A. is becoming much of a man. It won't be long before we break ground and plant seed. Now is the time to pray for the right amount of rain with a good balance of sunshine to make our crops grow well this year. Creator knows what we need without me having to ask. I do enjoy talking with him about it though.

Elihu walks out of a thicket across the field, carrying a half grown doe across his shoulders. He won't do it any other way. He can't. There's too much of the people painted blue in him, Ma says.

I yell, "Need any help skinnin' her?"

He shakes his head. "Not from you, Lummy. Last time you nicked me with the long knife Pa made you. I'll do it myself."

I shrug. "Suit yourself." I go back to nursing my coffee and thinking about what needs doing.

John A. hands Elihu a sharpened blade and walks over to get a cup of coffee. "I'll finish sharpening the rest of the knives here directly, Pop, if that's okay?"

"Sure, son. Just finish them today."

"Yes sir, I will."

It's been almost five years since I mustered out of the 1st Mississippi

Mounted Rifles. I recount the losses but choose to think on what we've gained and learned about friendship and honorable sacrifice through years of turmoil and destruction. Tears form, so I pitch the cold coffee on the ground and walk to the well for a drink of water.

I look out across the land that raised me and the vale set between two hills. It's like I'm seeing it again for the first time. I wonder what it was like when Grandpa Cloud saw the New World for the first time back in the 1661. My world is just as new today as his was then, and for that, I'm thankful. The freshness of newly turned earth, the smells of barnyard animals, the laughter of children, and the quietness of pine covered hills have captured my heart once again.

I can't help but smile watching Elihu slip a sip of good moonshine made by the Wood boys when he thinks no one's looking. Just like Pa used to do. Dan pitches hay down from the barn loft for the milk cows and playfully throws a pitchfork full at Elihu, letting him know all are wise to his secret. Children chase each other around the yard playing seek and find. Sounds of the ladies laughing and the smells of the their cooking up something good in the kitchen fill the air. Both make me hungry for more than food. It's family I crave.

I pray, "Lord, you've given it back to me better'n I deserve." Warmth wraps around me like a good quilt on a cold winter's night. Peace covers my soul.

Jasper rides in from his new home across the big cotton field to bring Ma some medicine. She's been feeling poorly of late and stays in the bed most days.

"Sit a spell, Jasper, and rest your weary bones."

"Don't mind if I do. Did you hear about the meeting at the Academy Building in French Camp?"

I shake my head. "You want some cool water?"

"Yeah, that'd be good."

"What's on your mind?"

"They're raising money for a monument to honor Confederate soldiers killed in the war. What do you think?"

"I think it ain't no different than havin' fancy church steeples and chandeliers in halls where God is supposedly worshipped. The money would be better spent to help the poor eat and weary farmers keep their lands."

"Can't disagree with that, but I'm going. I want to make sure George Washington's and Amariah's names get mentioned."

"You do what needs doin'. I ain't against it, but monuments are not what they fought and died for. A stone with carvings never tasted good when a man's gut is stuck to his backbone for want of somethin' to eat."

Jasper just sits, saying nothing.

I reach into my pocket to pull out the last ten dollar gold piece I have from Uncle Rube's treasure. I roll it between my fingers for a moment and toss it to Jasper. "Them boys deserve to be honored for the love they had for this county. Knowin' what they know now, I believe they'd be happy things finally got straightened out."

"Amen, brother, but you know there's still trouble in the air."

"Yeah, and it smells worse than an outhouse, I'm sure."

Jasper scratches his beard. "Can't do nothin' about it right now. "

"I don't want to."

"Well, I best get on home. Isabel will have supper ready. Love you, boy." Jasper stuffs the gold piece into his pocket and hops on his horse.

I reach up to shake his hand. "I'm glad you're my brother, Jasper. Don't be a stranger, and let's get our families together real soon."

He waves, disappearing down the lane. Soft footsteps plod up behind me. It's Ma. She's been staying with us for a week or so.

"Was that Jasper?" I nod. "Wish I could've seen him."

"He didn't want to disturb you. How are you feelin'?"

"Oh, I'm okay, son."

"Need anythin'?"

"No, but I got you somethin'. It ain't much. I put two nickels together, and Elihu picked it up for me in Bankston the other day. I wanted you to have this because it means so much to you."

She hands me a piece of neatly folded cloth. I shake out the new Union flag with thirty-seven stars that include the new states, Nevada and Nebraska, wherever they are." I stare at the flag.

"You know, Lummy, it never was about choosing between two colors, white and black, or even gray and blue. No, it was always about three. It was the red, white, and blue Stars and Bars that kept Negroes in chains, but it was the same red, white, and blue of the Stars and Stripes that finally set black people free, and all of us for that matter."

"Mississippi's star really is back on the flag, ain't it, Ma?"

"It never was really taken off." She wanders back into the cabin.

I lean my straight back chair against the log wall of our dogtrot cabin, savoring the moment.

Martha whispers from inside the cabin, "Go on, he'll tell you about it. You're old enough now."

John A. walks out onto the porch like a young soldier trying to show his confidence. He carries a familiar little box. He pulls up a stool to set between us. He settles into his chair and opens the box with black and white squares filled with many small lead playing pieces. I stare at the chess set. A thousand memories flood my mind.

"Teach me to play, Pop?"

I rub John A.'s head and help set up the playing pieces. "Sure."

Mary steps out with a little book like Gunnard carried in Vicksburg and Sheriff Barnett in Winn Parish. "Mind if I sit?"

"Not at all. What's that?"

"Someone needs put Tullos history to paper. Grave markers don't tell good stories."

John A. has the pieces set up on the board. "Will you tell me about the war, Pop?"

"I'll teach you to play. And tell you about a boy—no, about a *man*—not much older than you are now, who made this chess set for me one Christmas in Vicksburg."

My heart swells as peace covers me for the first time thinking on such things again.

"Pop, you ready?"

A rider barrels down the road to our farm like General Wirt Adams is on his tail. He wears a blue uniform.

I study the horseman. "I'm always ready. Go get my Henry rifle, would you please? Hurry."

The rider's horse slides to a sudden stop, and he trots over to stand at the bottom of the cabin steps. "You Lummy Tullos, sir?"

"I am. But I ain't no sir to you, son."

The young private salutes. "I need you to come with me, please, sir. By special order."

I spring out of my rocker quick as a bobcat on a swamp rabbit. "By whose authority?"

"President Grant himself, sir."

A TALE OF TWO COLORS

# JUDGED
## and found LACKING

A SHORT STORY

# THE STORY OF RAINY MILLS

## PART II

THE SALOON BARKEEP hung one arm on a batwing with the other holding the shotgun on Ratliff's former friends. "You won't be stayin' in Skullyville, I'm guessin'. Where you headed?"

"Louisiana, to find the man who should've given my folks justice and stopped Ratliff."

The barkeep looked back at Ratliff's former friends, then whispered, "I heard Ratliff say that a judge friend of his who lived in Shreveport moved from there to retire."

"You know where?"

"Ratliff once said he moved to Bellevue to start a newspaper of some kind. Said he was thinkin' about settlin' down there himself. The judge offered him a job as his personal security officer. He said if the judge owned the bank, most of the land, and what people read in the paper, he'd control the town and Bossier Parish. Ratliff planned on takin' the job. That is, until you showed up."

"Thanks for the information." Rainy looked around at the town. "Why are you here?"

"Everybody's got a past. Mine hasn't caught up with me here, at least not yet. If'n I was younger, I'd come with you. War's comin' on fast, and the Choctaws will line up with the South, I do believe. Folks are fussin' already about it. Some say the fight'll come even way out here."

"I pray it never does. Why the name Skullyville? Surely it can't be just about the government doling out money,"

"The Choctaws say it sounds like their name for money. Me? I heard a Choctaw witch hung a wolf's head at the edge of town to ward off evil spirits. The skull stayed there for years."

Rainy felt the wolf within calling him to Bellevue. "Thanks again." He flipped the barkeep a five dollar gold piece. "I was never here."

The barkeep bit the coin with his eyetooth. "Good enough."

The road leading east from Skullyville to Fort Smith offered no comfort. With Ratliff dead, the man who needed to pay next for his actions was the judge who let him get away with murder.

RAINY TURNED SOUTH from Fort Smith to find mountains with the solace needed to sort out his thoughts. Sipping his coffee in camp the first night, Rainy watched a shooting star blaze across a moonless sky.

"Isn't that a sight, horse?" His mount snorted and shook his head up and down. "I guess I should call you something other than horse.'"

The horse perked his ears up.

Rainy thought for a moment. "Homer. Yes, that's it. Your name is Homer."

The horse stared at Rainy like he had no sense.

"What? It's a good name. Homer was a historian and poet. He wrote some pretty good stories, too."

Homer pawed the ground.

"At least it'll remind me that I have a good classical education when I feel like an animal... like I did back in Skullyville."

Rainy got up from the fire to brush Homer down. "Let's not talk about that anymore tonight."

Homer nudged Rainy with his nose.

Sitting back down on his bedroll and pouring another cup of coffee, Rainy felt for Ratliff's throwing knife in his belt. He thumbed Ratliff's name etched in the smooth silver and bone handle.

"Ratliff used this knife to murder my father and hold my mother in place while he violated her." Encrusted blood along the hilt made him check the wound Ratliff left in his hip. It looked to be healing well, but it hurt something fierce.

"I have only one use for this evil blade." Rainy flipped the weapon point to handle, and back again. "I'll kindly leave this knife with the judge who freed the man that brought on the blood of my birth."

Rainy admitted to his horse, "Homer, it is a fine blade, sharp as a straight razor, and perfectly balanced. I guess I best learn how to use it."

Rainy practiced throwing the blade. In a short time, he got as good with the knife as he was with a pistol.

"ALL RISE. BOSSIER Parish District Court for the State of Louisiana is now in session, the Honorable Judge Jeremiah Waters presiding."

Waters gave a sharp rap on the desk with his gavel. "What's on the docket today, bailiff?'

"Everything is laid out there in front of you, Judge."

"Oh yes, yes, I see it now. Thank you."

As Waters examined the papers, Rainy slipped in the door and sat in the back row.

Waters grinned and slowly raised his eyes as a red-headed beauty, dressed in the latest Paris fashion, gave him a wink. He pulled his spectacles back up from the end of his hawk-bill nose.

"Miss Lacy Boyette, after reviewing your case, it has been dismissed due to a lack of evidence."

The court erupted in displeasure. A spectator chuckled and yelled, "I see now what made you come out of retirement, Judge Adulterer Waters."

Judge Waters slammed his gavel down. "That's enough! The burden of proof was not met in Miss Boyette's circumstance. Case closed." Waters pointed his gavel at the heckler. "One more word out of you, Sam, and I'll—"

The bailiff cleared his throat and shook his head at the judge.

Waters nodded to Miss Boyette. "Miss Boyette, you are free to go."

She frowned at Sam, blew Judge Waters a kiss, and twirled her parasol.

"Thank you kindly, Jeremiah. Stop by my establishment later tonight and let me show you how grateful I am."

As men shook their fists and cursed, Miss Boyette smiled and swung her hips from side to side on her way to the door. Judge Waters took out a handkerchief and wiped the drool dripping from his mouth. Sam shook his head in disgust.

Rainy gripped the back of the pew in from of him to keep from throwing Ratliff's knife straight into Judge Water's heart. He ground his teeth, whispering, "Evil as the man I just killed."

Sam elbowed the man sitting next to him. "Go on, ask him."

A farmer wearing homespun and a flop hat jumped up and yelled, "What about us, Judge? You gonna give us the same deal you just gave that whore?"

Miss Boyette stopped at the door and turned. "I resent that remark."

A man sitting next to Rainy who looked to be a well-to-do banker snickered, "I don't."

The bailiff shouted, "Here, here, sit down, or I'll throw you all out!"

Miss Boyette swatted the banker's hat down over his eyes, but grinned at Rainy. She kissed the air seductively and gave him a nod as an invitation. He turned back to the judge without acknowledging her. He'd spent too much time with such women. He had other things on his mind in this courtroom.

The farmer sat down hard and folded him arms.

Judge Waters readjusted his spectacles and leaned over the papers before him. "You, there! Farm boy! You owe Bossier Parish twenty cash dollars for overdue property taxes. Either pay today, or I put your farm up for auction on the courthouse steps this afternoon."

The bailiff chuckled, "If it ever gets to the steps, huh, Judge?"

"It'll never go on the block. I've already paid off the auctioneer."

The farmer gritted his teeth. "You'll do no such thing."

Waters leaned forward. "I'd be happy to take the taxes out of your holdings in other ways, if that suits you."

"What do you mean?"

Waters leaned back in his chair. "How is your oldest daughter doing these days? She's what, eighteen now? And still not married?"

"Leave my family out of this. I'll find your damn tax money somewhere, if I have to...."

Rainy spoke in a deep tone, "You won't have to."

The courtroom fell silent.

The farmer spun around to see Rainy rise and pitch a gold double eagle to the bailiff.

"Consider his taxes paid."

Waters craned his neck to get a better view of Rainy. "And who might you be, sir, generous to a fault?"

Rainy leaned up. "No fault here, Judge. Just doing what a decent man would do for a neighbor in need. Who I am doesn't matter. Not yet. But if you must have a name, just call me Robin Hood."

The courtroom audience erupted in laughter.

Waters glared at Rainy and snickered. "Like in the storybooks?"

"Yes, except this is no fairytale, Judge. You should know the difference by now. If you don't, you will soon enough."

Rainy slipped out the door and disappeared into an alley.

The farmer in homespun shouted, "Well, hallelujah! If it ain't ole Robin Hood still robbin' from the rich and givin' to the poor."

Waters barked at the bailiff, "Bring that man back here. I'm not done with him."

The bailiff laid the gold coin on Waters' desk. The Judge picked it and studied the shiny, newly minted piece.

The farmer took his hat in hand and couldn't hide his grin. "I'll be needin' a receipt for that, Judge Waters."

Waters slammed the coin on the bench, wrote out the receipt, and threw it on the floor.

The bailiff returned a few moments later and shrugged. "He disappeared, Judge. Like a haint or an angel, or somethin'."

"Get back to your post and shut up," Waters growled. "You'll find him later or I'll find someone who can. Next!"

Rainy found an out of the way café and settled into a corner chair. He ordered only coffee, not wanting a heavy meal to cloud his thinking.

The farmer whose tax he paid sneaked in the door and took a chair. "Thank you for what you did. You saved me and my family." After sharing Waters's exploits, the farmer pulled down his hat and went out the back door.

Rainy sipped his coffee and considered a plan. Tonight, he would put the past behind him—both Ratliff and the Judge.

THE MANSION WAS dark except for the flicker of a coal oil lamp lighting up Judge Waters's profile. Rainy sneaked to the window that was slightly raised. The bailiff, who also served as his henchman, listened carefully as Waters laid out a plan to find and quietly dispose of Rainy. With a nod, the bailiff slipped out a side door from the Judge's study and left in a gallop on his horse.

Rainy waited.

JUDGE WATERS FINALLY finished his paperwork about midnight and turned the lamp down, but not out. He rose to stretch to see a shadowy figure emerge from a dark corner.

"Who is it? What do you want?"

Rainy whispered gruffly, "Only one thing."

Waters mustered up his courage. "Yeah, and what's that?"

"You."

Waters sat back down in his plush leather chair, smirking. He leaned up and poured himself a whiskey and offered Rainy one.

"I don't drink with scoundrels."

Waters twirled the whiskey in his glass and threw it back, taking it all in one swallow. "You know all I have to do is yell, and my bailiff will come running, right?"

Rainy stepped into the dim light. "He left."

Waters leaned up, palms flat on his desk. "It's you—the stranger who stood up for that farmer. Honorable, I must say, but misguided at best."

"You'll never know."

Waters rubbed his hands together frantically. "It's a federal crime to harm a judge."

"And it's an eternal crime to take advantage of poor farmers, rape women, kill their husbands, and let murderers go."

"I never did anything—"

"That you didn't want to do, you bastard."

"Who are you, and what do you want?"

"Just an orphan whose father was murdered the day his mother was raped by your good friend."

Waters's eyes bulged. "No, it can't be. Ratliff said he had a son who—"

"And what do I want? You took the life I was supposed to have, and now I must take yours."

"I've done everything within my power to be fair and just. You can't do this to me."

"Do this I can. Do this I *will*. You're still twisting the law for your own profit at other's expense. I watched you let a whore off the hook and a poor farmer's dreams nearly go into the outhouse." Rainy spat. "And you call yourself fair and just. People aren't as dumb as you think they are. But you sure as hell are."

"What are you going to do?"

"Give you one consideration, if you do as I ask."

"What, what? I'll do anything."

"Stealing other men's land with their family's hopes and dreams is where we'll start."

"What do you mean?"

"You're going to sign all land deeds back over to the farmers from whom you stole them."

Tears formed in Judge Waters's eyes. "But I can't do that. I've already made deals."

"Deals I'm sure you're going to lose your ass on now."

"Please don't—"

"What's it worth to gain the whole world and lose your own soul?"

"I can't, I won't—"

"Either you will do it, or your family will die with you. You decide."

"Please don't kill me."

"You should've thought about that when you let John Ratliff off scot free after destroying my parents' lives, Thomas and Epsie Mills."

Rainy stared blankly at the empty shell of a man who sat before him. Waters's eyes darted here and there like a cornered mouse as he clawed at his face.

"You, sir, have been tried, judged, and found lacking. Choose your own sentence, Judge Jeremiah Waters."

Waters pleaded, "But I came to this town after the tornado destroyed it back in '51, and made something of it, damn it."

"Yeah, the farmer told me how you bought up all the land cheap because the good citizens couldn't afford to rebuild after the storm."

"I rebuilt it for them and—"

"Made slaves of them in the bargain. Now you boast of your good will in your own newspaper as you fill your pockets with somebody else's gold."

"How'd you know about that?"

"An acquaintance of your old friend told me."

"Where is Ratliff? He was supposed to be here last week."

"He won't be joining us, Judge."

"You killed him, didn't you?"

"The bastard who made me a bastard made his own bed. I just put him to sleep in it—for good."

Judge Waters lost control and darkened the front of his pants. He knew he was done.

Rainy stepped forward so Waters could see his face clearly. "What's it going to be, Judge? Your life, and I leave your family alone, or your life, and I don't leave them alone? Either way, your life is forfeit. I would hate to make your wife's last deed on earth be to sign those papers on your behalf, in your absence, of course."

Waters gasped, "Not my wife… I have grandchildren—"

Rainy slammed his fist on the desk as hard as the Judge did his gavel in court earlier. "My mother and father never got the chance to have grandchildren. And now, the days of you seeing yours are over."

Waters snatched open the top drawer of his desk to grab a pistol hidden there. Rainy kicked the desk so hard it pinned his hand. Waters opened his mouth to scream in pain.

Rainy pulled his pistol and stuck in the Judge's mouth. "Go ahead, cry out you coward. I'll kill everyone in this house and burn it down right now, do you understand?"

Waters nodded, sobbing and rubbing his broken hand.

"There's two ways this can happen, Judge, by my hand or by yours. Whichever you choose, the land deeds will be signed back over to their rightful owners."

Judge Jeremiah Waters looked to the rafters.

"Uh-uh, Judge. You're not getting off that easy."

"But my wife, my kids, my…."

Rainy sunk Ratliff's throwing knife into the oak desk. "I had no father and mother. Ratliff took them from me, and you let it happen, damn you. Now I live with that murdering rapist's blood running through my veins. That's almost enough to slit my own wrists."

Judge Waters stared at the knife. "What's the knife for?"

"You're smart, you figure it out. But first, sign those deeds and hand over the gold in that safe. Then you'll write a letter confessing the crimes you've committed. I want names and details. I'll have it printed in *The South-Western* in Shreveport. Just think, Judge, you'll be immortalized in the annals of history for all time."

Waters, head in hands, cried, "My God, what am I going to do?"

"There's only one thing left to do."

"What's that?"

"That knife there has a very fine edge, Judge."

Waters shivered. "I can't believe this is happening—"

"I'll have that drink now." Rainy noticed a new ten gauge shotgun standing in the corner behind the desk as he poured himself a drink. "Make sure you put the crime against my parents and their names at the top of the list, Judge."

Judge Jeremiah Waters completed the letter and shoved the papers forward. "I am finished."

"Yes, you are," Rainy whispered, throwing back the last of his whiskey.

Waters cried for a moment, then dried his tears. He took Ratliff's knife by the handle that was used to kill Rainy's father and hold his mother down as he violated her. He studied the name and thumbed the knife edge. He looked up as if to pray, then back at Rainy. "I'm sorry, son, for everything."

"Save it for the One who judges all things, Waters. You'll meet Him in just a moment."

Without a blink, Judge Jeremiah Waters slit his wrists.

Rainy stuffed the deeds and letter inside his coal black coat. He grabbed the shotgun and the money sack, then eased out the side door. Rainy heard the thump of Waters's body fall from his chair as he quietly closed the door. He laid the shotgun across his saddle and stuffed the sack of gold coins into his saddlebag.

Rainy rubbed Homer's neck and chuckled as he mounted. "A rather large donation will be made to the Natchez Children's Home by Judge Jeremiah Waters in honor of my parents."

Rainy rode to the farmer's house whose tax he'd paid. "You know what to do with the deeds. Put this letter in the mail to *The South-Western* in Shreveport one day after the law reports Judge Jeremiah Waters as dead." Rainy handed the farmer a gold eagle.

The farmer nodded. "I'll do it, and thank you." The farmer offered his hand. "Who are you, some kind of avenging angel?"

"Maybe once a death angel. But not anymore."

Rainy slipped away into the same darkness as the day his mother left him with the preacher on the orphanage doorstep."

RAINY BRUSHES HIS horse down, making sure his new set of clothes stay free of hair. "I like the quiet, don't you, Homer?"

A faraway locomotive whistle on the Vicksburg, Shreveport & Texas Railroad pierces the twilight. "Thank goodness it's going the other direction." Rainy places a feedbag on Homer. "There, boy, that should do you." Back by the fire, he stirs a stew that smells to be done.

A pack of coyotes sound off. Rainy eases his pistol from its holster. Homer snorts and stamps his hooves.

"I believe they're getting a little too close, Homer."

In the fading light, the tallest man Rainy's ever seen runs just ahead of the howlers, lunging and snapping at his heels. He dives into Rainy's camp as the coyotes slide to a stop, falling over each other. Rainy fires three shots, killing two. The rest of the pack disappears into the night.

The young man gets up and dusts himself off. He thanks Rainy for not shooting him and saving his life.

After a bit of small talk and food, Rainy shows off his fancy pistol.

The stranger marvels at the weapon. "I'm Lummy Tullos from Choctaw County, Missip."

"Where you headed?"

"Some place called Winn Parish."

Rainy smiles and pulls the ten gauge shotgun from a soft leather case.

Lummy asks, "Where'd you get that cannon?"

"Oh, I had ordered one just like it for a fellow you might know in Winn Parish. But to my good fortune, I happened upon a man who didn't need this one anymore. I have business to attend to in Shreveport. Would you be interested in delivering it to him?"

ANTHONY WOOD grew up in historic Natchez, Mississippi, fueling a life-long love of history. Not long after high school, he lived and worked in Alaska for several years. He returned to the South and ministered for nearly three decades among the poor, homeless, and incarcerated. Leading an effort that planted five urban churches inspired him to co-author *Up Close and Personal: Embracing the Poor* about his work in Memphis, Tennessee. He also authored a number of articles and stories about inner city ministry.

Anthony is a member of Turner's Battery, a Civil War re-enactment group, the Civil War Roundtable of Arkansas and serves as President of the White County Creative Writers' group. His short stories and poetry have won multiple awards and been published in *Saddlebag Dispatches, The Vault of Terror,* and *The Avocet: A Journal of Nature Poetry.* One of those stories, "Not So Long in the Tooth," won a Will Rogers Medallion Award in the Best Western Short Fiction category for 2021.

When not writing, Anthony enjoys roaming and researching historical sites, camping and kayaking on the Mississippi River, and being with family. Anthony and his wife, Lisa, live in Conway, Arkansas.

www.ingramcontent.com/pod-product-compliance
Lightning Source LLC
Chambersburg PA
CBHW050356260626
47156CB00003B/758